LOOKING FOR ELIZA

LOOKING FOR ELIZA

Leaf Arbuthnot

First published in Great Britain in 2020 by Trapeze
an imprint of The Orion Publishing Group Ltd
Carmelite House, 50 Victoria Embankment
London EC4Y 0DZ

An Hachette UK Company

1 3 5 7 9 10 8 6 4 2

ISBN (Hardback) 978 1 4091 8579 6
ISBN (Trade Paperback) 978 1 4091 8580 2
ISBN (eBook) 978 1 4091 8582 6

Typeset by Born Group
Printed and bound in Great Britain by Clays Ltd, Elcograf S.p.A.

MIX
Paper from
responsible sources
FSC
www.fsc.org   FSC® C104740

www.orionbooks.co.uk

*For Emma and
James, with love*

Chapter One

The moment Ada walked into the small supermarket on Iffley Road, she knew something sinister had happened to it since her last visit. Had the aisles moved three inches to the left? Had some zealous store manager set up a deli counter at the back, bunching up everything else in the shop? She grabbed a loaf of rye bread from the baked goods section by the flowers and walked vigilantly down the fruit aisle.

Something was very definitely off. She remembered visiting an earthquake room with Michael years ago in some London museum – there was a mock-up of a green-grocer's on level two, with a shopping trolley and all these fake cereal boxes everywhere, and every few minutes the whole thing would start shaking terrifically to give visitors a sense of what being in an earthquake was like. Ada had found the room mildly boring. Michael loved it and stood there for a long time, grinning along with the seven-year-olds whenever the quake began. At any moment, she felt, this shop too would start shivering; its tins threatening to spring from their shelves. This time Michael wasn't around to smile at the tremors. Ada squared her shoulders, trying to work out what was different. At the end of the aisle, where Braeburns turned to spring onions and leeks, each in their own solitary plastic pocket, she saw, at last, what had happened.

At the back of the shop, where Ada usually lined up with her basket by the chewing gum and snack bars, wondering whether it would be Adul at the till today or Fatima, or very possibly Kim – hopefully not – there were six machines.

They looked like cramped cashpoints. They were self-checkouts, each gleaming with twenty-first-century newness, lasers – for barcode scanning – glowing from their bellies like demonic eyes.

Ada froze. So the human tills had been replaced. Adul was nowhere to be seen. Nor was Fatima. Kim was there though, standing by the last machine in the row. She looked more glum than Ada had ever seen her. In beige moments at home, when the ticking of the clock in the sitting room seemed textured and malign, Ada liked to distract herself by marvelling at the herculean glumness of Supermarket Kim; a stringy thirty-year-old with turquoise pigtails and a reliably complicated constellation of spots on her face, who once told Ada in a rare two-minute confession that she lived over the shop with her mum, literally just above it, so she could take her breaks in bed with Nirvana on loud.

But now Kim was looking dejected. She was frozen on the spot like Ada, staring into the middle distance, the tip of one pigtail in her mouth. Only her lips were moving, ruminatively massaging the hair poking in, pulling more of it into her mouth as a camel might with a spear of grass.

Ada knew at once what Kim's brave new role was: to direct customers to the correct scanner. To check the IDs of the Magdalen schoolboys who ricocheted into the shop on Friday nights to pick up crisps and strawberry cider. To punch in her store manager code as and when required. To stoically rescan items that customers mis-scanned. To make sure that no one was logging pay-by-the-weight pistachios (expensive) as pay-by-the-weight peanuts (less expensive, but too salty). Kim was to stand by in silence, the green light of machines blinking enigmatically like Gatsby's pier, waiting for something to go wrong. If she was lucky the time would go fast.

Ada felt the bulk of a person move directly behind her. She realised she was just standing by the magazines with her rye bread, blocking the way. She stepped aside.

A young woman with pink hair and ripped jeans strode past her, carrying tea and a packet of crumpets. She seemed unfazed by the new checkouts. She went to the nearest one and scanned her items, throwing in a Twix at the last minute. Then she seemed to think better of it and put the Twix back on the shelf. She didn't notice Ada or Kim, who had shifted her weight and was pulling her other pigtail into her mouth with her lips. The young woman collected her receipt, stowed it carefully in a wallet and breezed towards the exit, leaving Ada agog at her nonchalance, infuriated by it, and envious too.

She realised she was dawdling. She also suspected she might be being melodramatic. This was modernity, that was all; she was just ageing, having trouble adjusting. This was what it meant to be a little old lady who lived on her own. She was playing her role so impeccably she should be proud of herself. These machines were the future: they were sensible and efficient, they would ease the queues that paralysed the shop's aisles, forcing customers to rotate around one another like arthritic dancers. If Michael were here, he'd encourage his wife to embrace the self-checkouts, to make a game of it. They'd miscategorise so many lemons as limes that Kim would have to come over to correct them, then they'd plead colour blindness and dodderiness and be forgiven.

Later, lying down on her bed in Swinburne Road with the curtains drawn, watching the mauve of her eyelids pop and blaze with frightful light, Ada realised it had been the combination of those two things that had set her off. On the one hand, the new machines, which meant a hardier kind of isolation, fewer opportunities for conversation and always, off camera, the chirrup and whirr of robotic presence nudging the human out. On the other, the lack of him there, the non-ness of Michael to frame the machines' arrival in a positive light. Ada hadn't realised how much she'd been relying on her daily trips to the shop on Iffley Road to supplement her human diet: Fatima's low laughs at the audacious predictability of Ada's groceries (milk, rye loaf, tuna, eggs); Adul's incomprehensible football babble (he supported West or East Ham); the other, less friendly shop attendants whose names Ada didn't know but who usually tossed a sentence or two her way, which she treasured and pocketed, and which kept her going until lunch. And irrefutably, no Michael with her to find advantages in the change, or see its funny side or, now she thought of it, as was equally possible, to rage at the implied job losses, at the obliteration of Fatima and Adul and the invasion of the machines even here, in their bour-geois corner of Oxford. Rage was better than her meek devastation, she realised, lying in her bed on Swinburne Road after she had burst into tears in the shop, by the magazines, waking even Kim from her trance.

It ended up being rather the event of both their days. Ada started crying and Kim took her turquoise pigtails out of her mouth. She came over to lift Ada tenderly from the ground where she'd sunk. She helped Ada out of the shop, as calmly as if this kind of breakdown happened regularly, and they stood by the lamp-post outside with the blue bike chained to it. They were silent for a time then had a quick chat, a light hug. Kim said that she would have to return inside and Ada nodded and left, bloodshot and embarrassed, to make the three-minute journey back to Swinburne Road and her yellow front door, which she unlocked with steady fingers, stepping through the dead house to the bedroom upstairs, listening all the while to the silence of the rooms around her and below her, as if even the walls were carpeted.

Chapter Two

'Swinburne Road?'

  'Yeah.'

  'Where's that again?'

  'Iffley.'

  'Near the fish and chip shop?'

  'Kinda. Closer to the supermarket.'

Eliza was shouting. She couldn't remember the name of the bar she'd ended up in but she liked it; it was badly lit and raucous, and the deal was, none of the drinks had set prices. The owner eyed you up, assessed from your demeanour, clothing and accent how much you could afford to pay for your whisky or whatever, and gave you a price. Most Oxford students – well-heeled southerners who couldn't hide their affluence as much as they tried to beneath Oxfam jackets – paid quite a bit, partly because the owner wanted them to stay away, preferring locals. But Eliza had learned long ago that she oozed hard-upness. Maybe it was in the angles of her face or her haircut, a pink bob she'd sliced herself, using her phone camera to check the neckline. Her Cumbrian accent probably helped, too; no one down here thought northerners had money. In any case, she'd paid £2 for every drink so far, and nothing for the olives, whereas the young woman Eliza was shouting her address at had dropped six quid for a vodka tonic.

Eliza had been at Oxford for five days now and was trying to throw herself into things. It was technically fresher's week, and you saw them everywhere – these shoals of children moving around the city uncertainly behind student volunteers tasked with taking them to this curry house or that club. Eliza was twenty-five but hadn't adjusted yet to not being unarguably young, and she was bemused to find herself noticing the roundness of the freshers' jawlines, the legibility of their unease. When she'd started her undergraduate course at Bath in 2009, had she looked as squashable? As cute?

The graduate equivalent of freshers' week was less of a thing. But Eliza was still going out as much as she could, beating down the reluctance that rose up her throat every night, ignoring the knowledge that she'd have a better night if she just, you know, stayed in bed. So here she was with Nat, an undergrad she'd met not three hours ago and had already kissed. They'd started talking in the smoking area of Cellar; Nat was mashed, she was pretty, she seemed to find Eliza funny. After four cigarettes on the trot, each drawn from the packet in Nat's backpack, they decided to go on to somewhere else. Nat ordered the cab; Eliza was grateful because she was skint. They kissed on the back seat like they were in *90210* and pressed their bodies into each other by the entrance to the bar. Nat grabbed Eliza's bum performatively, made her laugh. Now they were tucked in a corner by the window and their fingers kept brushing. Eliza's rough eczema hands were mannish, she felt, against Nat's cool soft brown ones, each painted silver at the end like she'd dipped them in melted necklaces.

'I'm more Summertown way,' Nat shouted over the music. 'I live with my parents.'

'Nice,' Eliza replied, as loudly. 'I've met a few grads who live there but the rent was mental so I didn't.'

'Yeah, the rent is mental.'

'I got a good deal where I am now.'

'Yeah?'

'Mm. There are building works going on. I'm the only tenant in the house – the whole thing is being redone, I think they found asbestos. They're gutting it. Except for my room. I'm there to make sure squatters don't move in.'

'D'you like it?'

'Yeah it's alright. It's not long to get into town.'

She brought Nat's fingers to her mouth and bit them lightly. Tasted salt.

'D'you get woken by builders?' Nat asked.

'Sometimes,' Eliza said. 'I try to be out the door by eight.' She considered adding that there was no hot water in her house. That she showered in the university gym along with the Varsity polo players coming back from training. That living on what was basically a building site meant getting used to a shit ton of dust, and that she'd taken to covering her narrow bed in a shroud of tarpaulin she'd found tangled by an Audi a few doors down; it stopped the particles of dirt from getting into her pillow and blankets. That she woke with a raw throat every morning and had to have lemon and water to loosen it.

But she didn't want to put Nat off, and anyway she was satisfied with how little she was paying for the room, how resourceful she'd been to find it: the developer, Nick, a local who'd got rich off the boom in Oxford property, had advertised the room deep in the bowels of a community Facebook page where he was clearly hoping the authorities wouldn't read it. Eliza had found the ad and called him at once; five minutes later the room was hers.

'God,' Nat bellowed. 'I'm never up as early as eight.'

Eliza smiled, shrugging. She thought about making a joke about early birds catching worms but realised it probably wouldn't be funny, so she said nothing. Nat started massaging her neck across the small table. Her arm was at a weird angle because of their seating positions but it felt good. Eliza told her so.

'You're doing a PhD, right? In Italian Lit?' Nat asked.

'Yep. Just started. They call it a DPhil for some reason. But yeah, basically I'm a creepy grad.'

Nat gave a mock scream of terror, like, 'Arghghgh!'

They laughed. The divide at Oxford between the undergraduate and graduate bodies was almost its own institution. Undergrads regarded doctorate and master's students as lank-haired dweebs who subsisted off lentil bakes and organic wine and who knew who the local councillors were. Grads pitied the littleness of the undergrads' world: their cliques, their debt, the lameness of their sporting societies, the shallowness of their academic programmes, the fact that they so seldom ventured outside the socially imposed perimeters of the city, never piercing through to real Oxford, its history, its politics, its less photogenic backwaters.

But sex was the great unifier. The principal lubricant of grad/undergrad fraternisation. It was socially acceptable, for instance, for an undergrad to pick up a grad on a night out or vice versa; it was even commended as a sign of openness. Maybe it would have been strange for a thirty-year-old physics researcher to hit on a fresher who had no idea of anything, but Nat wasn't a fresher and anyway, the codes were different in the queer scene; age was policed less, mattered less.

'So what's the DPhil actually on?' Nat asked. 'Wait, tell me when I'm back from the loo.'

She stood up and began to career to the bathroom, threading her slim body through the people crowding the bar. Eliza lost sight of her. She twisted to watch the road outside. A headlight bloomed white through the night. She swirled her drink. The ice tinkled. She decided she must look like a woman in an Edward Hopper painting; her back ramrod straight, her face unreadable, her body inscrutable beneath her black shift dress. 'I've been everywhere and seen everything and done everything,' she thought in an American accent. After this Nat would want to come back to Eliza's bedroom; hers wasn't ideal because she lived with her family. Eliza envisaged opening her bedroom door with Nat behind her kneading her neck or her earlobe. Eliza hadn't slept with anyone since Ruby; she wasn't sure, even eighteen months later, if she was ready, or maybe she'd just been conditioned to question whether she could be 'ready' for sex by magazines and TV. Whatever. She and Nat would tip into Eliza's bedroom. They'd be drunker then, they'd have kissed again on the pavement. Eliza would swoop at the tarpaulin on her bed, apologise for the sawdusty smell of the room and the mugs and the heaters and the cardboard on one of the windows. Nat would say she didn't mind, add that she liked Eliza's books or something and they'd kiss more, trying to demonstrate their range and desire, now lighter now harder, maybe this time against the bedroom door.

No, no. Not tonight. Eliza stood up. She placed her glass decisively back on the table. It would leave a shining circle on the wood. She put on her anorak, popped one final olive into her mouth and made her way to the door.

Chapter Three

Swinburne Road was like the trip step of Iffley, the southern patch of Oxford arranged around the ancient village that gave the area its name. Most residents didn't know the road was there. Even those who'd grown up in Oxford and remained there their whole lives struggled to place it. They'd frown when Ada said she lived there, narrowing their eyes as if their pension depended upon them successfully incanting the road's longitudinal coordinates, then finally they'd give up. Everyone knew the roads on either side – Fairacres and Donny Bridge – but Swinburne eluded all.

Partly it was the road's shape. Like a sloppy 'L', with a kind of crescent at one tip that obscured the entrance. Its unremarkable houses were to blame too: not the tart brick terraces that lined so many of the posh streets of Iffley but an assortment of white and beige semis. You could have been in virtually any middle-class suburb in England. There weren't many trees. The lamp-posts lining the road had once been notable – after sunset they glowed like hot coals, drenching the road in gold – but then the council replaced the orange bulbs with white ones and even night-time lost its mystique.

But there were worse places to live. There were several pubs within ten minutes' walk, an excellent fish and chip shop, a café and of course the supermarket, even if Ada was resolved never to shop there again. A few days after she burst into tears at the checkouts, she forced herself to go in to see if she could hack it; she'd been raised to get back on a horse if ever she fell off one. But it was too depressing. She rushed out of the shop almost the moment she walked in, deciding she would make her way through bits and pieces from the freezer until she found somewhere better to buy her groceries.

When she moved to Oxford with her husband a decade ago they hadn't put much thought into the address. They were following a job – Michael's – and by then Ada was writing poetry full-time, which was virtually as ill-paid as not having a job at all. His decision to swap a professorship in Manchester for one in Oxford had not been hard: already in his sixties, he'd been bemused to be offered a post in the prestigious Italian department. He'd not dreamed, like a few of his Manchester colleagues, of making it to Oxbridge – the Premier League of British academia – he was inclined to be content and not to salivate over hypotheticals or dreaming spires. Yet he wasn't lacking in imagination either, or ambition and a sense of adventure, and the offer piqued him, when it came.

Ada, for her part, was not surprised that Oxford came knocking. Michael was the darling of Manchester's modern languages department; he wrote a book every two years, and each was well received by the top peer-reviewed journals. He spoke on Radio 4 about the importance of literature and languages. His classes, on giants from D'Annunzio to Croce, Pirandello to Moravia, were the best-rated in undergraduate surveys; his lectures the most packed. Ada used to sit in sometimes – that was how they'd met; she'd watched a panel he was on at Exeter all those years ago and he'd directed his words entirely, or so it had seemed, at her. When she went to his lectures in Manchester, she saw the way the undergrads around her leaned forward to listen, tapping at their laptops to ensure his sentences lodged uncreased in the annals of their word processors. But it had always been a skill of Michael's, or his peculiar curse, not to notice his own quality. It was a form of tone-deafness: you could have bellowed words of affirmation at his face and he wouldn't have taken them in. And so the summons from Oxford came, for him if for nobody else, out of the blue.

Ada was happy to move. She liked Manchester but Oxford too would surely be pleasant. She packed up their life and friendships with goodwill. The books and art and crockery came with them; the furniture, bought for nothing in charity shops, stayed behind. They sold Ivy Cottage and the stable next door and found the house in Swinburne Road through someone in the Oxford Portuguese department who was off to UCLA. Got in before it was put on the market. They were lucky: Ada sold her shares, Michael scraped out the last of his savings and they found a way.

The day after moving in, they walked to the hardware shop on Magdalen Road and bought some paint. Michael chose the colour. Ada dug out two aprons and they spent their first afternoon in Oxford turning their new front door blistering yellow. It was an overcast day in August but warm enough. Michael managed to leave a kidney-shaped palm print by the knocker.

'Darling,' Ada rebuked him, her voice gentle. You could see the lines of his skin in the paint; the patch looked matte, while the rest of the door glistened wetly.

'When I die, you'll have something to remember me by,' Michael replied. Ada rolled her eyes but didn't paint over the mark. They spent the rest of the afternoon in the garden, picking cherries from the tree that had been kept in life by academics passing through the house before them. There were nettles around the base of the trunk. Ada cut them back, saving the younger leaves for soup. That night, she and Michael read and ate in the sitting room, cardboard boxes all around them like Tetris blocks.

Now Ada lived on Swinburne Road alone. Under the stairs, she remembered sometimes, was the tin of yellow paint; they'd only used half. After the door was finished, Ada suggested they throw the remainder away: they certainly couldn't use it on the indoor walls, their eyeballs would peel. But Michael insisted they keep the paint. It would do, he said, to jolly up the bench under the cherry tree.

They never got round to it, of course, and cast the tin into the cupboard. There it was still. Ada wondered sometimes if the gloop inside had hardened into a kind of radioactive spherical brick. She hadn't touched the paint since Michael had died. She was afraid of its distinctive tang, of its brightness.

In the months afterwards, when Ada felt less like her heart was being pulled from her chest through the small of her back, she came to be rather proud of how ordinarily her husband had died. At the kitchen table. On a flat morning in March 2014. A paper open on the table; a fiendish sudoku half done, biro in hand.

As his heart stopped beating, Ada was in a deep sleep upstairs. It thinned out as morning wove itself around her new situation. At eight, she woke properly and sat up. Soon she would hear the muffle of Michael's steps in the kitchen as he poured milk into a jug and prepared a cafetière to bring up to her. There were no such sounds today but that too was routine: sometimes Michael went for a morning walk to the river to watch the rowers pump past on the water. Most of all, he liked seeing the cox at the tip of the boat, bundled up and tiny, her voice – it was often a she – strident in the dawn air.

Ada found her reading glasses and shook out a fortnight-old copy of the *London Review of Books*. She picked up where she'd left off the night before: column three in a piece about the vagaries of the Arab Spring. For a while she tried following the thread of the article but it was no good, she'd need to start from the beginning; even the names of the movements' leaders were getting mixed up and she couldn't remember who was uprising against whom. Finally she cast the paper aside, feeling thick. She found her dressing gown and went downstairs. On mornings when Michael went to the river, she made them boiled eggs. On his return, they would eat them together in the garden, their laps weighed down with blankets they piled by the back door.

But this morning was different. Ada entered the kitchen to find Michael seated, not filling the kettle or scattering coffee beans all over the counter. His forehead was on the wood of the kitchen table as if, Ada thought unaccountably as she observed him, he'd been assassinated from behind by a Soviet spy. He was not moving. His coffee was warm. Heart attack, she discovered later. Killed instantly. Seventy-five. Younger than many but not so young Ada felt she had the right to complain.

Ada sat with his body for an hour, then surprised herself by standing up to call her sister. She spoke plainly, delivering the salient points of the story with no wet breakdowns. Eve came up to Oxford at once on the train. She lived in Brighton with her daughter Gwen, who'd been left by her husband eighteen months before. There were grandchildren: Ali and Tom, six and seven, beautiful creatures with white-blonde hair. They were growing too fast, Eve said.

She turned out to be a great help: emailing authorities from Michael's old computer, buying sleeping pills and bread, arranging for a note to be put in the paper. Ada sensed vaguely that she would come to appreciate her sister's efforts at a later point. She liked Eve though they were not close: as children they'd been sent to different schools – Ada was saved by the local grammar, Eve failed the eleven-plus so went to the comp. In their separate tracks they lost the intimacy of childhood. At one time they'd looked so similar they were mistaken for twins and they used to spend their time doing twin things, pretending to be one another, drawing matching moles on their cheekbones.

'It's a strange thing,' Ada informed her at the memorial.

Michael had had the good grace to die outside of term time so there had been no issues persuading Balliol, his college, to host the service. A hundred people came.

'What's a strange thing?' Eve asked, holding Ada's arm.

They were walking out of the chapel through the Fellows' Garden. The day was full of light and the spring flowerbeds, maintained by the college gardeners, were chattering with colour.

'Death,' Ada said. 'It's strange.'

They were nearly at the Buttery before either of them spoke again.

'D'you mean it's strange because you keep expecting Michael to walk through the door?' Eve asked softly. 'One minute he's here, the next he's . . .'

'I suppose,' Ada replied. She laughed. 'I suppose there's that. Of course. One does expect him to just turn up. But I'm also having trouble gripping what it is exactly that I've lost.'

During the memorial service, one of the organ pedals had jammed, sending a note resounding through the chapel like a foghorn. Everyone stopped singing 'How Great Thou Art' and whipped round excitedly to ogle the organist. The few children in the chapel clamped their hands to their ears and stared dolefully up at the ceiling. The note only ceased when the Provost hurried up to the organ and stamped on the offending pedal, dislodging it.

Michael, Ada knew, would have loved the disruption. He wasn't a believer but he'd been brought up in Dublin and accepted that religion ran deep in him like one of those secret springs beneath a city. There was no use resisting: unless he went to church regularly, he got twitchy. He recited his prayers; he inhaled the pew musk of cathedral buildings; he kneeled on their flagstones. But a hatred of it all ran deep in him too, alongside the tenderness, and he brought Quality Street to mass, disrobing golden pennies at the quietest moment. An organ acting up was just the sort of low-level rebellion he respected; he would have loved to hear such a cock-up at his own memorial.

'I get sudden stabs of him,' Ada said. 'Like when the organ broke in the chapel, I could imagine his reaction and I knew fully, for a second, the person that he was. But the rest of the time . . .'

She shrugged. Eve squeezed her hand. Ada could feel her nails printing half-moons into the palm of her hand.

Ada waded through the rest of the day as if enveloped in her own personal smog. Occasionally people or words pierced through: 'a wonderful man', 'I can't tell you just how . . .', 'the kindest'. When she looked up to link the sounds to their speaker, invariably they'd been reclaimed by the crowd. She was left holding the phrases in her hands, carefully, like injured birds.

She was glad of one thing: that she'd had the foresight to demand, on the invitations that were sent out all over the country, that guests wear yellow. Most obeyed but the lure of tradition was strong too, and they kowtowed to it by supplementing their vibrant clothing with black. Throughout the service, and at the bleak little reception afterwards, Ada had the impression she was in some sort of hive and that most of the bees were jostling towards her to buzz their condolence. The daffodil season was cresting too and every chest was pinned with flowers, their luminous heads nodding gravely in the close air.

Eve left for Oxford railway station the day after Michael's memorial. As the taxi waited for her outside, she asked if Ada would like to come with her. Stay with the family in Brighton for a while, be surrounded by noise and youth. There was space and Ali and Tom needed constant attention; there was no need for her to remain alone if she didn't want to.

Ada listened to the offer. At nineteen she'd learned that she would never bear children, and being around them for prolonged periods unsettled her even now. She didn't know who to be, what to make of their stares and sudden emergencies. She liked Gwen and Eve and the children but she missed Michael too much, she realised, to let go of their Oxford life yet, of their home, of its precise configuration of lamps and delicate ornaments. She'd kept herself together so far, partly to respect Eve's time and care. She wanted to luxuriate in her grief now. She said she'd be fine staying where she was. She said she needed to start afresh on her own, if such a thing were possible. She said no.

Eve nodded, kissed her sister on the cheek, stroked her hair and left. They spoke some time later, as leaves were nosing from branch joints in the cherry tree, until Ali leapt onto her grandmother's lap and the phone fell to the ground. Ada disconnected before Eve picked up the handset.

Chapter Four

Eliza had never ghosted anyone before. As she steeled herself to do it – to walk away from the bar while Nat was in the bathroom – she suddenly realised she hated herself for even considering it. It would be embarrassingly melodramatic to just cut and run while Nat was having a pee. She returned inside, sat down and crossed her legs as if nothing had happened. Nat came back from the bathroom. Her lipstick looked shiny. She didn't notice Eliza's hair was damp from the rain outside.

The night didn't turn out the way Eliza expected. She and Nat kissed for a bit where they were sat but it wasn't the sort of bar to get handsy in, so they soon felt weird about it and gave up. Eliza bought them more drinks. She stopped comparing Nat to Ruby, then stopped worrying about whether Nat would come back to Swinburne Road with all the implications that carried; instead she listened to what Nat was saying. All of it was interesting and most of it was funny. Nat was in her second year of history and was leading a group of students working to end university examinations, which they believed favoured 'peacock thinkers' trained to show off under pressurised conditions.

Privileged white men performed better in time-constrained situations than women did, so the reasoning went, only they didn't know as much; they winged it as they had done for fucking millennia. Exams were bigoted; off with their heads.

Eliza didn't think exams were bigoted but she did like the term 'peacock thinkers', and told Nat so. They said it to one another again and again in different accents, laughing and clinking their glasses.

Then Nat said she'd better get home. Eliza was surprised and relieved. She waited with her for the bus – she'd not imagined Nat was the bus type – and walked home. It was raining still but some of the weight had come off it. She pulled the toggles of her anorak hood tight, leaving a slit around her eyes. Her shift dress felt dry and warm underneath. When she got home, the buildings on Swinburne Road were dark. It was two in the morning and felt like it must be everywhere. Only the house opposite Eliza's, with the front door that glowed yellow in daylight, seemed alert; a room upstairs was lit. Eliza could make out the silhouette of a person standing by the window behind thin curtains. She watched the figure for a moment from the pavement, then fished her key out of her backpack, shouldered her way past the bags of cement in the front garden and opened the back door, the only way in. She walked up to her bedroom, her throat rough from the dirty air, and curled up on her bed.

When Eliza awoke the next morning she was momentarily disorientated by the crisp-packet crinkle of the tarpaulin she was lying on. Her phone was dead. It took her a minute to remember she'd left her bike outside

Cellar, the club she'd met Nat in. Footage from the night came back to her in bursts of movement and sound. She was still in her dress. She stood up and looked at her reflection, putting her phone on charge.

Her mascara looked clumpy but it would do. She gulped down some tea left over in a mug and pulled on her Nikes. New College, the college she was attached to as a grad student, was half an hour's walk away. If she wanted to buy a coffee before meeting the bursar, she'd need to jog. She crammed a mini-muffin into her mouth from the packet by the window, and left.

Outside, she looked curiously at number twenty-four opposite. She didn't know who lived there; Eliza knew none of her neighbours, but she remembered how ghostly the house had appeared the night before, its shadows and lit upper room, the person she'd seen behind the curtain. Now the building seemed ordinary, inconsequential. She swung her backpack on and began to run half-heartedly towards the centre.

Eliza first went around New College with her dad, Rich, a couple of months before getting an offer. They woke up at five and hammered down the A6 in the Volvo. Eliza's mother Flora didn't come – she and Rich weren't close, and the last time Eliza had talked to her mother, they'd argued: Flora had heard that Eliza had won £500 in an essay competition and she'd asked for a slice of it. Eliza had said no and they'd not communicated since.

Oxford was about a five-hour drive from Carlisle. Eliza didn't get carsick so much as car-trodden; more than twenty minutes in one made her feel weak and insipid, like she'd given blood. Rich wanted to chat the whole way down, to stop off for McDonald's and service station sprees, for the journey to become one big road trip. Eliza knew she ought to want those things, that it was lovely of Rich to be making the effort to drive her, that the petrol was expensive and he could have been finishing the Kanes' garden, but she couldn't bring herself to be warm and gossipy, especially after the dawn start.

'Crash Test Dummies or Meatloaf?' Rich asked eventually, holding up two battered albums, one hand on the steering wheel.

Eliza considered. 'Dummies, please,' she said, looking out of the window. She preferred to see the countryside from a car than to be actually in it. She kept her eyes peeled for walkers going through the fields: she liked imagining the idyll of their lives, their Agas and the trim dogs they named after characters in Shakespeare.

In Oxford they tried to see fifteen colleges in about six hours. Rich had left school at sixteen and was exhilarated; Eliza, not so much. She wanted to get into the university – its Italian department was excellent; if she completed her doctorate here, a career in academia might be within reach – but she couldn't untangle the knot of revulsion she felt at the whole Oxford shtick: the gardens, the wanky cello concertos advertised everywhere, the plinths and dead-eyed statues and rowing oars on display in college bars. It was like Bath on steroids. Rich wanted to banter with every porter, admire every oak, take Earl Grey and scones in every hokey tearoom lining the streets of the city centre. He kept squeezing Eliza's shoulders as they walked through this archway or that chapel, and soon the colleges and faculties garbled into one, a great bonfire of mahogany and wealth and honey-coloured stone.

'Why aren't you excited?' Rich kept asking. 'We're at Hogwarts! You love Hogwarts!'

This was true: Eliza had spent much of her childhood in Rowling's castle, watching Ron stuff his face with fried eggs in the Great Hall, dropping in on Hagrid near the forest. 'But it's like a Disneyland version of Hogwarts,' she tried to explain. 'It's like Hogwarts is the real thing and this is the fake version. None of the buildings look real. Even the cyclists look like they're actors in a period drama.' As she spoke, an Eddie Redmayne lookalike wobbled past on a Dutch cycle, a bunch of flowers in his front basket.

Rich shook his head, smiling. He didn't bother trying to understand. He'd begun to measure the difference between himself and his only child when she was four years old and it had only widened with every year. He was pragmatic, positive, robust; Eliza was puzzling, hurtable, prone to emotional crises Rich couldn't unravel. When Eliza got a scholarship to a boarding school in Surrey aged thirteen, his sense of alienation from the young woman she was becoming grew still further. She would return home from St Antonia's in the holidays and every time she felt more unknowable, more distant, and always less willing to reveal who her posh new friends were, what the teaching was like, whether it was a pain to go to chapel every day. Then her accent started to deaden; one Christmas Rich teased her about it, said she was talking like Princess Margaret, and Eliza didn't say a word for the rest of the day. He learned the next term at a parent-teacher weekend that Eliza was being hassled because of her accent: other girls hid her

belongings, made her say words like "Ow do' and 'butter'
until she could get her stuff back. Rich tried to persuade
Eliza to come back north, shine in a less academic school,
cut the snobs loose. She said no; the teaching was too good
to pass up. She knew that her father loved her extravagantly
and was proud of her difference from him, of her single-
mindedness and intellect, and that when he could only
look at Eliza and wonder at the fact that he had not a clue
what she was thinking, he felt a strange fizzle of joy, that
he could have played a hand in creating such an enigma.

They visited Oxford out of term time. Most students
they saw were grads. But there were one or two younger
students still in town too who'd stuck around to do tour-
guiding or 'telethon' as they wearily called it, where they
were paid to call up alumnae and press for donations. The
best tour they had was of Trinity College, where an Irish
student called Saoirse spent ten minutes showing them
the libraries, the music rooms and a few 'sets' (or as she
translated for them: bedrooms with living rooms attached).
She seemed so perfectly bored by the exigencies of the
tour that Eliza couldn't help but admire her; there was
something ghoulish in the happy-clappy students wearing
college stash and going wild for the Wi-Fi speed.

After a sandwich outside the Radcliffe Camera, they
visited New College. There were no guides hanging around
the entrance, waiting for prospective students to show
around, so Eliza and Rich visited the college unaccom-
panied. Rich read aloud from a pamphlet he'd picked up
by the chapel. By then it was raining softly, a breath sort
of rain, and the grass in the quadrangles shone as if every
blade had been licked.

'New College was founded in 1379 by William of Wykeham,' Rich read from beneath his umbrella. 'It often ranks first in the Norrington Tables. Lize, that means it's academically top dollar – you'll fit in!'

They chose random staircases to climb. The doors were heavy and old. Once, they found themselves in a student's unlocked bedroom; clothes were all over the floor and a snake was looped around itself in a glass tank. Rich and Eliza stared around, then the student himself appeared in a towel, his white torso sparkling from a shower. They apologised and beat a retreat to the second quadrangle, to meet with New College's head of Italian. His name was Davide Baleotti. He looked about forty, with boyish tufts of black hair. He'd grown up partly in the Congo and had gone down with polio; he moved now with a stick and a degree of awkwardness. Baleotti was well known in the tight-knit world of twentieth-century Italian literary criticism; Eliza admired him so much she felt nervous to see him in the flesh. He was, like her, an Elsa Morante fanatic, and reading him dissect writers Eliza thought she knew back to front was like walking along a forest path you loved, and finding it suddenly illuminated by lances of sunlight, motes of air swirling in the brightness.

Baleotti offered them the sofa by the fireplace. 'Your name?' he asked, resting his stick on his knees.

'Eliza Fender,' Eliza said.

She told him she knew his work; that she had studied Italian at Bath and was looking to start a PhD at Oxford in the autumn. She wondered if she was gabbling, Rich often told her off for her 'millennial mumble', and anyway most Italians had trouble with any accent north of London.

But Baleotti seemed to understand what she'd said. He launched himself upwards haphazardly and started rummaging around on his desk.

'This is your paper!' he cried. 'You are the Eliza Fender who did this?'

Eliza squinted. Then she grinned. The professor was waving a copy of the latest *Italian Literary Review*; two months ago the journal had printed her essay on Primo Levi.

'Yeah,' she said, not knowing what else to say.

Baleotti whacked the paper with his hand, so enthusiastically he looked almost furious.

'It is brilliant,' he cried. Shouted, really. 'It has been on my mind ever since the journal came out!'

Eliza felt her pleasure at his words unfurl luxuriously within her. She nodded and smiled and thanked him, Rich looking on in throes of excitement. Baleotti said that he would be seeing her in the autumn 'come what may'.

They tried to leave. Baleotti blocked the door, telling Eliza he had some books that she'd enjoy. In a great burst of energy he began acrobating over the columns of tomes teetering on this side table and that chest of drawers, and before long Eliza could barely see for the pile of books and DVDs that he'd put in her arms. She rested her chin on the top item, an eco-feminist reading of *Zeno's Conscience*, thanked the professor for his time and left, Rich in reluctant tow.

'He thought you were brilliant,' he marvelled as they walked back through the quad.

Eliza said nothing. The paper Baleotti had remembered

was a reading of Primo Levi's own readings, an explor-
ation of the books that had shaped him as a writer. She
wanted to continue working on Levi over the course of her
doctorate. That seemed possible, suddenly, and desirable,
and for the first time in months she felt puckish with a
sense of her own talent. She might have a direction at last.

They made their way to the Volvo. Rich was due in
the Kanes' garden the following morning. On the way
up, Eliza looked out for walkers again, for the bound of
their animals, the quiet conversations she could almost
overhear and certainly invent, about Russian novels they
were reading and the hot fish pies they were planning on
cooking for tea.

Chapter Five

One morning in October, Ada noticed that something had changed in the house opposite. The previous occupants had sold it to a developer who was gutting the building, but now someone seemed to have moved into the bedroom upstairs. Ada wondered vaguely if the new occupant was a squatter. Her interest in the street, once keener than she'd have freely admitted, was now minimal. Without Michael, Swinburne Road seemed cored.

She was reading on her armchair when she looked up, detecting activity in the house opposite. She rushed to the window, intrigued in spite of herself. A young woman was walking into the building, using a battered side door Ada assumed led to the garden. She watched, gripped, trying to judge whether the young woman was moving with any degree of furtiveness. Her pink hair certainly made her look like a trespasser. But no: it seemed she had a key. Ada felt slightly ashamed of herself. A second later, the girl was inside the house. Ada returned to her reading, pleased that something had happened and that she'd witnessed it for once, and wondering why it was that young people liked to dye their hair such eye-watering shades of unnatural.

That afternoon she roused herself for the first time in months to make a loaf of soda bread. She used to bake lots; feeding Michael had been almost a job in its own right, and above all he liked soda bread, preferably straight from the oven. As it was baking she composed letters she'd been meaning to write for weeks: one to Eve, her sister in Brighton, and a couple to friends who lived hundreds of miles from Oxford. She was out of practice: she received fewer letters now. In the weeks following Michael's death she'd never known post like it. That was what happened to newly minted widows, she learned; people liked to mark the occasion, to uncap fountain pens they rarely used and do something with stamps left over from Christmas.

In all, within a month of Michael's death she received sixty-two cards. At the time she wanted to know whether that was a decent headcount but she didn't have anyone in a similar situation to ask. She displayed the cards on mantel-pieces around the house, patiently putting them back up again when draughts tipped them shut. Letters weren't the only thing: the secretary of the Italian department, Alessandra, came round five weeks after the memorial to sort out bits of admin. She brought wine and a bundle of printed-out emails. 'These were sent to me and some of the rest of us in the department,' she said, once the worst of the paperwork was out of the way. 'They're about Mike. They're emails from his students, mostly. I thought you might want physicals.'

'Young people send letters less now,' Ada nodded.

'Exactly,' Alessandra replied. She was about thirty, from Córdoba, a kind woman with light brown eyes and jangly bracelets. Ada imagined Michael had spoken about her before. She looked at the A4 sheets. They didn't look like much.

'Are they nice messages?' she asked.

'They're lovely,' Alessandra said.

They spoke for a while about other things; funding issues, the department, building works dragging out near the faculty building. Ada found the conversation quite exhausting. Alessandra told her that she could come back to visit Ada if she wanted her to. She asked in a rush how she was managing; whether she had a 'support network'; if she was writing poetry (Ada's last collection, *Things Considered*, had come out a few months before Michael's death). Ada assured her she was doing fine, that she got out most days, that she wasn't writing but that it would come, that it was a blessing having the river nearby. The rowers. The houseboats. The fussy cygnets.

'Do you have plans to move out?' Alessandra asked, as she stood up to leave.

Ada looked at her blankly. She felt a coldness encase her chest. 'Why would I?' she asked.

Alessandra looked uncomfortable. They were in the kitchen. Alessandra's eyes flicked to the table; she must have known they'd been sitting where Michael had died.

'Well . . .' she murmured. 'Perhaps – it's a big house, and . . .'

'I'm going to stay put, thank you,' Ada said curtly.

Alessandra nodded. She was embarrassed. They walked to the front door. Ada extended a hand for her to shake. Alessandra pulled her into a hug. It was apologetic and brief, an angular affair of elbows and cheekbones. Ada felt invaded, she wished her body had been left to itself. Once Alessandra had smiled one final time, she left. Ada stood for a moment in the hallway, her eyes closed. Alessandra's bracelets tinkled down Swinburne Road as she walked to her car. Ada double-locked the front door and returned to the sitting room. The curtains needed closing and the lamps switching on.

Once the lighting was right, she set herself up in her armchair to read the emails. Leaving them to fester would be childish. To prevent herself from breaking down she tried to make it fun. She looked out for emails that were sent at night, looking to correlate lateness with incoherence. When she saw one sent by a Professor Macdougall from Dundee, she read it aloud in a Scottish accent. She laughed aloud at one email, which was by accident or intent in iambic pentameter. But the messages of goodwill quickly began to slur into one. Condolences were the same as sympathies, really; it was all very thoughtful, it was all very heartfelt. Lots of people were calling Michael Mike, which was vexing, and referring to his character traits in such slack-jawed ways that the words seemed unmoored from the man Ada was looking for in the emails. And none of the messages could address the issue that Michael wasn't in the kitchen at that moment, warming up yesterday's tortilla or watering the basil plant. Ada felt, for the first time since summers she half remembered as a child – when one week had the languor of a hundred – what it was like to witness time passing. To catch it in the act. It was like the last day of school, when you were burning to leave home and your dustball village but you didn't know where to go or who to become, and your life suddenly sprang out in front of you, vast and improbable.

*

The soda bread was ready. Ada paused the letter she was writing to Angus, a friend of hers from university who now lived in Liverpool with his family, and went to the kitchen to get the loaf out. The whole house was buttery with the scent of it. Ada knew it was the smell of contentment, of domesticity embraced. She put the loaf on the counter and sat at the table and wept. It was absurd to have made a loaf for herself: what would she do, eat it slice by slice until it went stale? She went to the bathroom to splash her face. By the loo was Michael's pile of pun books, their covers curling from the humidity of the room.

'You need to buck up your ideas, young lady,' Ada thought sternly as she looked at her sopping reflection. She and Michael had called each other 'young man' and 'young lady' ever since they'd reached their sixties: the more their skin crinkled and thinned, the funnier the joke became. 'Enough of this self-indulgence,' Ada continued. She gave her cheek a wet wake-up slap. It stung. The silence of the house reimposed itself. She walked upstairs, flexing her fingers to chase off the arthritis gathering in her knuckles, found her hairbrush and hacked it through her grey waves. She saw that the young woman who'd just moved into the house opposite was in her bedroom too, reading a book by the window. The sight of her consoled Ada for a moment. That woman, for all her youth, was on her own too. Once her hair was sorted, she cast about for something to do. But what did one do? It would be absurd to write a poem now; about what? She was in her nightdress, yet there was no obvious reason to change. She sat at the dressing table and watched herself watch herself. Her blue eyes looked greyer than they used to and she didn't have as many lashes as she'd once had. She thought perhaps that her cheeks had hollowed in the past few weeks; ho-hum. Once, Michael would have come up behind her, slipped his broad, warm hands under the cotton of the nightdress. She took it off and made herself take in her bare torso in the mirror, trying to look without contempt. Her chest was criss-crossed with lines, her collarbones practically cawed. She didn't know how to love the body she'd not thought of for years; that had been his business. She'd never had much in the way of breasts. He hadn't minded. She supposed she should be glad she'd stayed slender but she longed, as she looked mutely at her reflection, for there to be more of herself, more volume, more proof that she still took up space. The bed sprawled gigantically behind her; at night she was sleeping clamped to the left edge as she'd done since the start of her marriage, as if expecting one of Michael's legs to rocket out into the middle of the mattress. She picked up the nightdress and folded it up, found her gardening trousers and pulled them on. She would spend the day at the river, watching the rowers pull by.

Ada hadn't always been as isolated. The first few months after Michael's death were surprisingly busy. Once the memorial was over, people seemed to think she ought to be encouraged to cultivate a social life. Her first public outing was at Thomas Thomson's, the feted statistician, who invited her to dinner at his lodge. He'd been a friend of Michael's, a port and snuff sort of man, but nice, in his way. Ada was placed between a physics professor and a prepubescent choral scholar. Everyone present had clearly been briefed about her bereavement, so she wasn't asked a single question about herself. She ran out of things to say so she thought up topics of conversation by moving down the alphabet. She wasn't convinced it was a great strategy. After dinner, while waiting for Thomas's wife to give her a lift back to Iffley, Ada noticed that she felt exhausted, for all the world as if she'd spent the night doing vigorous exercise. She was out of social shape, that much was evident, but as she ran through the evening in her mind, doing what she and Michael always called the post-match analysis, she realised that she had had a horrible time.

More invitations followed. Will Grodz, a Petrarch specialist, alerted Ada to events happening at the university. Lecturers in the department remembered to send invitations to Swinburne Road. Everyone, Ada could see, was making the effort to perform their compassion. She was perplexed and rather amused. She found that it was possible, even enjoyable, to drag her ancient Clinique lipstick over her lips and taxi to the centre of town on a Tuesday evening. Having an event to attend allowed her to tick the day off as rather a success, whether she enjoyed herself or not. She would stand alone in some college atrium or lecture theatre, drinking warm white wine as bowls of vegetable crisps emptied around her. The room would fill with the roar of polite conversation. Sometimes there were canapés. Ada would stand by the drinks table, watching the waiters pivot in their funereal black. They moved gracefully. They were young and often from Portugal. There was beauty in the crystal grid lines made by the glasses on the tabletop.

Drinks were followed by a lecture or panel on some obscure tangle of interest in the Western canon. Many of the speakers were invited from other universities, some from as far as New Zealand, including once, a curly-haired chap who gave an unexpectedly groovy talk on the need for a 'politics of love'. Ada always sat at the front, handbag on lap, where there was never any danger of her not being able to hear. Mostly, she thought, it was a load of bollocks. Initially intelligible language soon gave way to academese. She couldn't make sense of it. Everyone seemed to be obsessed by gender; she didn't understand why. The lecturers spoke incessantly about the Male Gaze, unless they were referring to the Male Gays – it wasn't always evident. All art that looked doltish to Ada was declared to be erotic and aesthetic; all writers or sculptors in question were depicted as maverick disruptors ahead of their time.

She began to fear that it was she who was the cynical old bat, she the plodding pragmatist. Michael had been allergic to the jargon of the university public speaking circuit – his inner Irish iconoclast would come charging forth and he and Ada used to hold hands throughout the lecture, squeezing one another's fingers when they heard a buzzword they hated: 'liminal', 'framing', 'praxis'. Ada took to holding hands with herself, squeezing her own fingers at moments where before she would have squeezed Michael's. She considered her behaviour half pitiful, half comic; good material for a poem if ever she found the energy to write one. And in any case, it was comfortable and nice, holding your own hands. She hadn't known that until Michael's death, or not known it with clarity.

Ada had met a number of Oxford teaching staff over the years and some usually made the effort to come over to her when the talk was finished. She answered their questions as competently as she could, then, duty fulfilled, whoever had come over found an excuse to run for it: they got a top-up of booze or said they needed to relieve the babysitter. Ada saw her own solitude reconfigure itself at these moments. She was impressed by its instinct for self-preservation. She wondered if she would ever recover the ability to be engaging in conversation. Perhaps she should read some of Michael's pun books; reel in new friends with wordplay.

Just as she started turning invitations down, another of Michael's colleagues' grief took centre stage: Charlie Lanes, the Baudelaire critic, lost his forty-year-old wife to cervical cancer. It was a tragic, dreadful thing. He had three children under six and in the face of such biblical injustice people forgot the Irish professor's widow and her more plausible loss. It was assumed that Ada had friends in the area to look out for her, a baby boomer's garden to tend, grandchildren to dote on. People cringed at the notion of calling Ada up (what even was her landline) or worse, of arriving unannounced at her house to do anything so frightful as 'check in'.

Women of that generation loathed the mawkish, so the interior argument went. Better to concentrate on Charlie and his misfortune. Leave Mrs Robertson be. She was old. Her husband had been old. Death was the lot of the old.

Chapter Six

'I'm Eliza, hi.'

'Hey, I'm Eliza.'

'New College. You?'

'I'm Angelica. No sorry, you're Angelica. You just said that. Ha ha. Sorry. I'm actually Eliza.'

'You. Eliza? I mean – Eliza. You?'

Eliza thought she might have introduction fatigue. Or an allergy to people. She was seven days into her grad course at Oxford and felt completely wiped out. She'd snuck back to Swinburne Road to collapse onto her bed after a talk on student finance, and the temptation to remain on her front forever, her face plunged into her pillow, was strong. Even now, when she knew her room was empty, she felt it was crowded with people; that if she flipped onto her back a group of students and tutors in white coats would be leaning over her ghoulishly, taking notes on her condition or prepping needles to jab into her. Her night out with Nat felt like months ago. Eliza had not heard from her since she waved goodbye to her on the bus. She didn't know if she should message first; she was the older one but maybe that didn't mean anything. She didn't know the rules. At Bath, Ruby had taken charge from the off, been the one to ask Eliza out originally and then set the tone and rhythm of their communication after that. Eliza tried not to care that Nat hadn't got in touch but she did, and was surprised and a little excited that she cared, that she kept trying to remember the texture of Nat's voice, the stuff they had talked about, the shape of her nails when she brought them to her hair.

At least, Eliza told herself, she had a surfeit of distractions – virtually every waking minute since she'd met Nat had been spent pinballing between library inductions and faculty tours and consent workshops and status registrations, and every event presented a fresh onslaught of faces to take in, as if the people factory had gone into overdrive and was dumping excess stock in Oxford quadrangles. The hardest bit was remembering which name matched which subject and which origin story: was that brunette Sarah the volcanology researcher, or was she actually Sheera the psychogeographer from Wisconsin?

There was a silver lining: Eliza suspected, and had it confirmed by a welfare officer who cornered her at a welcome drinks, that everyone was 'going through the same thing' and that it was 'entirely normal' to find the start of your grad course 'overwhelming'. A more useful discovery was that talking about the difficulty of memorising new names was a sure-fire way of having a decent conversation. 'I'll probably not remember what you're called,' Eliza would say, and the eyes of whoever she was standing in front of would light up manically. 'Ooh but I'll not remember your name either!' they'd cry, and thus a more honest exchange could be attempted. The trouble with this approach was that sometimes the discussion spiralled into a perverse sort of amnesia competition: Eliza would say that she was the world's worst rememberer of names and her new acquaintance would throw down the gauntlet and say, 'No-no-nooooo! I am the worst with names!', and the exchange would go on from there, a race to the bottom, which usually ended up with someone seething something like, 'I've forgotten my own mother's name and have no idea where I live!' whereupon both participants would stand down, amazed by their incompetence and tired out by the entire conversation.

It was too much. Eliza wanted to be alone. She wanted a pistachio eclair; she wanted Sicily and lemons on a tree. She wanted her dad. She groped for her phone on the side table; she'd promised Rich she'd stay in touch. The jewel colours of the apps glowed like Haribo, giving her a fizz of energy. She fired up WhatsApp to send Rich a voicenote. She'd got him quite into them – they were like voicemails, she'd explained; the advantage of using them to communicate instead of telephoning was that the person receiving the message could listen to it when it suited them, rather than both parties having to pencil in an actual live call.

She was distracted by updates from Ellie and Jess, friends of hers from her master's who were now working in London, Ellie as a corporate lawyer and Jess in comms. Ellie had sent a photo of a burger; she was at work but the team had got Deliveroo. Eliza swiped until she found the burger emoji and typed it out a few times, alternating it with the tongue emoji. She didn't know what else to add. Jess had doctored a picture of a romantic Oxford spire, only she'd drawn Eliza on the top of it like Godzilla on the Empire State. 'Hahaha,' Eliza typed back. Then she turned her attention to Rich.

'Heya it's me,' she began, recording her voice. 'I'm lying on my bed in Oxford . . .' She paused. Tried to charge her voice with a bit of oomph. 'Missing you!' she said jauntily. It was no use, she sounded psychotic. She tried again. 'I'm tired and feeling a bit . . . flat. I've moved into a cheap room, which is good. Everyone here's interesting but . . . I guess I can't quite . . .'

She stopped speaking. She felt sort of stupid. She watched the recording pulse on, registering her silence. Rich wanted her to be having the time of her life at Oxford. He was desperate for it to be that phase of her twenties that she would treasure above all others. He'd known that Bath hadn't gone well: Oxford was his beacon of hope for her. She couldn't let him down. She needed more time. Another week and she'd have the halcyon days he wanted. It would be wrong to send him some limp fucking diary of doom from her pillow.

With a squeeze of the chest, Eliza remembered her final dinner with her father the night before he'd driven her to Oxford to start the term. They'd gone, as tradition dictated, to The Fryery. It was mild out, the sky hung with low yellow clouds, and as they walked to dinner they saw geese pass overhead in a victory formation. They sat outdoors at one of the aluminium tables. Neither of them would have thought to invite Eliza's mother. Halfway through the meal Rich rummaged in his jeans pockets and put a tatty envelope on the table.

'There's five hundred in there,' Rich said, fixing his eyes on his haddock. The battered tail had curled up in the fryer.

Eliza opened the envelope. She knew enough about her father's finances to be sure that this gift must have been in the pipeline for months, that he would have taken on extra jobs and done who knew what else to get together such a sum. There weren't just £20 notes in the envelope but tenners and two-pound coins as well. Whenever he'd been able to spare a bit of cash, he must have thought of her.

Eliza didn't know what to say. Her chest and her throat were full. She tried to cough; it suddenly felt urgent that she should cough. She willed herself to take her father's hand. It was right there next to the ketchup, but touching it might tip her into an emotional state she couldn't handle, and in any case she didn't think Rich would be able to handle it either (his eyes were glimmering, his lips pulled into a line that looked soft and boyish). But as Eliza tried to think of a way to show her gratitude, Rich suddenly covered her hand with his massive one. Relief sloshed through them both. They looked at one another, then looked away very quickly. Eliza didn't bother trying to turn the money down – Rich would have just said no – so in the end she picked up the envelope and put it on her lap.

'Thanks,' she said, reaching for a chip.

Eliza nudged her thumb over on her phone so that her message to Rich deleted. It was no good: her voice was betraying the bewilderment and exhaustion she was feeling. She didn't want her dad to worry that she wasn't coping. She swiped through her photos from the night before – she and the New College lot had gone out, this time under the wearying instruction to dress as 'Orwell's

Animals'. Eliza found a picture of herself with a pink snout on her nose that matched her hair. She was surrounded by other people in similar get-ups, heaving towards the photographer in some club. They were at odd angles, they looked like they were on a ship or something, clutching one another for support or to simulate closeness. She zoomed into the image to check that she looked happy. Yeah, she was smiling. She looked pissed, actually. Good. She pressed send.

Duty done, she turned back onto her stomach, hoping that she'd find the willpower to return to the fray. Gradually her resolve ground down. The white plane of her pillow was fresh with the scent of Bold 2in1. The sense that her bedroom was crushing with strangers receded. She told herself that she needed to be solitary, after spending so much time in the swirl and stomp of new people. As her heartbeat slowed so did the ticker of her thoughts, and a bird on the drainpipe outside joined the barking of a dog a few houses over to coax her to sleep.

Returning to Cumbria after Ruby had ravaged her heart, Eliza supposed that she needed to convalesce. She spent most days with her dad on jobs. She told him nothing of what had happened – he had never met Ruby or known of her existence – but Eliza found solace in the work they did together. They bombed all over Cumbria from project to project, the car weighed down with sacks of soil. Under her father's instructions, Eliza laboured. She moved pots from wheelbarrows to flowerbeds; she deadheaded roses; she gathered scrolls of eucalyptus bark for burning; she laid down patio slabs, like she was the queen opening endless town halls. They woke before dawn or just after, when the moon glowed pale against the strengthening light. Normally they gardened in silence; sometimes to the patter of BBC 5 Live. There was something soothing in the radio commentators' manner, Eliza found; something pacifying about their uncomplicated maleness. Eliza was mesmerised by the bathrooms and pantries and scullery rooms she saw while stepping through clients' vast houses to their gardens. It was another world, this affluent Cumbria, where brass saucepans gleamed in kitchens and gardens had swimming pools and quince trees and ivy-hung gates. She drank it up.

Rich had not been a gardener for long. Until the early 2000s, he'd worked at Cavaghan & Gray on London Road, a member of the meals hygiene maintenance team. Eliza remembered visiting the factory as a child – it was a red-brick structure, imposing and dour, though the air in the vicinity smelled of teatime. She'd hang about by the front gates reading as she waited for Rich to pick her up after his shift; around her the other Cavaghan kids played football or hopscotch, and the older ones smoked indolently in the car park, giving puffs to nine-year-olds in exchange for Rolos. As darkness fell you could pinpoint the teenagers by the lights from their fags. But eventually Cavaghan was restructured and Rich lost his job. It stung. The rest of the country seemed to be booming. The Iraq war was thundering away but so distantly it was barely audible in Cumbria, and the only domestic news that filtered through was of squabbles between Gordon Brown and Tony Blair. In Carlisle, even before the financial crash, things felt like they were crumbing up. Shops were closing, the care homes heaving with the infirm and forgetful. Motivated teenagers had always left for Newcastle or Leeds, but now all the youngsters were fleeing the moment they could.

Flora, Eliza's mother, lost her job too. She'd worked in a hotel on reception but was laid off because of dwindling guest numbers. For a while Rich scrambled to keep the sort-of family afloat. He had a puritanical streak that Eliza inherited, and would rest only on Sunday afternoons, when his great luxury was to watch telly with a crisp and pickle sandwich. The day Flora left for good, a Sunday when Eliza was eight, Eliza came home from the playground and found her father on the sofa, watching the television avidly. Eliza only knew something was wrong because the television wasn't on. Flora was nowhere to be seen. Eliza went to the TV and pressed a button, so the screen flared with colour.

Eliza's childhood was no more turbulent than those of many of the other Carlisle kids, but she and Rich had their moments. They were poor but not hungry; dissatisfied but not desperate; they had a car, if sometimes no money for petrol. Eliza's first memory was of when she was about five; they were living on Turnpike Road. Flora was still around then, though sometimes she went out so late she came home the next morning or not at all. The way Eliza remembered it, her mother stopped her as she was on her way to the toilet. It was summer. Bees were thudding into the window panes, reeling back and thudding again. Bending down to look Eliza in the eyes, Flora told her that they needed to save money. As a family. They were running out.

'So use two squares of loo roll to wipe up after a wee,' she instructed. 'And three squares for a poo. Not a square more.'

Eliza nodded, wide-eyed.

Flora had conceived Eliza at nineteen by accident. She never considered aborting; then, teenage pregnancies were routine and for a few weeks she was touched by the notion of being responsible for something so soft and dependent as a baby. She and Rich were not an item but he took the news well enough: he told his parents, by then well into their seventies, and made a cot with some wood he picked up at Ant's. He and Flora stayed with one another on and off for a few years, then other men and women wove in and out of the picture too, introducing themselves as Mummy or Daddy's 'new friend'. The best ones remembered to bring Eliza little presents: elephant key rings, sequin boxes, snap-purses that she stuffed with clip-on earrings.

Growing up, Eliza wanted a beautiful mother. Like the women she read about in books. Someone fragrant and blonde, with pearls and peonies in the dressing room. She wanted Flora to look better, to be better; to comb her horrible brown hair, to take her to Pizza Hut or the ice rink at Lockerbie. It would even have been nice for them to bake cupcakes together, like Verity did with her mum at weekends, coming to class on Mondays with Tupperware boxes of dry fairy cakes to be handed out to allies – and withheld from foes. Even before she left, Flora was not demonstrative, not naturally warm; after having Eliza she wanted no more children and saw her daughter as a logistical conundrum more than a small person to be cherished and fortified.

Yet one thing Flora did regularly do until she left was to take Eliza to the library on Globe Lane, because it relieved her of the need to keep an eye on her. It was a functional building that smelled of crayons and plastic book jackets. There was a rotating cast of grey ladies at the desk who admired the ribbon in Eliza's hair, slipped her chocolate digestives, asked her how school was going. She'd answer their queries then dash off to the books. She never spent much time in the kiddies' area – it was full of Lego and babbling toddlers – but towards the back was a special section for teenagers, and from the age of six, there Eliza could be found. Sometimes, as she read, a Mrs Butterfield or a Mrs Allen would pop over, tick her off for sitting in the teenagers' section and ask her what book she was on to. '*Charlotte's Web*,' Eliza would say. Or *The Hobbit*, or *The Wind Singer*, or *The Suitcase Kid*, or *Wild Swans* or, or, or. Only once did she have a brush with something unlovely: one Saturday before closing when Eliza was making swift work of a *Sweet Valley High* novel, she heard an odd grunting noise coming from one of the aisles nearby. It sounded like trotters and a snout, sorting through dry leaves.

Eliza closed her book and got to her feet, curious. She looped around one of the lines of shelves and saw a man in the strip-lit gloom of the biology section, dressed in a red jacket and walking boots.

The man looked at the thin, serious girl standing three metres away, and she looked back. Then they both looked down: he at his penis, which was in his hand, mauve and thick and veined; Eliza at the man's buckled stance, and the flesh pronging out of his trousers.

48

'Hello,' she said courteously.

The man sort of groaned and tried to turn away. He was holding his willy, Eliza realised. Satisfied she'd traced down the source of the noise, she returned to her beanbag. Jess and Elizabeth, the Sweet Valley High twins, were having boy troubles and she wanted to know how they'd resolve them. After five minutes she thought she caught a flash of red out of the corner of her eye; the man was making his way to the library exit. She heard one of the desk ladies say 'Goodnight', heard him say something in reply.

Chapter Seven

Ada had never been lonely before. It was an affliction like obesity or AIDS that blighted other people. She knew, from her daily reading of the paper, that it was a particularly modern phenomenon, that it was on the rise, that men and the old were especially susceptible, but as November frisked the trees of their greenery it became increasingly clear to her that she was falling prey to the spectre herself. One thought bothered her above all: if she died in her bed on a Tuesday, she might well lie undiscovered until the following Friday. That was awful. The sense of the gargantuan irrelevance of her own life and body returned to her every night as she tried to sleep, until at around two she would turn her bedside lamp on, rescued by the brightness that filled the room. She'd pull her knees as close to her chest as they'd come, then get up and stand by the curtains, stiff and cold, catching her breath, doing all that she could to contain her horror of the night, of the size of her bed and the scorch of its sheets, and the absoluteness of her own company.

In daylight she was able to recognise that she was not entirely cut off. Actually she was rather lucky. Though she'd abandoned regular social engagements she was in contact with a handful of people, not least her literary agent James. He was almost as old as Ada, bald as a nut, with eyebrows that were permanently raised in an arc of genteel wonder. He had a shabby little office on Gray's Inn Road in London and telephoned Ada a fortnight after her breakdown in the supermarket with the news that her latest collection, *Things Considered*, had been shortlisted for a poetry prize in Salisbury.

'It's a crappy little prize,' he told her, 'so you're under no obligation to go to the shortlist ceremony, which will probably happen in a Zizzi's or something. And you won't win, you're too old.'

'Oh,' Ada said.

'The winner only gets five hundred quid,' James continued.

'Which category am I up for?'

'Best Collection.'

'Not Promising Young Talent? Best Newcomer?'

James laughed. 'I've got the judges' comments in front of me here,' he said. Ada could imagine him sitting at his desk, boxed in by the manuscripts that were sent to him every afternoon. 'I didn't bother telling you I was submitting the book to the prize because frankly I didn't think you'd get listed. But the judges have written that they especially liked your poems on Ireland. They're calling them "terse" and "lyrical". So there you have it.'

Ada considered. 'Terse and lyrical is probably a contradiction in terms,' she said.

James chuckled. Then fell the silence Ada was expecting: a prudently weighted pause, intended to shift the conversational gears.

'And how are you coping?' he asked sombrely. 'I feel I ought to check now and then.'

'I'm fine,' Ada said.

'He was a wonderful chap, Ade.'

'I know.'

'Really smashing. I was thinking the other day.'

'There's no need to get mushy on me, James, we've known each other for too long.'

'I'm not being mushy. I'm trying to be nice.'

'I'm alright.'

'We must be coming up to the two-year mark?'

'Not yet. March next year.'

'Oh yes. I saw Miranda last week, she asked me how you were and I realised I don't even know what the bugger died of.'

'Weak heart. Packed up.'

'Ah. Did you know?'

'Yes. Had it for years.'

'I didn't know.'

'Well, I knew. And we both knew it might be a problem. He liked cream too much, I should think.'

She could hear James smiling. Michael had always been lovably fat; he'd use a quarter of a pat of butter on his toast without noticing.

'Well if there's . . . You're welcome to come to London and stay with us,' James said. 'We're still in Ladbroke Grove, the garden's been redone. The children are gone, thank God. Jan was saying she's not seen you in a decade. I think it must be true.'

'If there's anything you can do, I'll let you know. In the meantime, you let the Salisbury people know that regretfully I cannot attend the shortlist ceremony. I can't abide most people these days, it's boring of me. Tell them there's been a death in the family. Make 'em squirm.'

'That I can do.'

'And remember to send me my cheque if I win.'

'Of course.'

Ada could make out a seam of relief in his voice: he'd done his bit, flung out a few consoling words; Jan wouldn't have to make up the guest room. But she was touched by his concern all the same, and remembered it later, as she was raking the autumn leaves into a corner of the garden, pushing them into a great tawny pile that smelled of rot and rainfall.

James had been Ada's literary agent for over thirty years. He signed her a year before the publication of her debut collection, *Measure*. Over the years their relationship had worked well. James was connected and astute but lazy and forgetful; Ada was a good writer, but not a dependable or productive one; she didn't wake up brimming with verse that had only to be tickled from her pen nib to the page. Three collections' worth of poems would come to her in six months or she'd not write anything for two years. Once she had a sufficient number of poems in the bank, she sent off the best ones to magazines: *Magma*, *Granta*, *Ambit*. She had the impression editors were increasingly accepting her work out of pity – her style hadn't caught up with the times, she didn't have a pretty author picture, she often wrote in rhyming verse and loathed what she called 'blobby' poems that scattered words over the page like so many shards of glass. You could understand an Ada

Robertson poem after reading it once, even if it yielded a touch more on second, third, fourth readings.

But she had once known fame and favour. There had been a period in the nineties where Ada looked to be breaking into the big time. A few poems, including 'Washing Up' and 'Burley Park', were hurried onto the English GCSE syllabus after a push for more women writers, and she had a whirlwind year talking at literary festivals with the likes of Wendy Cope, doing interviews on Front Row, coquettishly denying she'd be the next poet laureate. James, busy with more lucrative clients, didn't push her to become the public figure she might have been.

Then it all died down. Her next collection, *Beetles*, was greeted with courteous dismay by the critics. *The Times Literary Supplement* called it 'muddled, but not without charm'; a sharp young writer from the *Guardian* lamented its depiction of married life as 'unreconstructed', and *The White Review* searched for a 'fresh' depiction of beetles in its pages and found 'not one'. The collection sold fairly well, for poetry, but there were no more pleas from BBC producers for her to feature in that year's programming; no letters from English departments at private schools asking Ada to come and 'lead a seminar for our delightful girls'. She spoke at the odd festival but in smaller tents, to increasingly cobwebbed women. Ada pretended not to find the damp squibness of it all discouraging but of course she did: it had been amusing to find herself a literary somebody, it gave one food for thought, material to recycle into yet more verse.

Once it was over and she was back in the trenches with all the other half-known poets, she took to referring to her period of fame as her *annus horribilis*. She kept it up until everyone, apart from Michael, was convinced that Ada had hated being a successful poet, that she had abhorred the limelight, that she was too refined, too resolutely literary, to want to make a dime out of her poetry (the grubbiness!), or to satisfy the gurning critics. She put it out that when some lugubrious grown-up schoolchild told her that they had studied one of her poems in class, she felt demoralised. On the contrary: on being told such a thing Ada felt a little burn of awe, and would tell Michael about the encounter the moment she got home.

Just as her career as a poet was on the wane, Michael's in academia went berserk. His field was twentieth-century Italian literature, and both subjects suddenly became hip, much to his bemusement. Swanky American universities paid him handsomely to talk about things he'd been working on unnoticed for years, and so he and Ada came to know New Haven and Boston, Greenwich Village and Princeton; the glamour of American fall, the cinnamon stench of the stateside bakeries. Summers were for trips to Turin. Michael fell in love with the grim little city, tucked between the Alps and the Superga hill; he was fixated by its incongruous grid system and silent broad avenues, by the confluent rivers and *Star Wars* dome of the Mole, Turin's old Jewish synagogue. Italians from Turin were not like Italians from other parts of the country: they were more like the English, ironic and suspicious; you got the feeling that they had less sex and ate less olive oil than their southern counterparts.

It was in Turin that Michael came to know Primo Levi. Or rather, he began to understand him in the mountains surrounding the city, as he and Ada walked through their brown-green brush as Levi had as a boy, long before he was sent to Auschwitz. Until then Michael had regarded Levi as an august chronicler of the Holocaust, but not much more. He learned in Turin that he was also a poet of the outdoors and of nature, an adventurer and a gossip, a memoirist of range and ambition, a generous man, a complicated man, a serious writer.

Ada had a picture of Michael and her on one of their Turin trips. It must have been taken in 2002, or the year after. They were wearing faded shorts and walking boots; they both looked sunburnt and happy, their heads in matching purple caps. In the photo, Michael was holding a copper-wire owl the size of a hand that he had bought off Carlo, the son of one of Primo Levi's closest friends. Ada was holding a copper-wire owl too. Hers had been wound to look like it was pricking its ears, whereas Michael's was shown opening its wings, as if it were about to launch itself skyward. Together the animals made a pair – the left wing of Michael's owl curved perfectly around Ada's smaller model, anchoring them to one another when they were placed side by side. The industrial wire making up the animals' bodies had been twisted by Levi's own hand years before he died, by which time he'd started making many such sculptures, dotting them around his study. The owls were the most expensive items Michael had ever bought and looked perilously spindly, like they could be flattened by a severe stare.

'Hold your owl to the camera,' Ada remembered Michael instructing her as they posed for a German tourist armed with Michael's camera. The wire body of the animal felt warm in Ada's hands under the mountain sun.

After the picture was taken they ate lunch on one of the rocks just visible on the left-hand edge of the photo. They had focaccia, crumbly black sausage and figs, finishing up with swigs of wine from the water bottle in Michael's rucksack. The owls stayed on the rock as they ate, interlocked. Every so often Michael would toot with pleasure at his new treasures, laugh in delight at their expressions. Then Ada decided it was time to get walking again, and Michael returned the owls carefully to his bag.

Before Michael's death the photo lived in his study. Since, Ada had moved it to a little table in the sitting room. Directly in front of the picture, she'd placed the owl that looked like it was listening to something. The second copper figurine, the one Michael was holding in the photo, was missing. It had disappeared in the house move from Manchester to Oxford. A few days after they'd painted the front door and unpacked the smaller items, Michael suddenly said that he'd not seen the second Levi figurine since leaving Manchester. He'd stored it away in its box; had Ada unpacked it?

'No,' she replied simply.

'Shite,' Michael frowned.

They began to search, initially calmly, then in a frenzy. The removal men had put a few boxes in random cupboards and soon they were all open. Slumped in the sitting room after their hunt, Michael and Ada speculated that the second owl had perhaps fallen into some cranny of the moving van. Michael looked close to tears, his colossal body reduced. In all the years after, he never found the strength to tell Carlo that one of the figurines was gone. Ada learned not to mention it and for both of them, knowing that the second copper owl was alone somewhere gave them more pain than they liked to acknowledge, even to one another.

Now the solitude of the little creature on the table seemed starker than ever. It caused Ada such suffering that she learned to stop looking at it. Her gaze would skip from the rug to the lamp to the mantelpiece, never pausing on the picture frame housing those two cheerful sunburnt people, or, right in front of the photo, the burnish of the singular copper-wire owl, irredeemably bereft of its partner.

Chapter Eight

The beginning of term was buried and the great tide of people that had threatened to submerge Eliza had finally pulled out, leaving her feeling weak and strung up with seaweed. A number of students she'd liked most on first meeting seemed to have vanished with the receding water. Gone was Joseph Kay, the music DPhil with bleached hair who'd told her his compositions used sounds like weeds coiling and fridges breathing; gone too was Zelda, the French photographer from Lady Margaret Hall. And Tommy, the biology post-doc, what had happened to him? Oxford had eaten them alive.

On the whole, Eliza's first term seemed to be going uncannily smoothly. Her night out with Nat turned out to be one of her latest, the only time she went to bed without removing her make-up. By November she had mastered skills crucial to surviving at Oxford: where to buy sandwiches, when to rebel against the town's one-way system, how to establish whether someone looked familiar because Eliza had already met them or because they were a freaky fusion of faces she'd seen at other points in her life and since half forgotten. It was fashionable not to love

Oxford, especially among pockets of the graduate popula-
tion who decried its colonial past and the male-pale-stale
cast that dominated its elite. Eliza accepted these flaws
and others as true and unedifying but she began to be
beguiled too by the butterscotch light that drew tourists to
the city in their coachloads, by the cobbled passageways,
by the jutting banality of the shopping malls. She was
even fond of Swinburne Road, if not her death-trap room,
and learned the rhythms of those who lived around her:
the Sikh family on the left, the boy who played football
on the street, the frail older woman opposite whom Eliza
glimpsed from time to time, when she opened her yellow
door to water her window boxes.

Baleotti, Eliza's tutor, invited her to his house for dinner
once a week. He lived in Jericho with his wife Cosima, a
professor too. After every visit Eliza would return home
with books digging into her through her backpack; there
was always this novel to read '*immediatamente*,' or that
underrated Ukrainian film to watch. They talked in Italian.
Slowly her tongue became suppler as it learned again to
shape the generous Latinate vowels. The last time she'd
spoken Italian at length was when she and Ruby had lived
together in the cramped attic of a palazzo in Venice on
Eliza's year abroad. At home they'd spoken in English,
in which Ruby dominated, but in the city's canals, Eliza
reigned: you had to speak Italian or be treated like a
tourist, and Ruby couldn't speak a word. Eliza found it
oddly empowering, being the conduit through which Ruby
asserted her will, though Ruby, resentful and aware that
her power on the street was weaker than it was at home,
compensated when they were alone together. She made

Eliza download an app that tracked her movements, and would monitor the screen as Eliza walked back from class; if she dawdled too long, or accepted a classmate's invitation to have a gelato, Ruby gave her a call.

At Baleotti's, Italian became as plain and limpid as water. The professor would ask Eliza what she had made of his most recent load of pimped-out books and films, they would go from there into a cultural hall of mirrors. Keeping on top of it all was draining and after a heavy session, when Baleotti had to lend her an extra canvas bag to carry tomes Eliza couldn't fit in her backpack, she cycled home feeling like Bruce Bogtrotter, her mouth full of the richest chocolate cake, her cheeks bulging and her teeth blackened, but expected of course to eat more.

Not long after Eliza had begun to get used to Oxford life, a darker truth began to shine through the novelty of it all. She saw that she was an intellectual fraud in academic drag. Sure, she was clever enough to be on the grad programme but her comet had a short tail; it would disappear into the night. She'd not read a word of Dickens, or of Dickinson. She didn't have a complicated relationship with Judith Butler. She could have jotted all she knew about the civil rights movement onto a Post-it. There would be no professorships at Brown, no keynotes, no Wikipedia entries. The competition was too fierce. The more grads Eliza met, the more certain she became that she was a pedestrian thinker, a dull pebble on a diamond beach. Nearly all the British grads were from the Home Counties and many assumed that because Eliza was northern she must be studying something correspondingly dour like engineering or physics. When she revealed she was in the Italian literature department they looked mildly offended, as though it hadn't crossed their minds that a northerner could read novels. At school, Eliza's northernness had cut her out from the crowd, mostly in a bad way, but it didn't even make her interesting at Oxford: there were people getting their doctorates who were actual refugees, who'd studied at night in war-torn countries and found their way to the university anyway. Eliza's story by contrast was one of cloying privilege.

She had read too much woke content not to be aware that feeling like an imposter was normal, but knowing that was no help: she felt like an imposter anyway. It was like being told by your doctor that the migraine you were dying of was all in your head, the flagellations of your own kooky psyche: fine, cool, but it didn't ease the symptoms.

'I don't have enough of a past to make me a genuinely independent thinker,' she told her friend Judy over dinner.

Judy was an English literature grad student at New College too. They saw one another a few times a week: they would grab food in the canteen or go to talks. They liked each other in a loose, vague way; mostly they sent one another links to good *Guardian* articles.

Judy didn't respond. She was working her way through a pile of boiled carrots. Behind her in the dining hall, exuberant undergraduates were joshing and hooting, chucking fries at one another. The portraits lining the room looked on sourly.

Eliza continued. 'Artists, or really good ones, are knotted up by some dysfunctional relationship that drives them, makes them compose stuff with psychological heft,' she said. 'But the closest I have to that is – I dunno, me and my mum; we've never been that close.'

Judy continued to chew contemplatively. Eliza tried to work out if even her first point was true: was it fair to call her and Flora's relationship cold? Probably not; Flora had called her last week, they'd had a five-minute conversation. 'But even that's not catastrophic,' Eliza cried in frustration. 'My mum told me recently that she had a new crush – she confided in me! People with icy mothers are not called up by them and told about their love interests!'

Judy cut the end off one of her carrots and pushed it to the side of her plate.

'Aren't you going to eat that?' Eliza asked, distracted.

'It's grown one of those hairs,' Judy said.

She pronged the carrot and lifted it up. Eliza looked closer. A ropey ginger hair had sprouted from the tip.

'Furry fucker,' she said. Judy snorted. They started to laugh.

Leaving the hall, Judy told Eliza that it was lazy to suppose that she needed more trauma in her past to think in the present with clarity or creativity: the tortured artist trope was so knackered it almost sent her to sleep. Eliza saw that Judy was right.

Yet as the weeks passed her disquiet grew, along with a new misgiving: that there was absolutely no point in going ahead with her studies. 'If I complete my doctorate,' she whispered to Judy the next time they met (this time in December at the Ultimate Picture Palace; the film was about to start), 'there's little chance that anyone, including me, will benefit from my having done so.'

Judy gave Eliza a Delphic smile. 'Same here,' she replied. 'Obviously the work we do is mad abstracted. We're basically building sandcastles on a made-up beach.'

'Don't you feel shit about the fact that once you've written your million-word thesis,' Eliza said, 'it may only be read by twenty people and will have no practical application at all?'

Judy shrugged. 'Most things people do leave a negligible trace. Why should I be different?'

The film began. They were watching *Roman Holiday*, some remastered version. An aerial shot of the Vatican trembled into view. Eliza saw what Judy meant. It came to the same: of course their doctorates wouldn't electrify the fucking world; who were they to want to make such an impact, to expect that they could?

As they left the cinema Eliza was gripped by another worry. 'Do you think I'm being self-indulgent and entitled, fretting that there's no underlying point to what I'm doing?'

Judy was looking for a bin for her popcorn bag. 'Yes,' she said. 'I mean, don't you?'

Eliza considered. 'Yeah,' she replied. 'But that's not enough to stop me from having these existential crises when they occur, it just makes me hate myself even more for having them. And then I get stuck in a loop of hating myself for hating myself.'

'Sounds tiring.'

Eliza nodded. They hugged one another goodbye. Judy cycled off and Eliza walked back to Swinburne Road, messaging Ellie, who was at work and would be until the early hours: they were closing some deal. The night was treacle-dark, the sort of night that murderers wait for. Eliza's hands were cold. As she walked, she tried to quell her dread of being imminently back in her bedroom, surrounded by books she'd not read and windows that were scummy with dirt, though she'd traced daisy and penis hieroglyphs into the grime.

During her first week in Oxford after Christmas, Eliza was in Tesco when she felt someone look at her from the hummus shelves. Her name was Pandy and she'd studied at St Antonia's too; they'd been close for a time in Year Eleven but the relationship had cooled when Eliza became the target for the sharper-tongued girls in their class. Pandy, self-protective, had seen she needed to make less compromising friends. It was odd and a little embarrassing for them both to cross one another: once they had got on well enough to gossip deep into the night, quietening only when the matron swept through the dormitory with a torch.

In fact, Eliza regularly saw St Antonia's girls around Oxford. Parents sent their children there on the under-standing that it would turn their cygnets into Oxbridge swans, and the school generally succeeded. Whenever she ran into an old girl, or a SAG as they were known in the private school network, Eliza hated it, because she had hated St Antonia's and seeing its ponytailed missionaries chilled her; nothing she could do would ever let her escape its shadow. Yet St Antonia's had drummed into its pupils the necessity of good cheer, so when Pandy cried, 'Lize!' as if they hadn't seen one another for years, as indeed was technically true, Eliza responded in kind.

'Pandy!' she whooped.

They chatted for a bit. Pandy was still clearly entrenched in the SAG crowd. She and Tilly, Mia and Molly were going back to school for a chapel service the next day, would Eliza join them?

'Tomorrow?' Eliza repeated, startled.

'Yep, it's a Sunday,' Pandy said.

'Oh.'

'Well, you up for it?'

'Sure,' Eliza heard herself say gamely.

The following morning came around too soon. The 'crew' Pandy had mentioned all lived in Oxford and so she was giving everyone a lift. Eliza was the last to be collected. She stood in the middle of Swinburne Road at 9 a.m., waiting for Pandy's car to arrive. She thought she glimpsed the woman who lived opposite peek at her through the curtain and couldn't blame her: she must look odd, standing stiffly on the road. Eliza was hoping to eliminate the possibility that she'd be asked to give her schoolfriends a tour of her house; they'd be appalled by the squalor and dust, and the news that she was essentially squatting would spread around the St Antonia's network in about five minutes of HS2 WhatsApping.

At last, the vast snout of Pandy's Land Rover appeared at the end of the road. Tilly, Mia and Molly were in the back of the car, a row of appealing blondes. Eliza got in the front. She regretted agreeing to the expedition at once. The girls hadn't seen her since school, though they'd kept abreast of her movements on Facebook and through the gossip mill that had kept clanking on since they'd all left after sixth form. They were nice enough, but so curious. These young women had known Eliza as a teenager, they knew her roots and her weaknesses, that she'd attended St Antonia's on a full scholarship, that her mother had never turned up for sports day, that her father had worked in a food factory of all places, before being laid off (poor chap). As Eliza willed the questions to end she suddenly recalled Molly, now graceful and likeable, pointing out aged fourteen the 'irony' of Eliza's father's name. 'He's called Rich?' she'd giggled as they lined up outside maths. 'Rich? Hahaha!'

Eliza could barely remember who she'd been at school, what she'd looked like, what she'd spent her time doing, but these oracles seemed to know all, to remember all.

'So you did turn out to be bi!' Mia trumpeted when Eliza was quizzed about her love life. 'We all knew it!'

Eliza smiled blandly. At St Antonia's many things were socially permitted: you could steal and self-harm, betray and sell coke, but you could not like girls. It was deemed a contagion: one lezzer in the boarding house might infect the others, so the unspoken rule went, and pupils were always on the lookout for signs of deviancy.

'Did your Bath girlfriend break up with you then?' Pandy asked casually, her eyes on the road.

Eliza was stunned. She didn't know word of her relationship had reached this far. 'Yeah,' she said. She felt something shift in the atmosphere of the car; all four women were powerfully interested to hear more.

'Why?' Mia asked.

Eliza wanted to get out. Roll down the motorway verge like some budget Tom Cruise. 'You'd have to ask her,' she said, as lightly as she could. 'We met in, like, the first week of Bath. I was in my first year, Ruby was in her third. We got together at the start of term, and it ended when I was doing my master's.' She fell silent, hoping that would be enough.

'And are you cool about it now?' Mia asked.

'Mia fucksake, stop interrogating her,' Tilly said.

Eliza looked at her, surprised. She didn't know Tilly well: she'd been shy at school, geeky and musical, until in sixth form she'd become really beautiful basically overnight and so was rushed into the elite girl group running their year. But whenever Eliza and she had spoken, Eliza remembered Tilly hadn't been a dick, even when she was kicking around with the cool crowd, actually she'd stayed pretty nice.

'Thanks, Tilly,' Eliza said.

'There's no need to tell us about it, honestly it's not our business,' she replied.

'It's OK, I should learn to be able to talk about this stuff. If only to warn you all how to behave more wisely in love, ha ha.'

Tilly didn't smile. Eliza considered. 'Ruby and I had quite an intense relationship,' she said.

'What kind of intense?' Molly asked.

'Intense, I dunno. We became a couple pretty early on. I was finding the whole university thing a bit much, I couldn't find my groove, work piled on the moment term began, I couldn't get my head around how town was laid out – just went from the faculty to the supermarket to the library and back round in this infernal triangle. Ruby was an escape from it. We became one of those couples that – you know – disappear off the scene completely.'

'What, she like, locked you in the house?' Mia asked.

Eliza shook her head equably. Fuck Mia.

'Nothing like that,' she said. 'It was more . . .' She wanted to say 'subtle' but couldn't bring herself to. 'Ruby just— her company made me lose appetite for other people.' She stopped. She found it strange to be saying these things aloud, it was the first time she had articulated it to another person, but she carried on, chased by the need to finish what she'd started. 'Ruby made me believe things that I realise now are off-centre, I suppose, like that I'd not find anyone else, that I was a cold person, that she could put up with me where others couldn't, that I was crap at like giving head and stuff, that I couldn't handle my own money. She used to take it from me and give it back to me in bits, like an allowance.'

There was a silence. Everyone seemed to be regretting the subject having come up and was trying to find something jaunty to say.

'I bet you're great at giving head,' Pandy ventured.

'I dunno, let me know later,' Eliza said. The others laughed.

'So how did it end?' Tilly asked.

'I started my master's, still at Bath but living with Ruby, and I began to think that maybe I'd sunk too much of myself into her. That I'd not had the university experience I'd been sold by TV and films and whatever, that maybe I wanted to go out, be drunk, be preposterous, do the undergraduate thing. So I tried to pull back. Hang out with new people. I made a few friends I still have now. But Ruby didn't like the new dynamic.'

It was an understatement. Eliza remembered when she'd announced just before the end of their final Christmas term together that she wanted to go to the Bath Abbey carol service.

'It's candlelit,' Eliza told her.

Ruby was making a vegan curry. 'A carol service?' she repeated. She gave Eliza this look, so charged with contempt that Eliza took a step back.

'I'm not going to spend an hour of my life praising a god that doesn't exist and shoring up a religion that has basically spent the last two millennia repressing women,' Ruby said. Christianity was a 'virginity cult', she went on; Anglicans had always hated the queers; there was no way that they could go to a fucking carol service, she'd rather cut her clit off. So they didn't go. Eliza ended up downloading an album of carols onto her phone, listening to it when Ruby was out.

'In the end,' Eliza concluded, 'in my second term of my master's, Ruby got bored of me.'

'What?' Molly asked.

'Why?' Pandy demanded.

'No clue,' Eliza replied. She was exhausted now. 'She tried to break up with me, I wasn't ready for it and was living with her so I asked to stay, and then she brought some guy back when I was in the house and they fucked downstairs, then she broke up with me properly. Lol. After that, I went back to Cumbria. Handed my dissertation in from there. Did supervisions and stuff on Skype.'

There was a short silence.

'Well babes,' Molly said. 'Ruby sounds like a shitshow.'

It was such a stupid comment, so millennial and beery, that it cut the tension.

'I'm really sorry,' Tilly said, once the laughter had subsided.

Eliza looked at her. Tilly was sitting by the window. She looked back at Eliza steadily. Her voice sounded genuine. Something in her expression made Eliza believe there was some actual fellow-feeling there. 'Thanks, Tilly,' Eliza said. The questions came to a close.

The rest of the day passed nightmarishly. Apart from a flash new geography block and a few new teachers, school was unchanged. The main part was a grand ivy-covered building constructed in the 1830s, converted not long afterwards into a Protestant schoolhouse for nine sisters. Now the institution's 800 young ladies could, for £40,000 a year, enjoy two lakes and a stables, a fitness suite and tennis courts, a pool and a ballroom where boys in black tie were summoned from Harrow and Eton for monthly discos, and the young ladies' aim was to get fingered on the dancefloor without being caught by patrolling pastoral staff.

A third of Eliza's school year turned up to the reunion service. They filled four back rows, while the rest of the pews were taken up by the school's current pupils in their starchy Sunday uniform. Eliza knew that the girls in front of them must look as they all had back then, but of course now they seemed impossibly small and breakable, their wrists the wrists of infants.

The ceremony began. There were prayers for 'the seniors'. There was a collection and a sermon on microplastics. The organist led the congregation into hymns that Eliza had intoned on repeat for five years, and as the rafters filled with praise, she looked along her row of overgrown schoolgirls, all of whom were bellowing the beloved songs at the tops of their voices. She felt almost aggressively alone. They'd all stayed in touch since leaving school; Eliza had not, she'd worked diligently to put her school memories from her mind. And of course Eliza's cohort seemed to be doing far more impressive things than she was by now, for the school educated well. Tilly was at the Home Office, Mia was a human rights barrister, Molly was an artist. Asked again and again what she was up to, Eliza saw her answer – 'a doctorate on the author Primo Levi' – grow wan under the spotlight, and she began to feel ashamed of her work, of its futility and smallness. What did it mean, exactly, to be preparing to write a treatise on a dead author? What would it change, who would benefit? If Eliza succeeded in becoming an academic, wouldn't her work just go into further educating people like these young women, who waltzed into the best universities and got the teaching they felt was their birthright, alongside even more entitled young men? One or two of the SAGs Eliza spoke to knew about Levi but they were only interested in one thing: the way he had died. 'Suicide, yep?' 'So the Nazis got him in the end?' 'Did he jump or was he pushed?'

After a cello recital and plea for donations from the headmistress, the seniors had one final tea in the Pankhurst Parlour, then Eliza got into Pandy's Land Rover and they drove back to Oxford. Eliza tried to participate in the merry gossip but she lost track of the names and fell to looking out of the window. The black night was masking the countryside. The white lights of cars panned towards them from the other side of the motorway.

They got to Swinburne Road at nine. Eliza was bemused at how happy she was to be back. The house's renovations were reaching new levels of industry: the entire first floor had been peeled back and bundles of cabling were piled in great hairballs everywhere. The moment seemed perfect for some LCD Soundsystem; she listened to the band when she felt particularly alone. Two minutes in, she had to pull off her headphones: the lead was singing about all his friends, about how whatever happened, they'd be there, talking shit and getting high together. She tapped and swiped to find an alternative. There was a Radio 4 documentary on Boko Haram that seemed promising. When it was finished she found the next one on Isis brides. When that was over she felt as listless and silenced as she had wanted to feel. She stood up to brush her teeth at the browning sink by the window. It was late, maybe three. The street looked oddly fake under the antiseptic light of the lamp-posts, and in the house opposite, Eliza saw, just as she had the evening she kissed Nat, a figure standing on the first floor behind thin curtains. Their bodies were mirroring one another. It must be the elderly woman she saw watering her window boxes sometimes, unless it was her husband or child. Eliza watched the silhouette for a minute; she wanted to go over and knock, see who the person was, have the sort of conversation that was only possible when it was as dark as this, as quiet. Then she noticed her mouth was full of toothpaste. She rinsed at the sink, washed her face, checked her phone and went to bed. The following morning she noticed that a deep inertia had settled in her bones, like a yearning for sleep.

Chapter Nine

'Ade. You're being completely ridiculous.'

Ada was in her sitting room talking to her sister Eve on the telephone. It was a Sunday morning. The landline was clamped to her cheek; her other hand was holding the lace curtain open a little – there was a pink-haired young woman standing on Swinburne Road, bang in the middle as if she was hoping to be struck by lightning.

Ada had told Eve about her breakdown in the supermarket a few months ago. She'd not gone to another shop since. Eve couldn't believe it: how had Ada survived for so long?

'The freezer,' Ada explained primly. 'The farmer's market. Long-life milk. High-quality cocaine.'

'Go to another bloody shop!' Eve cried.

Ada considered. Actually, that wasn't such a bad idea. She let the curtain fall back into place, then whipped it open again when she heard a car pull up just outside. A Land Rover had appeared. Ada could make out three chattering young women in the back and saw clearly what was going on: here were five best friends, setting off on a road trip to a feminist socialist acupuncture retreat in the Cotswolds or something. Lucky girls.

'Ali, get your fingers out of your Coco Pops,' Eve said. 'Right. Ada, I have to go. Please go to a shop today. Please.'

'Fine,' Ada said.

And so she started buying groceries again, not at the supermarket but a few doors down, in a smaller shop owned by bearded men Ada supposed must be Muslims. It was an Aladdin's cave where you could buy any number of dates and figs but where staples like spring onions and butter were touch-and-go. The first time she went, Ada was cheerfully informed that the shop hadn't ordered milk so none would come for a week.

'Right,' Ada said, startled. She bought double cream instead and spent the next few days swirling it into her coffee, like a recovering anorexic.

She missed Adul and the others from the supermarket but liked her new gang more. The shopkeepers were kind to her there. They called her Miss Robertson, made jokes she couldn't understand but laughed at politely, and she always walked out with something peculiar in her canvas bag, like tahini or kumquats, plucked firm and vibrant days ago from trees in the Middle East. Her cupboards began to fill once more, and anyone rooting through them would have thought they belonged to a Bahraini chef. She didn't know how to use her new ingredients, but they imbued the kitchen with a sense of possibility and ambition, and anyway, making dishes she'd once served to Michael – shepherd's pie, lasagne, kedgeree – was out of the question, so she tucked quite happily into fattoush and hummus, lamb cooked in molasses, baklava.

And yet, she was lonely still. And she had time on her hands, and money in spades but no sense that it could be spent to make her happy. It was better to open the garden door to invite the breeze in; even if it dotted the kitchen with rain, it revived her, bringing in the wet-earth smell of outdoors. The gore of fresh widowhood was gone now. There was no more admin, no more operatic weeping. She simply missed her husband. She wanted her old life. There was one small comfort: she'd not suspected, before Michael's death, quite how much more of human nature there was left for her to explore, but the discoveries since had been frequent, and they'd been remarkable. First of all: that friends of one's husband's did not count as friends of one's own. Secondly: that people would do anything not to talk about death; they conceived of it as a hobby of the old or unwell. Thirdly: that becoming a widow was something you became every morning; that there was a bland and precious non-time between waking and realising, waking and remembering. When Ada opened her eyes (earlier and earlier it seemed) she tended to feel fine, chirpy even; then things settled into their correct ghastly order. She had lost her love. On her worst days Ada would become a widow multiple times; upon waking, but then again in the afternoon when the clamour of a family laughing on the pavement alerted her to her isolation. She aspired to 'take to poetry', as James had advised her on his latest call, but even the idea of doing so felt silly, like trying to pacify a rampaging elephant with a lute. She was not equipped to prospect beauty from the dumb fact that Michael had died, that he had left her earlier than she would have liked, that she wished it had not happened.

There was no use rueing that he wouldn't have liked her to give up; he wasn't around to like or not like things, that was rather the point. And yet still, as her second January without Michael ground on, Ada started to feel ashamed of her behaviour: other people lost their entire families in fell swoops and seemed to get by. One of them had to die first; why not him? Seventy-five wasn't that old, but it was no reason for Ada to wait around glumly to be claimed too.

One morning as she settled down to watch TV after breakfast, she stopped, realising what she was doing. She covered her mouth in horror. She'd become one of those people that watched daytime television. She had developed a crush on Holly Willoughby. Before Michael had died she'd not even known the presenter existed, but frequently now she thought of Willoughby's shining hair and milk-shake lips. What was more, most evenings she settled down to watch a battered DVD of *The Wedding Date*, a film even she could see was inane, about a bouncy American who hired a stud to accompany her to a wedding in England, to deflect questions from relatives about her still being single. Ada didn't know why she kept watching the film, other than it made her laugh and cry (mostly cry, particularly in one loopy scene when the lead hunk ate an anchovy as proof of his love of the leading lady).

The person Ada thought she was would have to stretch and warp to accommodate these startling new tastes. Continue the way she was going, she warned herself bale-fully, and she might start searching through her attic for antiques. Her appetite might roam beyond the quiet little terrestrial shows she currently gorged upon – she could become, what was it, a 'Netflix subscriber', or worse still a 'gamer', losing herself to the violent shoot-em-ups that seemed to absorb teenage boys. Things were at crisis point.

Ada vowed to electrify her quiet existence. The day after her conversation with Eve, she opened the curtains to a victorious blue sky. It was frosty out, the grass crunchy and silver. As the kettle whirred, Ada gave herself the psychological pat-down she'd become accustomed to performing every morning. Had she dreamed of him, of their lost life? How tolerable would her own company be today, as the prospect of afternoon ballooned before her, blank and unfillable as morning? Actually, she realised, today she felt pretty good. Tea in hand, she opened the back door into the garden. The freezing air struck her face like a pail of water. It was just the sort of morning that used to make Michael roar with pleasure, demand that they go for a walk that minute. Well, she thought, she would walk to him.

He was buried at a Victorian cemetery twenty minutes' walk from Swinburne Road. The last time she'd seen his grave was when his coffin was lowered into the ground a week after his death. Ada had been aware of a great crowd around her, many of them Irish relatives Michael hadn't seen in years. The coffin was tinier than the man had ever been. Since the burial she'd thought of returning to the cemetery but had held off – perhaps because Michael had always been agnostic about how his body would be dealt with, or because Ada feared that visiting the spot would be the seal on an identity she was not ready to assume.

Ada bought lilies in the first open newsagent she found. The roads were oddly quiet. At one point a fleet of university runners in Lycra flashed past, so quick and efficient she wondered whether they'd been a mirage. Michael's grave was by the Remembrance Garden. Ada stood looking at his granite headstone for a long minute; it was so new it looked tacky. It made Ada feel like she was on some Hollywood set where only the fronts of buildings were real and stonework was made out of polystyrene. She'd not brought anything to put her flowers in; they'd wilt without water. She cast about for a jar or coffee cup. There was nothing. She'd come to be close to Michael but this random stone meant nothing; even his name seemed unfamiliar.

She tried to busy herself with a spot of weeding around the headstone. The ground was so cold her fingers froze and she stopped. She decided to leave. As she made her way back to the street she passed another woman her age, kneeling at a grave that can't have been much older than Michael's. The woman was dressed in black (Ada hadn't thought to) and tears were running fluently down her cheeks. Their eyes met. Ada couldn't hold her gaze. The grave behind the stranger was hidden beneath a flower cortège spelling out the word 'Grandad'. Normally Ada would have found it vulgar but she had no cynicism left in her, no fight, and she nodded fearfully at the woman and walked out of the cemetery feeling shaken and old and alone, as the heatless winter sun made the pavements bright and the car bonnets glint white.

At home, she saw that she'd forgotten to leave the lilies on Michael's stone. She cut their stems at a diagonal, put them in a vase and stirred a sugar cube into the water. Her fingers were quavering and she couldn't bear the patter of her own mind; she longed for it to quieten and knew she needed to make a change. This half-life would be the death of her.

*

The next day Ada decided to write a CV. It was her first, though she'd written her author biography before for poetry collections. By now she knew a thing or two about Google and she discovered that it was a treasure trove of advice for things like CV-building. By early afternoon she had a first draft. It filled two pages – JobSmart124, a contributor on a jobs forum, advised keeping the document to under two A4s – and Ada was pleased with what she was able to conjure up. She centred the text and put it in Comic Sans to make it friendly and legible. She put the First that she had got at Exeter University all those years ago in bold type, underlined, size fourteen. Some sites advised pasting in a photo of herself, so she looked for one by searching her name online; to her shock there was a grainy picture of her talking on some panel at Cheltenham years ago. She didn't know how to crop the photo so she left it as it was, hoping that whoever read her CV would know that she was the poet on the left, not the one on the right. She printed twenty copies and went on a walk around town to distribute them.

Her first stop was the Magdalen Arms on Iffley Road. The only person about was a woman wiping a table near the entrance. She looked bemused when Ada asked if the pub was looking for a bartender, then softened as Ada handed her one of her CVs.

'I have zero bar experience,' Ada said. 'But I like a drink and I'm ready to learn.'

The woman thanked her and said that she'd keep the CV 'on file'.

'Righto,' Ada said briskly. 'My telephone's on there. I'm always in the house.'

She enjoyed her job hunt. People were nice enough, though there seemed to be no vacancies, even at the snack bar which had a sign in the window saying 'Vacancies'. At a café near the covered market, having given her CV to the bearded young man behind the counter, Ada was taken aback to see him rummaging around for something to give back to her. She took it and brought it to close her face to read; she wasn't wearing her specs. It was an Age Concern leaflet. There was a couple on the cover in M&S-type jumpers, smiling cornily and having a grand old time. Before Ada could say a word, the barista offered her a 'cup of tea and a nice slice of cake on the house'. He was leering at her compassionately, his hair in a stupid bun on top of his head. Ada wanted to knock his tortoiseshell glasses to the floor. She snatched her CV back and left.

She ended up at Sylvie's on Iffley Road, a café she used to go to with Michael. She had a surprise when she walked in: the inside had changed. A cat rushed up and began rubbing himself on her legs. A waitress in her forties came over to the table. Ada ordered a Lapsang Souchong tea, noticing that the young woman she'd seen standing in the middle of the street was sitting opposite her reading a book, her pink bob tangled around her face. They were drinking the same tea, Ada could see from her teabag label. She stood up impulsively, wanting to say hello, then she realised: she'd not thought of applying for a job here.

'Do you have any vacancies?' she asked the waitress.

'Afraid not,' she replied. 'Is it for a grandchild?'

'It's for me.'

'Oh!'

'I've been coming here for years and thought it would be nice to work here.'

'Wonderful idea. I'm Kate. New owner.'

Ada gave Kate her CV and sipped her tea daintily while Kate read it. The cat jumped onto her lap and began purring extravagantly. Ada didn't much like animals but this fellow was rather fine, and so soft it seemed barely possible. The arthritis in her hip was painful after her walk around town but the hot drink and sit-down were helping.

'So you're a poet?' Kate asked.

'Yes,' Ada said.

'How come you want a job?'

Ada considered. Nobody had actually asked her that question. She decided on the truth. 'My husband died, I'm stuck in the house, I don't think I'm exactly flourishing on my own.'

Kate looked at her.

Might as well go on, Ada thought. 'I don't get out as much as I ought to, friends that I assumed were mine and Michael's turned out to be either crashing bores or uninterested in me, and I miss him terribly but I know I need to strike out on my own. Everyone bangs on about staying active, having a social life. It supposedly makes one live longer, though at this stage I'm not sure I'd like to.'

Kate's arm twitched, like she wanted to take Ada's hand. Ada watched her placidly. Kate suggested that Ada pop by next Friday for a trial run.

'I'd love to, thank you,' Ada said.

The following week she arrived at the café at 10 a.m., dressed in black as instructed. As well as Kate, there were two other waitresses on duty, Sophie and Lucy, both twenty. They'd clearly been briefed about Ada and looked at her curiously, as they might a moose that had walked in and ordered a flat white. At first Ada enjoyed herself. The other two waitresses didn't note down orders so Ada followed their lead, but soon she got into a horrible muddle: had that couple ordered hot chocolate and a bowl of granola, or tea and hot cross buns? Every time someone put in an order, another customer would flag her down and the interruption would nudge the first order from her mind. She began noticing that customers were giving her the same deadened smile. After what felt like hours, Ada fled to the bathroom for a rest. She put her elbows on her knees. She checked her watch. It wasn't yet noon. Every part of her body was aching. She was so motionless, so comprehensively wiped out, that the automatic light in the bathroom switched off and she was plunged into darkness. She had to wave her arms madly to make it turn on again.

Kate was behind the till. Ada walked over, ignoring customers trying to hook her attention. 'I'm not managing very well,' she said.

Kate nodded kindly. Ada felt like a berk. 'I'm sorry,' she said. 'I'm finding it much more tiring than I anticipated.'

'It is exhausting, you're right.'

'Thank you for giving me a go. It was most open-minded of you.'

'My pleasure.'

Kate motioned to Lucy to cover the till and they went and sat at a free table. 'So what'll you do next?' Kate asked.

'Well, given I'm not cut out for employment, perhaps I should start my own business,' Ada mused.

Kate grinned. 'Great idea! I recommend it. I started this place after my divorce and it's been pretty tough, but wonderful.'

'I do keep reading about start-ups,' Ada said. 'Uber and so on. They all seem to be run by teenage boys. Maybe I should give that a go, infiltrate the market.'

'Why not?'

'Not much to lose.'

Ada smiled and told her she'd be back soon for another Lapsang tea. Kate said the next one would be on the house. Ada returned to Swinburne Road. She would spend the afternoon setting up her business.

Ada had watched enough films and TV by now to know that in order to successfully launch a start-up you needed to be dressed in sportswear. In Manchester years ago she'd resolved to get fit and in preparation went on a spree in John Lewis. She'd worn her purchases – fluorescent-pink leggings with a fluorescent-pink top – three times as she lugged herself out of the cottage for a jog; then her resolve weakened and the clothes made their way to the back of the cupboard. Inspecting them now, Ada was pleased to note that the outfit was in good nick. It was strange to recall why she'd last worn the clothes and how differently she was hoping to use them now. The leggings felt loose on her shins and thighs but tight around her waist. Her body, too, had changed in the intervening years.

There were A3 sheets in a roll in Michael's study. Ada set herself before them in the kitchen with a permanent marker. She didn't know quite how brainstorms worked but assumed they involved freedom of association so she wrote down whatever words came to her in large black letters: bakery – technology business – PR agency – cab company – chocolate factory – modelling agency – and so on. Then she set about listing the pros and cons of each.

Soon it got dark. The evening outside was black and malignant; erratic gusts kept rattling the kitchen windows. Ada wasn't getting anywhere; she needed fresh air. She pulled on one of Michael's old coats and some crocs over her thick socks, and left the house. Swinburne Road was empty though Ada could see televisions shuffling their colours in blue living rooms. The house opposite was still being renovated. There was a room upstairs that was lit; she could see the young woman from Sylvie's staring at the open shell of her laptop.

On Abingdon Road Ada heard two people arguing. The voices were shrill. She followed the sound until she saw a mother rowing with someone that looked like her daughter, aged six or seven. The girl seemed to be unwilling to carry on walking down the street.

'I don't want you,' the child was crying. 'I want her!'

Ada stopped ten metres away. This sort of commotion never happened in Iffley, or if it did, it was behind closed doors. The woman and girl seemed too absorbed in their argument to notice Ada standing there.

'Kimbie, Gran isn't here,' the mother was saying, again and again. 'She's not here, darling. She's not coming back. I'm sorry, she's not here.'

The girl shook her head and stamped her feet. She was weeping, her small face pink and burnished, her fine brown hair sticking to her wet cheeks. The woman had tears on her cheeks too.

'I want to see her,' the girl was saying over and over. 'I'll only go if Gran's there too.'

The exchange continued in circles. The January cold pressed in. Ada stepped forward. The light from one of the lamp-posts lit the reflective strips on her leggings, and the woman and Kimbie noticed her at the same moment.

'Can I help you?' Ada asked. Her voice was trembling. As she spoke she realised she had no idea what she was doing. 'I'm sorry to interrupt.'

The mother's face hitched up, pulling itself into a public-facing shape. 'No, thank you,' she said composedly. 'My daughter Kimbie's missing her gran, who lived with us.'

Ada understood that the grandmother, whoever she was, had died. She looked at Kimbie. The child looked wary but she had stopped crying in the face of such an apparition, a wacky old lady in pink clothing, crocs with socks and a gigantic Barbour.

'I'm very sorry to hear your grandmother died,' Ada said gently. Kimbie stared. Then she hiccuped and wiped her eyes with the back of her hand. 'It's awful when people we care for are taken from us,' Ada added. 'It's so unfair.'

Kimbie nodded.

'Did you like her?' Ada asked.

'Yeah,' Kimbie said. 'I liked her loads and now I don't get to see her and I hate it.'

'Yes.'

Kimbie seemed to collect herself a little. She took a deep breath, her tiny chest juddering with the ghosts of sobs, but she didn't cry. Ada pointed out that it was quite a chilly night and that if her gran had known she and her mum were out in the street on a night such as this, she'd not likely have been happy about it. Kimbie nodded.

'I'd like to be with her again,' she said. 'That's all.'

'I understand,' Ada said.

Kimbie's mother stepped forward. She thanked Ada and took her daughter's hand. They walked together down the road towards their house, the girl glancing back every so often at the lady on the pavement, who looked at her too until Kimbie's mother chivvied her into their house and they disappeared.

By the time Ada was back at Swinburne Road, she knew what her start-up was going to be. She poured herself a large sherry, shook out a fresh sheet and wrote in large capitals in the centre, 'RENT-A-GRAN'.

She was going to rent herself out as a grandmother. She might not happen to have the grandchildren that would make her technically qualify as one, but no one need know. Whoever felt they needed a benevolent elderly woman in their lives could have one: she'd set herself up as a sort of hybrid Mrs Doubtfire and Mary Poppins, with Maria from *The Sound of Music* thrown in, minus the singing. People would pay her to be grandmotherly with them. Perhaps her start-up would let her connect to people in unexpected ways, like in *The Wedding Date* when the woman who rented a boyfriend ended up falling for him and vice versa; Ada could weave herself into the fabric of Oxford, become indispensable to someone again – now that she wasn't to anyone, she knew it was the most precious feeling one could have. And weren't there entire Japanese families that hired themselves out like theatre troupes, so that solitary city workers returning to their remote villages during the holidays could keep face, bring home a courteous wife?

At midnight she stood up and surveyed her work. She was rather amazed by the state of the kitchen: there were sheets of paper all over the table and empty packets of Cheddar crisps everywhere (she'd been too preoccupied to fix up a proper supper). Using Michael's laptop, she conjured up Microsoft Word and composed an advert for her new company. She'd seen similar signs all over Oxford – PhD candidates looking for guinea pigs to experiment on, linguistics professors paying for interviews – and many had phone numbers in flappy vertical strips at the bottom, so that interested passers-by could walk off with the relevant contact details. Ada didn't know how to do vertical writing, so in the end she fudged it by typing her address, email and home telephone number at the bottom of the sheet. 'Any interested parties,' she typed out with a finger, 'should contact me directly.' They could jolly well note down her details if they wanted her.

She decided not to illustrate the advert with a picture of herself, but instead searched 'grandmother' on Google Images and found a photo of a ravishing white-haired beauty in a cream polo neck. She and the model didn't look in the least bit similar but she hoped people wouldn't mind when they met the real her; perhaps her charm would make up for it. She printed 100 copies and took the pile of adverts upstairs. The paper was warm and heavy as a baby's head, and smelled gratifyingly starchy. She laid the pile on the pillow next to her and fell asleep the moment she got into bed, stretching herself out in the middle of the mattress, still in her pink sports outfit.

Chapter Ten

The week after Eliza's school chapel service, she slept with five different people on five consecutive nights. She'd not done that before and part of her wanted to tell everyone she knew just to be able to revel in the abundance of it. She could see exactly what she was doing, that it was playbook damaged pixie girl behaviour, fundamentally uninteresting and foreseeable, but she couldn't rouse herself to care; a sense of weight and joylessness had settled on her since the day at St Antonia's and she was trying to give it the slip. As long she didn't get an STD or an actual baby, she'd probably be OK. Four out of the five nights she was drunk, the fifth night sort of high (a girl in the queue at Plush offered her some MD and Eliza accepted the crescent pill graciously, swallowed it with some cherry Coke). She didn't feel out of control so much as reluctant to spend nights coughing dust in her room on Swinburne Road.

The next week, Eliza did it again. The sex was so-so but every encounter gave rise to moments of oddity, of memorable specificity, that Eliza treasured. The Old Etonian she hooked up with on Tinder on the first night had a gecko, of all things, that he seemed to genuinely cherish; then there was the guy the next night who hit on her at The Chester. He was called Stu and he lived on a canal boat. He held her down while he fucked her, pressed her neck into the pillow, but not so hard it made her feel scared. After they finished he gave her the tour, showed her how adapted everything was for the narrow space; even the bookshelves had been carefully shaped and the kettle gleamed like it had just been polished by Mr Tumnus. They ate biscuits and lit the tiny coal fire, read copies of the *Mirror* by its light.

'Are you tired?' he asked. It was past two.

Eliza looked at him. Something in his voice made her wonder if he meant 'tired' in a deeper sense than just sleepy.

'Yes, I'm tired,' she said.

She could hear the relief in her voice. Relief to have been asked.

There was silence all around. Eliza wondered what Stu would say, whether he'd accept her invitation to talk about how they both were, really.

'We'd best be going to bed then,' he said, standing up and stretching.

Eliza nodded. He lent her some boxers for pyjamas. She slept deeply after weeks of fitful nights, her body rocked by the boat. She watched Stu's face as light moved into the room the next morning and a rabble of geese chattered on the water. It was strange to be in bed with another person, to see the warm bulk of a chest rising and falling. Stu awoke. Eliza looked away. After breakfast he offered to take her downriver to a wrecked nunnery. She said she'd better go. Stu nodded peaceably, smiled when she told him she'd return. They knew it wasn't true.

Having sex with men was less enjoyable than with women, Eliza found, but it was safer: she was not in danger of thinking of Ruby as it was happening. With women the experience was more sensual and communicative, more about finding a connection and making sure it was maintained for the benefit of both; with men, her body felt seized from her, its use ferreted out and put to work. She liked how legible the sexual dynamic with a man could be; they wanted this or that and she could provide it. She began to see her body differently, with more respect: for all its inadequacies it could gratify other people, take them out of themselves, give them the break from themselves that she was seeking from her own interiority.

The only time she brought back a woman to Swinburne Road was a disaster. Her name was Todd, she was a politics student at Catz, a friend of Eliza's friend Jess. Eliza knew that Jess was worrying about her in London and that she'd got it into her head that Eliza needed someone in Oxford, a girlfriend ideally; Todd was a lesbian. Eliza was reluctant to meet Todd, embarrassed she was being set up; she wanted disposable people only just now. But in the end she found Todd quite interesting. They went to a few bars and ended up in Eliza's room. They kissed on the bed. Todd started moving her hands up Eliza's tights, trying to take them off. Eliza wiggled her hips, trying mechanically to take off Todd's clothes too though she felt too tired to have sex, and she was fighting to contain a sense of despair building in her chest. Soon they were naked. Eliza saw with horror that Todd's body was covered in moles, just as Ruby's had been. They looked very similar, she now understood why she'd been attracted to Todd in the first place. The two women were even built the same: tall and strong, pale, with small breasts and thick thighs. Eliza felt ill. She'd drunk too much. She remembered the last time she and Ruby had had sex – it had happened a fortnight before it all ended, they'd lounged together in their bedroom in Bath for hours, Eliza coming again and again.

'You'll miss this,' Ruby had told her. Her lips and chin were wet. 'You'll never have it as good as you do now.'

Eliza hadn't known what to say.

'I'm sorry,' she said, trying to cover her bare skin with her duvet. 'I'm sorry.'

Todd's lips were clamped around Eliza's left nipple. For a moment their eyes met. Then Todd drew away.

'What's up?' she asked.

'I don't think I want to do this,' Eliza said. She pressed herself against the bedroom wall. 'I know that sounds stupid, I'm sorry.'

'Um, don't worry.'

Todd didn't ask further questions. Eliza was grateful. It was long past midnight, the darkness booming in from outside. There didn't seem to be anything else to talk about. Todd dressed quickly and left. Eliza was glad when her body was clothed and out of sight, though she felt guilty too. She poured herself some Night Nurse, the green liquid thick and incandescent as a potion, and let it clobber her to sleep.

Eliza told Judy about her promiscuous phase in mid-January. The days were dour and brief. Judy laughed, called Eliza's buccaneering a 'roaring rampage of revenge'. She'd been seeing a post-doc from Jamaica called Sam for a couple of months now. He was nice. He'd started joining her and Judy's dinners, along with their friend George, a grad Eliza met by chance outside the modern languages library, smoking surreptitiously like her under a leafless wisteria. A few times a week Eliza was lured out of her trough of unease, as she rolled her eyes at George's jokes and watched Sam and Judy chat agreeably, hold hands under the long college table.

Once or twice she tried to talk to the three of them about her work: they were doing DPhils too and knew better than anyone what that entailed. But Eliza learned not to mention her studies – she was meant to be investigating the notion of impurity within Levi's books yet all her ideas seemed obvious, undergraduate marginalia barely worth typing out. Whenever she tried to explain what she was looking into an image of the author would return to her: of Levi at his desk in the Corso Re Umberto in Turin, his fingertips pressed together, his expression enigmatic. She was missing something; the man she thought she knew felt alien, like they'd been having a conversation and she'd lost the ability to understand Italian.

'Can you talk to your tutor about all this?' George asked her one afternoon when she tried yet again to explain her block. They were in the New College library.

Eliza frowned. 'I should do,' she said. But she couldn't face the prospect of another load of books and films to sift through before their next meeting. She'd not seen Baleotti since long before Christmas, despite him extending invitations to have tea or attend the constant lectures and round tables happening at the university. Eliza was embarrassed for Baleotti that he thought she was an intellect worth engaging with. If he wás offended by the cooling of their relationship, he didn't show it, and one afternoon he asked by email if she might be interested in helping organise a conference on the literary scene in seventies Turin. Eliza accepted reluctantly, unable to shake the impression that she was radically misusing her time, that she wasn't cut out for academia, that any day now Baleotti would see the flesh beneath the mask and cease to invite her to things or seek her feedback on this novella, that opera, that poem.

Eliza knew she should 'talk it out' or whatever, so she did what she could. She sent endless WhatsApps to Ellie and Jess, her friends from Bath; they were sympathetic but distracted, both caught in the London spin: brunch, Bumble, galleries, vegan markets. On a whim Eliza told Judy and Sam that she was going through 'a bit of a low patch'. They were in Spiced Roots, a Caribbean restaurant in Cowley. The music was loud and the waiters were dancing jubilantly behind the bar as they made cocktails. The tables flanking them were so close Eliza could have eaten her neighbours' food.

'What kind of low?' Judy asked gently.

'I dunno really,' Eliza said, grinning. 'I suppose I'm probably lacking in direction, purpose, joy, all the usual. It's probs just a quarter-life crisis. Also I'm skint, which is why I'm just having a side dish.'

Judy and Sam watched her silently, their faces bearing the same expression of compassion.

'We can cover you tonight,' Sam said.

'Nah, nah,' Eliza replied.

She squashed her remaining nub of plantain with the back of her fork. The caramelised mash squirted up between the prongs. She felt dumb for having torn through so much of her savings, but Oxford was way more expensive even than Bath had been – the books and rent and Wi-Fi, the random bits she needed for her room, the pub trips that seemed not to weigh on the budgets of other students but which decimated hers.

'Are you talking to your dad much at the moment? Maybe you should go home for a weekend,' Judy suggested. Early on in their friendship Eliza had sketched out the situation with her mother; Judy knew they weren't close.

'Maybe,' Eliza said. With difficulty, she added, 'He's being quite distant at the moment.'

She didn't know what was going on. Rich wasn't picking up her messages with his normal promptness. It wasn't like him to be anything other than extremely keen to speak with her, normally she had to fend him off. He'd mumbled at one point on the phone that something was going on with Flora, but when Eliza had asked him what, he didn't elaborate. It had been years since Flora and Rich had been a couple anyway; they barely saw one another. In December Rich had seemed alright – he and Eliza had spent Christmas Day with Tony, an old Cavaghan mate, bought a load of canapés from Iceland and parked themselves in front of the TV. But something was troubling him now.

Sam suggested that Eliza help out with a sandwich run he organised for homeless people in Oxford; it might help her escape 'the bubble', give her a sense of perspective. Eliza had no choice but to accept: of course she had the free time; of course it was the right thing to do.

She was disconcerted to discover that the sandwich run did actually help. For a few hours twice a week she felt useful. It wasn't really about giving homeless people sandwiches but about talking to them. The students that passed them multiple times a day literally did not see them, though tourists were a little better, more likely to find change in their wallets. The second time Eliza did the run, when she was giving a sandwich to a man called Daz outside Worcester College, a cab drove past with a couple of undergrads in dining gowns inside. One of them leaned out of the window and screamed, 'Corbynista cunt!' His face was crazed, watching Eliza talk to Daz. The car was gone so quickly she didn't have the time to return the middle finger he had shaken in her face. She turned back to Daz, shocked. His expression was unchanged. 'Happens a bit,' he shrugged.

She took a seat next to him, pushing her back into the golden stone. She tried to dismember her fury, as the college clocks rang 8 p.m. An old lady walked past and dropped a couple of quid into Eliza's lap. That made Daz laugh. His voice was threadbare. 'You worked for that,' he said. Eliza started to laugh too. The air from their throats tufted silver-white in the cold. She stayed for an hour, talking to Daz about the IT business he had set up in the early 2000s. Then she said she would have to get on. He nodded, raised a few fingers as she walked away. She wondered if she was being moral, doing this homeless run thing, or if she was just using it to feather a sense of herself as a caring person. She wondered if it mattered why people behaved morally, more that they just behaved morally. Rain began to fall, then thickened into wet snow. Finally it dried out into fat, gorgeous flakes the size of bumblebees. Eliza watched the snow float down in the halos of lamp-posts. She walked back to Swinburne Road, hoping the flakes would settle on the pavements, but they didn't, they melted at first touch, leaving them dark with water.

A couple of weeks later Eliza was outside Waterstones when she was handed a leaflet by a couple of activists. One was a skinny black guy of about eighteen; the other a white woman in her late twenties. She was wearing an EU flag draped over her backpack that made her look like a rabidly Europhile snail. The pair of them were obviously campaigning for Remain in the upcoming referendum; Eliza didn't need persuading but she stopped anyway: she was on her way to a meeting about Baleotti's conference and she felt like dawdling.

'Vote to keep Britain strong?' the young man asked her timidly. He was one of those diehard introverts who'd found a cause he cared about enough to induce him to talk to strangers.

The woman began asking Eliza about her feelings on the EU. From her accent Eliza thought she must be Spanish. 'I'm Remain, I'm Remain,' Eliza said. 'Save your energy.'

The woman laughed. She had thick glasses and a lovely voice, low and fissured and lived-in, like she'd gone out a lot when she was young but had turned her life around since then, become a cello player or something. Her irises were pale jade, Eliza noticed, ringed by a line of dark grey or blue. Warmth blushed through Eliza's body.

'I'm Paola,' the woman said.

'Eliza,' Eliza said, then laughed.

'What's funny?'

'Oh, I dunno, saying my name I suppose.'

She grinned loopily, then tried to dial the voltage of her smile down a bit: maybe she looked unhinged. They stuck out their hands for the other to shake, then raised their arms into a more modern wave. It was awkward. Eliza thought they must look like Lindsay Lohan in *The Parent Trap*, Twin One and Twin Two doing that synchronised handshake by the lake. She asked how the campaigning was going.

'Pretty well,' Paola said. 'Oxford at least is a cert.'

Eliza said she wished she could feel as optimistic: in Cumbria, it was a different matter. Even her father at Christmas had mused that the country ought to 'take back control', and when Eliza had sat up straight (they were watching *Call the Midwife*) and asked him what the hell that meant, he told her huffily not to have a 'millennial meltdown'. They both sat in silence after that, the TV sloshing them with noise; a baby was being born with an umbilical cord looped around his neck. Rich was so rarely rude to his daughter that they were both shocked, too busy absorbing his words, replaying them, flexing them this way and that, to say much else.

Then Rich apologised, said they were both entitled to their opinions, that Eliza might be right, but that it did seem from where he was sat that Brussels had done diddly-squat to help Carlisle out, and that he'd rather decisions were made on this island than in some foreign city he had zero intention to even visit. Eliza listened, hoped she understood, worried later about what it might mean if she hadn't understood.

She tried to evoke all this to Paola, as a warning that in some parts of the country things weren't moving the way it looked down south, but she wasn't good at telling stories: by the end the people expected another hump in the narrative, a punchline to round it all off. She finished and saw that Paola was watching her smilingly, imagining more was coming. Eliza saw too that her lips were full and dark, the colour of cherries when you bit them.

'D'you want to campaign?' Paola asked. 'We're looking for more people.'

'I'd love to,' Eliza heard herself reply enthusiastically.

Leslie introduced himself uncertainly as a biochem undergrad from Tooting; Paola said she was from Madrid, doing a master's in international relations. They weren't working for the official campaign but for some Oxford grassroots thing. Paola asked Eliza where she lived, looked pleased when she discovered it was on a street they'd not leafleted before.

'No one's heard of Swinburne Road,' Eliza said.

'Oxford's full of places like that,' Paola remarked. 'Secret places that you'd not know exist.'

Eliza wanted, very suddenly and very much, for Paola to show her every single secret place in Oxford that she knew; they could cycle to each one, every day or one per week to eke out the pleasure of it.

'Saturday work for you?' Paola asked.

'Yep.'

They swapped numbers. Then Eliza gave Paola and Leslie a wave, separating her fingers into a zany *Star Trek* V. Leslie grinned in recognition but Paola looked confused, like she didn't understand the reference, so Eliza made her fingers go normal again. Paola obviously hadn't watched *Star Trek*. Well, that was fine: they'd watch it together.

A little giddy, a little cold, she walked off, realising as she wove in and out of the tourists that she'd forgotten about the conference meeting, that it was well under way now and that Baleotti would be disappointed in her for skiving; but for now: Paola, Paola, and the fizz in Eliza's chest, and the white sun overhead, slamming the pavements with brightness.

Back in her room, she flipped open her laptop to find a crestfallen email from Baleotti. It was polite but suffused with concern for her, worry that she was feeling 'a bit lost in the DPhil'. Why had she missed the meeting about the conference – was it all too much on top of her work, was she keeping afloat, was she coping? Eliza didn't know what to say so she put it in a starred folder in her inbox and tried to forget about it. But his instincts were right – every day that week her work felt sludgy; she spent hours in the library but couldn't concentrate, she kept checking her phone, swiping through photos of her and Ruby from years ago. She ate up the endless Instagram stories being posted hour by hour by the St Antonia's girls, refreshing Twitter and the BBC news website as if she had a stake in any of it, could change any of it. Meanwhile the image of Levi in his study, his expression inscrutable, began appearing in her dreams and in the grey zone between sleeping and wakefulness, when Eliza was aware of light pooling in her bedroom but was not ready to confront it yet, to accept its invitation. By Friday Eliza hadn't replied to Baleotti and she'd barely done any work. She resolved to avoid hotspots where people from the Italian department tended to hang out – the faculty, the library, the Eccola café on Trumpington Street.

The following morning arrived and with it, the date with Paola. The freezing spell had broken; for two days Oxford had been battered by rain. Some of the villages further out were preparing for flooding; meadows were sopping and rivers all over the county coursing by like rapids. Eliza met Paola outside the supermarket on Iffley Road. It wasn't raining yet though the clouds were full and violet.

'Where's your flag?' Eliza asked.

'I thought if it rained, it might get heavy on my back,' Paola explained.

As she spoke Eliza remembered the way her face worked, and that she was one of those people who smiled almost whenever she talked. She was relieved to discover that she definitely fancied her. The jade of her eyes hadn't been some implanted memory.

They began knocking on doors at the end of Swinburne Road by Donny Bridge. It felt like a bit of an act, self-conscious and grandiose. Eliza had assumed they'd just be slotting leaflets through letterboxes. People opened up their houses suspiciously or not at all, and when they discovered the pair of them were Remainers they softened: at least they weren't having to see off a couple of Jehovah's Witnesses. Everyone said they were for Remain, at which point Paola urged them to 'get out and vote' on the big day, to which they replied that they had every intention. It felt like being a popular MP doing a glory lap of a local stronghold.

Ten buildings down, they came across a household that was voting Leave. Eliza said a few vague things about how Britain would have more influence by being part of the bloc, and as she spoke she could see the couple's eyes sliding in and out of focus, now bored, now engaged, now bored again. She didn't think she changed their minds. 'Ah well,' Paola said as they left, squeezing her hand. They continued to hold hands after that.

Eventually they reached Eliza's end of the road. It started to pour. Black puddles bloomed like oil spills on the tarmac. They stopped at the house opposite Eliza's with the yellow door. A woman answered. She was slight, in her late sixties, Eliza estimated, with grey hair that she'd piled on top of her head with a clip. Her skin was thin and flecked but radiant too, as if there were a lit bulb somewhere beneath. She looked shocked to see the pair of them sopping on her doorstep, Paola's glasses bobbled with raindrops. Eliza wished she could see inside the house; who the lady lived with, clues that might reveal how she spent her time. Most of all she longed to see the room upstairs where she'd seen that figure standing late at night by the curtains – was it the woman in front of her now, or some Boo Radleyish other?

Before Paola could launch into her spiel, the woman cut in. 'It's not an Age Concern thing, is it?' she asked suspiciously. 'I'm coping perfectly well, thank you.'

'No!' Eliza said. Paola produced a leaflet.

'Oh, you're here to talk about Brexit,' the woman murmured. Some of her frostiness subsided. 'Well,' she said. 'I'm undecided. I don't think I should've been asked to have a say.'

'But since you have been asked . . .' Paola said, 'perhaps it's worth engaging?'

'You're right, of course,' the woman said. She looked uneasy; she was holding the door as if a gust of wind might precipitously slam it open. Eliza had the impression that no one had visited her at home for a long time.

'Thank you for coming by,' the woman continued. 'I'm encouraged to see that you care about all this, quite right, but I must get on.'

This sort of thing had happened a lot. Eliza and Paola thanked her and turned to go. Then the woman asked them to wait: she had something to give them 'in return', she said, her voice light with excitement. They waited for her to fetch whatever it was from indoors. It turned out to be a printed-out piece of paper with a picture of a ravishing elderly model on it, who definitely wasn't the woman they were standing in front of.

She explained that it was an advert for her business. 'Fold it up nicely so it doesn't get wet,' she instructed them; surprised, they did as they were told. The lady thanked them for dropping by, then retreated into her house. They heard her lock the door. As they braced themselves to cross the street through the downpour, Eliza glanced at the woman's living room window. She thought she could see a darkness behind the lace curtains, a shape or a shadow, fingers parting the material just a little to check they were leaving. And on it rained.

Chapter Eleven

'You're hiring yourself out as a granny?' Kate repeated, aghast.

'Yes,' Ada said equably. She was in Sylvie's.

'Isn't that a bit – bonkers?'

'I don't really think so.'

'What about your own grandchildren? What do they think about it?'

'I don't have any.'

'So, sorry, people who want a granny to attend their christening or whatever will call you up?'

'I hope so. Or they'll email me, or write me a letter. I even have a mobile now, I got a pay as you go. Clients can text me if they wish.'

'Why on earth are you doing it?'

'I want to. People barely even see me when I walk by; you'll know what I mean in twenty years. I want to make my life enjoyable and I think by starting a business I might manage it.'

'What if people think you're a . . .' Kate lowered her voice and looked around. 'A prostitute?'

That made Ada sit up a little. 'I'll break it to them that I'm not. I'm sure they'll survive.'

Kate collared Sophie and Lucy, the two waitresses Ada had worked alongside during her shift. 'Ladies,' Kate said, her tone plaintive. 'Listen to what Ada is planning.'

Ada explained. Lucy's eyes widened. Sophie clapped her hands. 'Sick idea!' she exclaimed.

Ada intuited that 'sick' denoted something positive. She raised an eyebrow at Kate. 'You see?'

Kate didn't look convinced.

'If it goes really badly,' Ada continued, slightly irritated, 'here's what I'll do: put a stop to it. I started Rent-a-Gran, I can bloody well end it.'

Kate rolled her eyes. 'And anyway,' Ada added, 'I've been putting my ads up all over Oxford for weeks now and still not got a single call, letter or anything. Perhaps this will be the start-up that never was. The flop. There are lots like that, I've read about them in the papers. They get all sorts of investment anyway.'

Returning home after tea, Ada found three voicemails waiting for her on her landline. The first was from a journalist from BBC Radio Oxford, asking her about the 'intriguing business proposition being advertised all over town'; would Ada consent to be interviewed? She deleted the message. The second voicemail was some sort of prank call from what seemed to be a rabble of drunk teenagers. She deleted that too. The third was from a woman who introduced herself breathily as Valerie Edgcombe. She lived on Warwick Street and said she was interested in 'hiring a granny as soon as possible'. Her voice sounded like it could break into giggles at any moment; as if she couldn't believe that she was making such a call. Ada opened a packet of pork scratchings to celebrate her first prospective client and worked on summoning the courage to call the woman back. Valerie picked up on the third ring. Ada cleared her throat and introduced herself.

'Oh!' Valerie gasped. 'You! Oh! Gosh.'

'I received your voicemail,' Ada continued smoothly, trying to sound like a pro. 'And I'd be happy to be of service.'

'Well!' Valerie said. 'Well! Gosh!'

She fought to recover her poise. 'It's not for me, it's for my son. Can I speak in confidence?'

'Of course.'

'He still lives with me but he's thirty-four. He's called Little Hen. Henry, strictly. He's a wonderful squish but my husband Simon and I do worry he'll remain with us forever. He's utterly useless, poor bub. I've tried to teach him how to cook and things but we just row and he storms off.'

'How awful,' Ada said, meaning it. 'That must be very hard.'

'Oh, it is,' Valerie replied. 'He's totally undomesticated. He's essentially a cave child.'

'Does he have a job?'

'Goodness me, no.'

'Does he have interests?'

'I daren't ask.'

Ada thought she could sense why Little Hen might be having trouble leaving the nest. 'And how do you think I can help?' she asked delicately.

'I was sort of hoping that you might teach him the basics,' Valerie said. 'Even just to boil an egg. Anything you deem appropriate. That way he may find a girlfriend, become independent.'

Ada considered. Perhaps the lad needed rescuing from his mother. 'I'll do it,' she said.

They talked logistics – payment, timings and so on. Ada decided to charge £10 per hour. She imagined she'd be breaking the law by not paying tax on her takings but she didn't care; it seemed unlikely she'd ever make enough to meet whatever threshold the taxman currently demanded, and in any case she didn't think she'd be caught. If the business took off, she'd blow her earnings on something preposterous, like a convertible.

'Just one other thing,' Valerie said. 'Would you mind pretending you're a friend of mine?'

This was more complicated. Ada didn't want to deceive people; her aim was to help, not hoodwink. 'Do you think Henry would not agree to meet me if he knew you were paying?' she asked.

'Oh, no no no,' Valerie said, aghast. 'He'd never do it. He'd be humiliated, he'd say it was "cringe". But if he thought you were a friend of mine I'd put up to it, he might behave a little better.'

'Won't he have seen the adverts I've put up?'

'He doesn't leave the house much. I drive him to Cineworld, but that's about it. I doubt he's heard of, um, Rent-a-Gran. How similar do you look to the photo in the advert?'

Ada swallowed. She felt a strong urge to cackle.

'Not hugely,' she said. 'Who shall I say I am? I'd like to keep my first name, at least.'

'That's fine. Pretend we met at my book club. Henny knows I do that every week. We last read something racy. But maybe say we read *Atonement*. If he asks. He's not frightfully sexual. Wouldn't want to traumatise him.'

'Righto. I'm Ada, your friend from book club. I simply love Ian McEwan.'

And so, two days later, on the first Friday of February, Ada made her way to Warwick Street to meet Valerie and her son. She packed a couple of aprons into her handbag for the cookery lesson. They were splodged with yellow paint: the last time they'd been used must have been when Michael and she had redone the front door a decade ago. The fabric still smelled of paint, and of dust and moths from the cupboard where the aprons were kept. It took all of Ada's resolve, as she was preparing to leave the house, not to stay in the kitchen, pressing the silly aprons to her heart.

But sentimentality wouldn't cut it. She forced herself to leave, avoiding looking at the copper-wire owl in the sitting room and the framed picture behind it. Outside the air was glass and cool, wrung clean by a morning of rainfall. Valerie lived on Warwick Street in a portly red-brick house; it wasn't far to go. Ada walked up the long road, counting down until number sixteen came into view. She checked her watch and waited for a minute until it was four on the dot, then rang the doorbell. She felt thrillingly naïve, like a governess in starched clothing arriving at a gothic house, possessions in tow, a life of Latin and quietness ahead of her.

A woman about ten years younger than Ada opened the door. She had a bob of dyed red hair and was wearing a flowery blouse over a wool skirt. She'd applied two

bold streaks of terracotta blusher to her cheekbones. Ada
thought her head looked interestingly cuboid. The woman
was smiling. She smelled of pencils.

'Hello,' Ada said.

'Are you the gran-for-hire?' the woman whispered.

'I am,' Ada said. She felt the overwhelming impulse to
click her heels together officiously.

'Oh goodness, I'm so glad you're here, I'm Valerie,' the
woman said. She talked even faster than she had on the
phone, fully double Ada's speaking speed. 'So good of you
to come, this is quite mad of course but I'm so happy to
meet you, gosh aren't you nice in your nice neat coat, it's
funny, I felt nervous but now I don't, seeing you there
you look exactly as I'd hoped, isn't it chilly, oh, Little
Hen will adore you I'm sure, how kind of you to come
all this way.'

'Not at all.'

Valerie ushered her into the house. Everything had a
print or a pattern or a doily or a bonnet; there were about
twelve lamps in the living room alone, each draped in
beads or boas. Valerie's husband Simon, she said, was at
work. A surveyor. Back at eight. Little Hen was upstairs.

'Henny?' Valerie called up. 'My chum's here for your
cookery lesson. Come down, sweetheart, when you're up
to it!'

Ada heard an inchoate yell from upstairs. They walked
into the kitchen. Ada wondered if this was how the sexually
adventurous felt when they attended their first orgy: horribly
embarrassed and rather excited to see how it all turned out.

Ada had decided to teach Henry how to make an
omelette, a puff pastry tart and a chocolate mousse. She

started sorting through the ingredients laid out by Valerie for her on the kitchen counter. Valerie hung around, staring at her, anxiously polishing this surface or that tap, asking Ada again and again if she had everything she wanted, if she was 'in the market for a cup of tea' or a 'biccy'. Ada stopped wanting to laugh and began to feel rather concerned for the woman. At last they heard the thump of feet on the stairs and Valerie jumped. 'I'll be off,' she chirruped.

She had agreed to leave the house while the lesson went on: Ada had explained on the phone that she wanted to interact with her son on their own terms. Now that he was on his way downstairs, Valerie made several attempts to exit the kitchen but kept returning to ask Ada another question – was she really 'all set', did she not want an orange juice – until Ada heard her son in the hall groan 'Muuuummmmm, just goooooo,' and Valerie, waving and babbling, left the house.

And so Little Hen entered the kitchen. He was no child, but vast and bearded with Viking red hair and an ancient Nokia T-shirt stretched over his chest. The rest of his body was curtained off by a turquoise sarong.

'Hi,' he grunted.

Ada saw he had strips of lavender under his eyes; his skin looked uncooked, like he'd been indoors for a decade.

'Hello, I'm Ada,' she said.

She stuck out her hand neatly. Henry shook it, not meeting her smile. He stumped over to a cupboard, got out a bowl and filled it with Coco Pops. He was on the point of pouring in milk when Ada said sharply, 'Hang on, I'm here to give you a cookery lesson, don't eat now.'

Henry looked slightly surprised. He returned the milk to the fridge, his ears reddening. Ada saw he was wearing hand-knitted slipper socks, one with 'Little' embroidered at the toes, the other with the word 'Hen'. She felt sorry for him. 'Would you mind if we had a conversation before we begin?' she asked gently.

'No,' Henry said.

'We'll keep it short.'

'OK.'

'Would you like me to call you Henry or Little Hen?'

'Henry.'

'Who does the cooking here?'

'Mum.'

'Do you help her?'

'I lay the table.'

'Do you help her cook, though?'

'No.'

'Does your father?'

'Sometimes he grills stuff, in the summer. Sausages.'

'Do you think it's unfair that only your mother does the cooking?'

Henry paused at this. 'Probably,' he said.

'Can your friends cook?'

'Some of them.'

'Would you like to cook for them?'

'Er. Yeah.'

'Do you think it would be nice to cook for your mother on occasion?'

'Yeah, if she let me.'

'Well then, shall we get to work?'

'OK.'

Henry seemed energised by the straightforwardness of the conversation. Ada told him that the best way to start would be to break some eggs into a bowl for the omelette. It transpired that he knew full well how to make omelettes: he'd spent four years at Nottingham University and had had to fend for himself there. His mother simply refused to believe that he could raise a finger to sustain himself. Ada asked if he'd ever made a soufflé; Henry said that he hadn't. So they began doing that instead, talking haltingly all the while. He was lovely, Ada realised, if lavishly underconfident. When she showed him how to beat the egg whites with a whisk, he offered to do them for her. Then he decided there must be an electric whisk in the kitchen. He began looking through the cupboards, in the manner of an inquisitive alien exploring a human residence for the first time. Eventually he gave up and beat the egg whites into peaks manually, marvelling at how long they took to stiffen.

They had a pleasant few hours. Henry was capable of being charming and interesting, so long as he didn't think that attention was being focused on him, so Ada made sure she kept busy, and over the clatter of chopping and stirring they talked properly. It was hard emotional labour that required constant vigilance in case she spooked him back into his reticence, but she found to her bemusement that she was equal to the challenge.

'Are you happy living at home?' Ada asked, as she showed him how to peel tomatoes by pouring boiling water over their shining red backs.

'No,' he said. 'I'm in limbo here.'

He explained that he'd wanted to become an actor since he was a kid and spent a few years trying to get it off the ground in London, until he was dropped by his agent and dumped by his girlfriend and returned home. That was four years ago. Now he didn't know what to do. No job seemed interesting enough to bother with. His life had fallen apart just as his friends' lives had clicked into shape – marriage, babies, all that.

'What sort of life do you want?' Ada asked.

Henry considered. 'A normal sort,' he said eventually. 'I'd like to live self-sufficiently.'

'A girlfriend?' Ada asked.

Henry looked at her coyly through his ginger eyelashes. 'Yeah, I guess.'

'Do you talk to your mother about this kind of thing?'

'No.'

The soufflé was ready. Henry could barely believe how much it had risen. He took it out of the oven and set it on the table proudly. They ate it there and then.

At seven, Valerie returned. Ada had set Henry onto the washing-up. His mother asked him if it had gone 'alright', her fingers fluttering to her neck. He nodded, said he'd had a nice time, recounted what they'd cooked. There was a tart ready for dinner later.

'Would be nice to have a few more lessons,' Henry muttered in Ada's direction, shy now that his mother had returned.

Ada glowed. She said she'd love to come back. Valerie watched the exchange agog. When she noticed that Henry was boiling the kettle to soak the soufflé pot, her hand flew to her mouth. Ada got out her diary and suggested she return the following Friday. Henry agreed. As Ada was getting her coat, Valerie slipped a few notes into her hand. Ada felt guilty, in an abstract sort of way, but pocketed the money; she'd worked for it after all. Then Henry came into the hallway in his washing-up gloves to say goodbye.

'So you'll come back next week?' he asked, looking at Ada's shoes.

'Yes,' Ada said.

Behind him, Valerie was staring at them both avidly.

'Have a think of what you'd most like us to cook,' Ada said.

'I've wanted to master Bolognese for a long time.'

'I used to make it for my husband, I'd be delighted to teach you.'

Ada gave Henry a shimmering smile. He smiled back. Valerie kissed Ada goodbye, a quavering peck on both cheeks as one might thank Mother Teresa for dropping by. Ada left the house, amused and touched and close to laughter, her heart frothy, her eyes filling intermittently with tears that she had to blink away impatiently, thinking of Henry in his washing-up gloves, and the drink he was fixing his mother that very minute, under Ada's encouragement.

Chapter Twelve

Spring was on the cusp of easing winter open. Trees around Oxford that bloomed early were pushing out their white flowers. There was a tree on Portman Close whose branches were so heavy with moon-pink petals that Eliza wanted to gobble it whole, or hold it or destroy it, until one morning as she detoured to walk past the tree, she saw a gathering of teenage girls worshipping the only way they knew how, by posing at its trunk, their heads lilting to the left, yanking the branches downwards to kiss the blossom as they were photographed by one another's smartphones. Eliza stopped visiting the tree after that, then chastised herself for her snobbery and made herself continue to walk by it on principle. Then the flowers fell.

It was a week after Eliza and Paola had first gone leafleting. Paola arrived at Swinburne Road with the intention of picking Eliza up to go on a walk, but the rain began to fall furiously, lances of water zipping onto the tarmac and rebounding back up, and they decided to stay in Eliza's room instead.

Eliza was a little ashamed of the state of the house, but her bedroom at least was cosy and warm. They stood at the window for a while, watching the downpour, saying things that are said in heavy rain. Then they sat on the bed. As they spoke they moved closer to one another, in nudges and shifts and quiet readjustments, like settling birds. Paola started stroking the underside of Eliza's wrist with her fingertips. Eliza felt a thrill move through her. She couldn't do much more than watch her wrist be touched, the vein green-blue and ticking silently. She wanted to run her hands over Paola's skin, she wanted to measure the warmth of her body with her own. Paola had taken off her coat; underneath she was wearing a black T-shirt and high-waisted jeans. She was flat-chested, her skin a light caramel. Eliza saw her own hand reach out for Paola's left one and wrap around her loosely closed fist. It opened at Eliza's touch like coral. Their bodies were angled oddly on the bed; sort of slumped amorously against the wall. All Eliza wanted was to lie flat and be kissed. Neither of them knew what subject they were talking about, it could have been anything, and at last Paola leaned in, tucked a strand of Eliza's hair behind her ear, brushed her lips with her bitten-cherry ones. The kiss was soft and light. She tasted of croissants. Eliza thought of Ruby and the last time they had kissed. She wondered if it had felt as weightless as this, as full of grace.

Paola ended up staying the whole afternoon. It was so apocalyptically wet outside there wasn't much to do, she said, but 'watch Netflix and chill'. Eliza laughed at the euphemism. She lent Paola a pair of pyjamas and they made a pot of Lapsang Souchong, then cut Eliza's hair. Paola palmed the pink curls on the ground into a ball and released them into Swinburne Road through the window; they were swept off by a riffle of wind. They spoke a lot about the advert that Eliza's neighbour opposite had given them, advertising her services as a rentable grandmother. There was a picture on it of the most gorgeous elderly woman imaginable. 'Need a gran in your life?' it read jauntily. 'Now you can hire one!'

Paola thought it must be a joke; Eliza was convinced it was legit. 'But who would pay someone to be their gran?' Paola demanded. 'You'd have to be end-of-the-world lonely.'

Eliza didn't say anything. The curtains opposite were drawn though their peach brightness suggested someone was in the house. 'She's probably the lonely one,' Eliza said.

As evening fell they fired up Eliza's laptop and watched a few episodes of *Gossip Girl*, repeating Blair's best lines to one another in lopsided American accents. At eight Paola said she was hungry.

'I've got crisps,' Eliza suggested.

Paola shuddered Spanishly. She lunged across Eliza's bare legs for her phone, saying she was getting them Deliveroo. They had fun choosing what to eat. Eliza hoped she wouldn't have to pay – she only had about two hundred quid left in her account and she didn't think Rich would approve if she blew some of that on a takeaway – but when she offered to go halves Paola insisted that the meal would be her treat, and Eliza gave in.

The food arrived. They unpacked the ramen and gyoza and watched a film about shark attacks. The actors were toned and gorgeous, with glow-in-the-dark teeth and short shorts, but when the sharks bit they screamed like hell. Paola and Eliza tuned in and out; kissed, touched one another, chatted idly. There was something addictive about Paola's scent, sweet and grassy, like a meadow in late summer. When Eliza tried to explain, Paola collapsed into giggles, saying an ex had told her once that she smelled of ponies. At midnight she took a taxi home. It was a wrench. Eliza folded up the pyjamas she'd left behind, crumpled the rubbish from their meal and got into bed. The sheets were warm from their bodies, the linen suppler than usual. She fell asleep at once.

They arranged to see one another the following weekend. Before that, unendurable days of vigilantly calibrated WhatsApp. Eliza could barely concentrate; she'd still not apologised to Baleotti for missing the meeting and she had skived all other Italian department events too. She started following Paola on Instagram and regretted it: her photos were of good-looking people Eliza didn't know in places she didn't recognise. The images conveyed a social life so rich and blithe she worried it wouldn't map onto her own quieter way of being. Paola followed her back, which was charitable given Eliza had only ever posted three photos. One morning Eliza woke to find that Paola had liked all three, even one of Ruby years ago stretched out on a pier in Venice. Eliza knew it was dumb to be pleased by the affirmation but she let herself be pleased anyway. It was like waking up to a stocking on Christmas morning, feeling the weight of it on your feet.

On Friday Paola suggested they go swimming the next morning. Eliza was reluctant: bikinis were death, she had thrush, she felt like she'd been cold for about a hundred years, she didn't like getting wet. Paola insisted they'd have fun and Eliza, keen to show she was up for anything, said yes.

The next morning Paola sent her a location to cycle to. The sky was bare, a cored blue. Eliza biked along the river, watching the rowers heave past, the coxes bundled up in coats at the tips of the boats. There were swans smoothing upriver too, and walkers on the pocked path by the water. Everyone seemed to have someone else with them. Eliza left her father a voice message, wobbling perilously as she tried to hold a handlebar with one hand and her phone with the other. Rich's remoteness had all but increased lately; he was behaving unlike himself – shiftily, mysteriously, according motives Eliza couldn't quite make out. She had asked him multiple times to call her up but he seemed unwilling to do it; claiming busyness or forgetfulness. Eliza speculated he didn't want to talk because of what his voice would betray: it was easier to conceal emotions in typed-out messages.

After ten minutes she arrived at the dropped pin. She looked around for some sort of outhouse that might contain a municipal pool. There wasn't one, but Paola was standing by a disabled ramp leading up to a small red-brick building. Eliza locked her bike up, feeling nervous; Paola looked lovely even from afar.

'We'll have to walk onwards for a bit, but we're nearly there!' Paola called.

They hugged, padded out by their thick coats. Eliza wanted to kiss her but she didn't know if it would be presumptuous; they'd made out before Paola got in her cab last Saturday but that had been night-time, in daylight the rules were different.

They walked across a field, heading, as far as Eliza could tell, for the middle of nowhere. Her trainers soaked through in seconds; the grass was glossy with dew. She was glad she'd brushed her teeth. After a couple of minutes Paola announced that they'd arrived. It took Eliza a while to make sense of what she was looking at; it seemed that she was just facing a broad section of the river.

'It's a pool!' Paola said.

Eliza began to see. The two banks were unnaturally straight, boxing the current in, and two metal ladders descended into the river. The pool was man-made – but further ahead, it was being topped up ceaselessly by a backwater of the Thames. Sun was crackling off the surface in bright flakes.

Paola explained that it was a Victorian bathing spot that had been built in the early nineteenth century and abandoned in the sixties or something. Eliza began to appreciate how beautiful it was; half reclaimed by nature, with reeds and other plants growing in the pool itself. After days of rain the current was strong, and downstream the water crashed into a sort of weir. There was nobody there but them.

'The water changes colour every day,' Paola said.

Today it was silvery blue. It looked very cold. Eliza realised she didn't want to take this any further: entering the river would be out of the question, she'd probably get hypothermia. They dropped their bags on a patch of grass encircled by brambles, Eliza scrambling to work out how to not swim without looking lame. Paola pulled a swimming costume out of her backpack, chatting happily.

'I'm not sure I can do this,' Eliza said.

Paola laughed. 'You'll be fine.'

'No, properly, I'm not sure I can. I'm not a good swimmer.'

'It's not as cold as it seems.'

Eliza felt the beginnings of panic. 'I'll drown! You'll have to fish my body out.'

Paola grinned. 'If you die I'll just run for it. No one will know I led you here.'

Eliza smiled begrudgingly. Paola began to change. Eliza was calmed a little by her nudity, radiant in the morning light.

'You'll be glad you did it,' Paola insisted, wriggling into a dark red swimsuit.

Eliza nodded doubtfully. She forced herself to change too, into the horrible black bikini she'd bought in Primark when she was sixteen. She looked down at her body, marvelling at how plain and lardish it looked. They walked to the pool edge. The ladder leading in seemed ancient, all rust and spindle, as if it could clunk into the river at any moment. Paola dropped her towel and went down the steps without a fuss. Yet even she gritted her teeth as she released herself into the water. The force of the current swept her off but she soon returned to Eliza by beating her arms in a love heart shape against the shove of water.

Eliza, hating everything, began to step down the ladder. The water was even more freezing than she'd imagined, a vicious cold that stripped her skin. 'Jesus fuck!' she yelped.

'Just launch off the ladder,' Paola said. 'Don't creep in, it's easier.'

Eliza did as she was told. She let go. Struck out. Dipped her whole head under. When she broke the surface she could barely breathe and felt herself being swept down-river, like a branch in a tidal wave.

'Aim towards the ladder,' Paola shouted.

Eliza tried to breaststroke upstream. It was hard work; the water had an animal force, relentlessly trying to palm her towards the weir. She had no idea what might happen there; whether blades or whatever would chop her up. She remembered that she was meant to be on a romantic date, and found the strength to whoop or yell something exhilarated. She sounded addled. Paola swam up to her and kissed her hard on the mouth. Her lips were cold but her tongue was warm and she looked different with wet hair, her eyelashes dark with water. They swam for a couple more minutes then got out and lay on the grass.

'I'm frozen,' Eliza croaked, once her body had stopped shaking.

'Imagine it's a forty-degree day in Portugal,' Paola replied. 'All you want is an ice cream, it's so boiling you can't even think.'

'It's not a forty-degree day in Portugal. I don't want an ice cream.'

'It's hot. It's gorgeous out. You're looking for your sunglasses.'

'I know where they are. They're in my cupboard in Swinburne Road. Because it's freezing and I don't need them.'

Paola laughed. 'Doesn't your skin feel good now? Mine's tingling.'

'I can't feel my skin.'

'You can!'

Eliza could, it was true. It was prickling; it felt almost singed. Her body was ringing with endorphins. She knew she was grinning idiotically. Paola pulled herself onto

Eliza's stretched-out body. Her body was light and cold, her swimsuit low-backed. Last Saturday Eliza had noticed that Paola had a way of holding herself still for unendurable seconds before she would finally lean in to kiss her; she was doing it again, until just as Paola was about to touch Eliza's lips with her own, they heard a phone ring nearby. Paola rolled off and rummaged through Eliza's bag for her mobile. She took the call, mouthed 'Someone called Flora' at Eliza and tossed her the phone.

'Lize?' came Flora's voice, on the other end of the line.

'Hi,' Eliza said. She wondered why her mother had called. They seldom spoke; when they did it was usually about something logistical.

Eliza immediately detected something tinny in her mother's voice, like fear. She sat up. 'How are you?' she asked. 'It's my mum,' she mouthed at Paola. 'I'll be one second.' Paola put her thumbs up and started towelling herself dry.

'Lize, I'm in a bit of a sticky one,' Flora said. 'I'm in a bit of a sticky one, in a bit of a sticky one, in a bit of a—' She sounded frenzied, like she'd called to say her hair was on fire.

'What's the matter?' Eliza asked. She'd not heard her mother sound as bad as this in years.

'I'm in a fix, Eliza, I quite want your help, love, I quite need your help.'

'What's wrong?'

'Have you got any money?'

Ah, Eliza thought. Right. A different sort of cold began to pool in her torso. 'Um, why?' Eliza asked. They were on familiar terrain. Flora had long since developed a habit

LEAF ARBUTHNOT

of asking for the odd bank transfer from Rich, colleagues
or whoever else seemed likely to give. Eliza had got the
same treatment when she went to Bath; Flora discovered
she had a maintenance grant and requested a slice. And
then another and another.

'Doesn't matter why I want it, doesn't matter, have you
got any?' Flora said.

'I have about £150,' Eliza said resignedly.

'D'you mind if I borrow some?'

'Er, a bit,' Eliza replied. She didn't want to say more
aloud, in case Paola worked out what she was agreeing to.

'A bit but not a lot?'

'Um, not, like, a lot a lot.'

'So you'll transfer it today?'

'On my bank app.'

'How long will that take to appear in my account?'

'Not long.'

'Will you not tell Rich?'

'Why not?'

Eliza thought she knew: Flora must have already asked
him for money. She felt exhausted. A ragged sadness
unfurled in her like night blossom.

'Just don't tell him,' Flora said. Her voice sounded
starched. 'Or I'll return the money.'

'OK, OK. Why d'you need it though? I thought you
were working at The Anchor?'

'Not anymore.'

'Oh.'

'Right, I have to go.'

'Oh.'

'You'll transfer the money?'

'Yes. Are you alright?'

'I'm alright, I'm alright. Are you alright? How's Bath?'

'Oxford.'

'Oxford, Oxford. It's alright, is it?'

'It's fine.'

'Fine. Good. You'll transfer the money today?'

'Yes. I've said. I'll do it now. It won't take too long to move over.'

'Thanks. OK. Fine. You'll transfer it today. Right, good. Bye.'

'Bye.'

Eliza put the phone in her bag. She stretched out on her back, the grass icy against her skin, taking a savage pleasure in how cold she was, in how extremely her body was suffering. Paola watched her contentedly. Nothing, for her, had changed. She made to kiss Eliza again but Eliza sat up, said mechanically that she needed to do something for her mother, that it wouldn't take long. She didn't want to look at Paola or tell her what was happening. Presumably she had a mother who didn't ask for this sort of thing. Paola got to her feet and pulled her jeans on. Eliza tapped away on her phone, as the water raced by, under the bridge and into the deafening weir.

Chapter Thirteen

The day after Ada's cookery lesson with Henry, she received a number of other business-related enquiries. It felt like a monsoon after months of drought. The first message seemed a little tawdry – a man called Sir Julian left a voicemail on her landline while she was in the garden. He cleared his throat portentously and announced his name with the tone of a man liable to get goosebumps at the sound of it. 'I'm looking for companionship,' he oozed. 'I'm a fellow of means, and I'm sure you'll find my fees satisfactory and your duties enjoyable. I've never had complaints before.'

Ada began to laugh. Sir Julian paused broodingly. 'The picture you included in your Rent-a-Gran advert is entrancing,' he said. 'I very much wish to rent you, so to speak. I too have erotic capital. I am seventy, but trim. I am a Glyndebourne regular. I should be flattered to take you. We could make as passionate adversaries as twilight companions, you and I.'

Ada stopped the message, wriggling her toes. Her next potential client seemed less objectionable. She received an email from someone called Dr Akhi Bajwa, who explained that he was a Sikh architect running a project in Thrupp. He was about to marry 'a beautiful girl from the sort of family mentioned in the Domesday Book', and he wanted lessons in 'proper English manners' to help him fit into the dynasty. There were courses in London that one could take at Debretts and so on, but they seemed corporate and slick; a real English grandmother might do the job better. Ada telephoned him immediately.

'I'd be delighted to finesse your manners,' she said. 'Though I'm sure they're top-notch.'

'You are mistaken,' he replied gravely. 'I am a buffoon. I have been known to show the contents of my mouth to those condemned to dine opposite me.'

'We all do that!'

'I do not wish to do so again. I need your help. I fear I need it urgently.'

They organised to have tea at the Randolph the following week. 'And will your fiancée be coming?' Ada asked delicately.

'She will not,' Akhi said. 'Tamara is at her parents' in Gloucestershire for the weekend.'

Ada nodded. Another secret-keeper. 'Four o'clock?'

'Perfect. I shall wear a lemon bow-tie for you to recognise me by.'

Ada arrived at the Randolph a trifle early and found a table by a window facing the Ashmolean. She felt nervous and kept smoothing the material of her frock, an ancient Jaeger shift dress she'd bought in the eighties and worn twice.

'Are you Ada Robertson?'

'Yes,' she said, looking round. Her second Rent-a-Gran client had arrived.

'Please call me Akhi.'

Ada shook the man's hand. He was a small man, with a straight nose, light brown skin and a blue turban. He was wearing a powder-pink suit and a shirt striped peppermint green, with a rather magnificent yellow bow-tie. He moved with such grace that Ada immediately sensed they would founder upon a major issue: he had excellent manners; his entire being was the embodiment of elegance. He even smelled nice – sage, perhaps, or bergamot.

A waiter came over to take their orders. Akhi indicated with an arabesque of the hand that Ada should choose first. 'High tea for two, please,' she said, trying to channel Lady Catherine de Bourgh.

'I quite agree,' said Akhi approvingly. 'And a bottle of champagne.'

They began to talk. It felt like a date, Ada noticed with a thrill. She could feel uncomfortable if she chose to; instead she leaned into the delicious fiction of it, sensing herself expand into her role. She was an etiquette mistress. She should behave like one. She sat up straighter, poofed her hair, imagined that her middle names were Eleanor and Genevieve, that she'd been raised at Blenheim and was singularly qualified to tell an educated man how to be even more polite than he already was.

'Have you lived in Britain long?' Ada enquired.

'Three years,' Akhi replied, unfolding his napkin. 'I'm from Calcutta.'

Ada wanted to ask how he had come to cultivate such flawless manners but couldn't see how to pose the question without sounding prejudiced. These things were so hard to judge now.

'My father was fascinated by the UK,' Akhi said. 'I grew up in a house crammed with Wodehouse, Waugh, Saki, Delafield. He raised me to be British, and now that I'm here I'm beginning to see the shortfall between what I believed the country was and its reality.'

'Ah,' Ada said. 'Yes. On the whole we're a disappointing tribe.'

'My books only refined me up to a point. I fear the façade will crack.'

'That you'll have a *My Fair Lady* moment at a racecourse and forget yourself?'

Akhi smiled. 'Precisely.'

Ada began to do what she could for him. Her priority was to shake up his stiff manner, because as she pointed out, 'casualness is all the rage at the moment.' Cucumber sandwiches were not to be eaten with cutlery but with one's hands, lustily; milk was to be added to a cup after tea, no matter how dainty the china. It was commendable to stain one's napkin but not to allow food to freeride in one's teeth; tap water was preferable to bottled, which was the penurious aristocrat's nemesis. It was always a good idea to say you went to Lidl 'for the wine', even if you only ever shopped at Waitrose.

Gradually the talk moved away from manners to Akhi himself: his upbringing in India, his job, his bemusement at English habits. He was enchanted to discover Ada was a poet.

'Well,' qualified Ada, 'I've not written a thing in ages.'

'What's stopping you?'

Ada considered. 'I don't have anything to say.'

Akhi cut a scone in two. 'Cream before jam?' he asked.

'A hotly debated question,' Ada smiled. 'I put the jam on first, myself, after some butter, but you can do either. It's important to develop a strong opinion on the subject.'

Akhi shook his head and spooned some jam onto his scone. 'So you don't think you have anything to say,' he repeated thoughtfully.

'No,' Ada said. 'Nothing interesting happens to me now. Other poets do more, think quicker, write better. I'm not sure readers want bags like me. They want photogenic graduates from East Anglia with tattoos and attitude, writing about – I don't know, takeaways, multiculturalism, sexual assault. I can't do any of that. Of course I've been groped but I can't seem to mind very much, is that so awful? I prefer writing in rhyme about subjects that are now seen as hopelessly traditional – birds, rivers, Oxford. My husband, our life.'

Akhi bit into his scone.

'Pile it higher,' Ada told him sternly. 'Greed when one is eating scones is vital.'

Akhi spooned on more cream. 'Have you tried writing about things you never used to write about?' he asked.

Ada tried to think. 'No. I've always just written what came naturally.'

'Why not give new topics a go?'

Ada shrugged. Why not push herself to explore different subjects? She wasn't sure she knew how to. One didn't write poetry in themes; it wasn't like school where you chose your classes and off you went. Poetry was slipperier, something altogether more enigmatic. She almost started explaining that but then realised how pompous she would sound. She felt tired out; now that the conversation had moved on to her she wished it hadn't. This man didn't know her and she didn't know him. Their attempt to connect, to help one another despite understanding next to nothing about each other, struck her abruptly as desperately sad.

The champagne arrived. Ada fought to recover her good cheer. She began tossing Akhi imaginary scenarios – how would he behave at a funeral, at a gallery opening, at a Christmas lunch? Little fazed him, even office lift etiquette: he knew to keep his eyes on the doors, to comment blandly on the weather or the time the lift had taken to arrive. Ada began to sense that Akhi knew himself that his manners were beyond reproach but that he needed encouragement and friendship, that he was terrified of his wedding and the commitment it meant to a country he'd read so much about but which seemed far from the idyll he'd envisaged. He was scared that his marriage would mean life as an exotic animal, ceaseless questions about his provenance, his accent, his turban. Ada said what she could. She liked him. She learned a good deal. Hours passed. They finished the champagne and ate everything on their tiered tray. A waiter came by to inform them that the table had been reserved for dinner. Ada saw that she wanted her own company now, its silence, her room and the amber glow of her bedside lamp.

'Your manners are perfect,' she told Akhi. 'It's been a pleasure meeting you.'

He shook her hand. 'You too,' he said. 'And please send me your new poems, when you come to write them.'

Ada smiled a little tightly and left. Akhi remained at the table, waiting for a card reader. From the pavement outside

Ada could see him crisply, like he was lit by a spotlight. She wondered what he would do with his evening, and with all the time before him now. She knew she might not find out. It would be her cross to bear: to drop into people's lives and never discover how they turned out, which turns they took on the road.

There were no cabs about so she walked to the bus stop. Ada felt rather stupid in her prissy outfit and wished she'd brought a scarf or sensible shoes to change into. The bus arrived, brightly lit as a supermarket. It reassured her. Fifteen minutes later in Swinburne Road she poured herself a sherry and sat in the sitting room with a pad of lined paper on her lap. There was a familiar stirring in her, a kind of held-off anticipation; it was a poem in embryonic form. She found a pen, trying not to become agitated: she knew that desiring too much at this stage could kill a poem outright. She started to write, just a few words, then more. She crossed it all out, wrote another few lines. The copper owl in front of the photograph of her and Michael seemed to be watching her write, its golden mesh delicate in the lamplight, its ears flicked upwards like it was waiting for music.

Chapter Fourteen

Eliza wasn't sure quite what changed in the way she saw Paola after the trip to the Victorian bathing spot but something shifted, very slightly. After she was asked for money by Flora, she and Paola went to a community café near Tumbling Bay for breakfast. Eliza wasn't hungry; she was skittish and could in theory explain why but the moment to divulge never quite arrived, and in any case Eliza was beginning to sense a fundamental incompatibility clarifying between the two of them: that she was a dusk person, a navy or indigo sort of person, and that Paola was more straightforward, the sort of person who naturally liked other people and doing wholesome things like spending time outdoors. Paola's personality was more noon or 10 a.m., a solid primary colour that knew what it was; whatever was scrambling into being between them would never work. Eliza worried it might be condescension or vanity that was making her dismiss Paola as unambiguous – perhaps there were subtleties to Paola's personality that Eliza was too self-absorbed to detect; maybe Eliza was being grand, thinking she was different. But whether that was the case, it came to the same: as far as Eliza could tell, Paola was what-you-see-you-get, and she could only stand by as her enthusiasm for their entanglement diminished.

They drank bowls of warm milky coffee. They shared a slice of lemon polenta cake. Paola's lips were as full and dark as they'd ever been; she was as pretty. Their hair was wet. It should have been romantic, it should have been faltering and lovely. The bill came and with it the moment to decide whether to spend the day together. Eliza said that she had a ton of work on, that she had better get going. Paola, detecting the true reason, said smoothly that she was in the same situation, that she needed to go back to Trumpington to collect some books.

Outside on the disabled ramp, they hugged and parted. They messaged one another a little over the next few days but soon they stopped asking one another the questions that were eking the conversation out. Eliza could tell that Paola felt dismayed by what had never come to be; that she was unsure of what exactly had caved in, and so soundlessly. Eliza didn't know what that was either. When they bumped into each other around Oxford they spoke animatedly about how the referendum build-up was going, though the awkwardness of their botched romance made them both shudder the moment they were alone again, wish they hadn't seen one other, wonder how the glitter had come to crumb off it all, whether it was right that they'd let it.

A few days after Eliza's trip to Tumbling Bay she decided to go to Carlisle. She sensed Flora would be bemused, even derisive, if her daughter tracked her down with the articulated aim of finding out what was 'wrong', that would imply a softness to their relationship that didn't exist. But Eliza couldn't shake off the memory of the fearfulness of her mother's voice on the phone. And there was also Rich: Eliza hadn't had a proper conversation with him in weeks. A train would almost empty her account but she needed to find out what was going on.

The journey went quickly. Outside, the countryside looked macabre and ill-intentioned, the fields grey with cold, though every so often a tree in blossom burst into view like a firework. There were no seats in second class so Eliza decided to sit in first. She felt laughably affluent, her leather seat so big and buttery she kept sliding around. There were lots of men in suits, consultants by the look of them, scurrying at their laptops like they had important tasks to do. If she had her computer, Eliza reflected, she could do some work on her thesis; she'd barely touched it for a fortnight. She was telling herself she was taking a well-earned break, but knew she'd not earned it at all, and every so often a flash of Levi's face would slip into her mind, severing her line of thought, his eyes unreadable behind their wire-rimmed spectacles. Lately another image had started to dog her too, of the author on his bike as a teenager, years before he was sent to Auschwitz, zooming along an Alpine road perched on the edge of the abyss.

At lunchtime the train arrived. Eliza loved Carlisle station, a big Tudor-style building whose grandness was at odds with the scruffy town itself. The station wasn't far from the place she and Rich had moved into four years ago on Buchanan Road, a rented two-bedroom bungalow with a stone-slab patio at the back. Eliza had decided not to tell Rich she was coming – he was expecting her at Easter so it might be a pleasant surprise. He took

Mondays off as clients wanted him to work through the weekend, so chances were he'd be home. As Eliza walked she was bemused to find herself becoming excited about her imminent apparition, like a showgirl rocketing out of a cake; she was too cynical to pull off this sort of stunt usually. As soon as she and Rich had eaten lunch and caught up, she would go over to Flora's.

Nothing seemed to have changed on the road since she'd been back at Christmas. Even the parked cars looked like they were in the same configuration. It was, actually, pleasant to be back in this docile place; it felt rooted, fastened in time. She rang the doorbell of number forty-nine, smiling in spite of her hunger. She heard nothing and rang again, wondering if her father was at the shop. Then she began to sense movement inside and imagined Rich walking through the kitchen, scratching his head with his great raking scrapes.

The door opened. It wasn't Rich. It was Eliza's mother. They stared at one another.

Eliza couldn't process; there was no logical reason for Flora to be in the doorway, therefore she probably wasn't. Flora lived miles away in a crappy sublet; she and Rich hardly spoke, especially now that Eliza was too old to require much in the way of joint parenting.

Eliza waited patiently for the body and face of her mother to rearrange themselves into someone that wasn't her. Flora recovered from the surprise quicker, noting how thin her daughter looked, how haggard and unlike herself.

'New dress,' Flora said. 'New jumper.'

Eliza looked down at her body. It might as well have been someone else's. She was wearing a loose black dress with a polo neck over it and a camel corduroy jacket.

'They're not new,' she heard herself say.

She continued to stare at Flora. It was irrefutably her. She was wearing an oversized T-shirt and nothing else, though it was lunchtime, and her brown hair was crazy around her face, the cheeks a clean rose like she'd been exercising.

As Eliza worked to understand what was going on, her eyes roved over her mother's body; she seemed different somehow.

Then she saw. One of Flora's hands was cupping her belly. She was pregnant.

Eliza stared at her mother's stomach. She could not feel or hear a thing, she just looked. For a long minute the two women faced one another.

Slowly things slotted into place so neatly that Eliza nearly sighed in satisfaction. Of course. Yes. Of course. Her mother was expecting a baby. Rich's baby. They were together. They had got together again. Eliza may have stated the fact aloud. Banal expressions started filing through her head like station announcements. Baby on board. Bun in the oven. Banged up. Flora didn't move but looked down at her body too and nodded imperceptibly. Some subterranean part of Eliza was gratified to note that her mother's expression was nervous.

Eliza heard feet slapping on the tiled entrance towards the door. Rich appeared by Flora's side, a towel around his hips, his torso gleaming. He shouted Eliza's name, but the sound was strangled and weird. Eliza stepped back at the noise. Rich looked horrified, his massive face crinkled with concern and guilt. He stepped around Flora to give Eliza a hug. She endured it. He was damp. Sweat, not water. She tried to enervate her body so she felt less rigid to him but she couldn't manage it. She contemplated disconnectedly that this was the kind of thing that happened in films about teenagers coming of age; their parents messed up and it was traumatising but ultimately it ended up being good for the adolescent in question because they realised that the two adults they looked up to most were human and wrecked like them, and they were released into the world with a sharper sense of how things really were.

'Let's go inside,' Rich said.

Eliza was grateful for the steadiness in his voice. She thought of just walking back to the station, leaving these people to their bad decisions. But her body was unresponsive and she was almost amused to feel it follow her parents obediently into the sitting room. Steve the goldfish was still alive at least, drawing figures of eight in the hairy green water of his tank. It was in this room that she and Rich had hunkered down at Christmas with Tony, eating canapés, watching films back to back as Steve patrolled his underwater castle.

Eliza sat on the floor by the TV, folding herself up as small as she could get without rolling into a ball. She wanted someone to kneel by her and stroke her hair; she wanted someone to tell her in a deep Aslan voice that everything would work out. She thought unaccountably of Ruby, of how wilful she was, her way of taking everything in hand. She longed for her, for the daily abdication the relationship had offered.

Flora sank onto the sofa. As she lowered herself Eliza stared at her stomach hungrily; it wasn't blowout distended but possibly a little fuller than normal, cute almost. Eliza felt ill with emotion, unsure yet what her feelings were composed of but conscious of their intensity. Rich sat next to Flora in his towel. They looked like a couple. Their hands were close to one another as if they hoped they might touch. Since they'd broken up for good when Eliza was eight she'd seen the pair of them together many times – but they'd never looked like this, like some sort of fucking unit.

The inevitable conversation got under way. Half a year ago, Flora and Rich explained, they had started seeing one another more than they used to. All that shared history, the Cavaghan years, bringing up Eliza and so on, made them more comfortable with one another than they were with other people. They connected. Things started happening. When? Oh, four months ago. They didn't use protection as Flora couldn't have dreamed she could still get pregnant. (At this point Eliza fought not to roll her eyes or say 'Spectacular' or something similarly disparaging.) Flora found out six weeks ago that she was expecting a child. Didn't know the sex. She didn't have a job, she was running out of money and she was ashamed of it, which was why she'd asked Eliza for the bank transfer; she was sorry for that, she'd slipped into habits she was trying to bury for good. She'd moved in with Rich, it was temporary but they were going to continue seeing each other because it was just working. At this point Flora glanced at Rich and he took her hand, smiling quaveringly. Eliza thought he looked like a gummy grandfather.

'So you are actually keeping the baby?' she demanded.

Flora nodded, so tenderly, with such maternal coyness, that Eliza actually had to grip herself to stop from crying out.

'You're forty-six years old,' she said.

'I wasn't ready to have you,' Flora said. 'It shouldn't have happened. But I'm ready to have this child.'

Eliza heard her father add something, trying to temper the blow of Flora's words, perhaps he was trotting out the story she'd heard a million times before that Flora had been basically a child when she'd conceived Eliza and that any coldness or aggression she'd shown to her daughter after had originated from that fact. Eliza thought later that she may have reminded them at this point of the many times they'd been shit as a couple before, that if they tried it again they would argue and be spiteful and come close to attacking one another as they had done daily for the first eight years of Eliza's life; but the next day, going over what had happened, Eliza was hazy about where she'd drawn the line between what she'd thought and what she'd put into words.

It was easier, she found, to look at her mother; she was used to her betrayals. She couldn't look at Rich. His eyes were on hers, his worry for her its own microclimate; she could tell how rabidly he wanted her to show him a sign of love, he'd take the leanest scrap but she wouldn't give it. Even Christmas had been a sham; he'd been sleeping with Flora by then and hadn't had the balls to tell her.

By six, Eliza was reaching her limit. Her parents were explaining themselves over and over. Rich tried, twice, to hug her. Flora accused Eliza of being ageist and suggested that she show a modicum of enthusiasm for what was about to happen to them 'as a family'. Eliza replied that she hadn't been aware until today that Flora considered their trio a family; as far as she was concerned it was a duo, her and Rich, for the simple reason that Rich had made an effort to raise her and Flora hadn't. And anyway, Eliza added, she didn't think on principle that forty-six was too old to have a child, but there was little reason to believe that Flora would make a better mother this time round. Flora said nothing to that. Eliza's shock subsided, giving way to something more subdued and rigid, until she announced that she was going to make her way back to Oxford. Rich looked wretched; Flora nodded peaceably. Eliza went to the kitchen to grab a banana for the journey. She snuck a box of cereal into her bag and a pack of chicken breasts from the fridge. She wasn't sure why. Rich offered to drive her to the station. She was exhausted and couldn't be bothered to fight; she said yes.

'I'm sorry I didn't tell you,' Rich said as they drove down Buchanan Road.

'Yeah,' Eliza said.

'I was going to, Lize.'

'Yeah.'

The irritating thing was that she was beginning to feel uncomfortable with the teenagishness of her own reaction; that she could have handled this whole dumb fiasco better.

'I know you're hurt,' Rich continued.

Eliza didn't want to cry so she bit her thumb hard. 'All good,' she said.

'I know it must seem hard that, I don't know, we're starting the family we never had a chance to, when you were born.'

'Lol,' Eliza said. She couldn't find other words. She wanted to be tucked up in bed, she wanted someone to take care of her, she wanted everyone to start behaving better, to be better. She bit her thumb harder, hoping the skin would bruise or break or something.

They got to the station. Eliza gave her father a kiss on the cheek. His eyes lit up for a second, then as she pulled away he registered her expression.

'I love you,' he said as she got out. The 'you' was cut off by the car door closing. Eliza walked into the station like a tin man. A train was due in ten minutes. She put her headphones on and waited. She looked in her bag and saw that her dad had given her forty quid. She sat in first class again, though her ticket wasn't valid, and moved to second when a ticket inspector asked her to. She stared out of the window at the night. Every so often the darkness was beaten back by supermarkets and towns, fizzing light like synapse activity in some vast black brain. From Birmingham she got a coach to Oxford. She arrived at Swinburne Road at one in the morning, her phone out of battery. The cardboard she'd wedged in her broken bedroom window had been sucked out or in; rainwater was soaking the library books on her desk and pieces of lined paper were frisking around the floor in the breeze. She got into bed. Her eyes were wide open under their closed lids as the wind blew in from the street and the white light from the lamp-posts made her feel she was sleeping in a computer.

Chapter Fifteen

As spring continued opening up the trees on Swinburne Road, Ada's diary began to fill. There was Henry to cook with every week, but soon Akhi emailed to say he would love to see her again too. Other requests came in daily. She learned that roughly one enquiry in four led to an actual booking: much of the interest in her services came from men who obviously thought she was indeed, as Kate had warned, some sort of OAP sex worker. Ada wasn't offended; in fact it was rather gratifying to be shown that many men liked the idea of going to bed with an older woman. All the same, she was not in the least bit tempted to acquiesce to their demands and replied graciously to each one, saying that she wasn't selling sex but that she wished them the very best for the future. A few days after her first tea with Akhi she was texted by a woman called Camille who said she needed help with her children; would the Rent-a-Gran advertised in the chippy on Iffley Road be interested?

Ada thought carefully about whether to accept. Her life had been starkly child-free: she'd told Michael she was infertile soon after they got together; he'd said that as the oldest of six siblings, he'd had his fill of childcare in Dublin.

Later, when the relationship had settled into itself, they had wavered once or twice on the childless road – Michael was moved to tears by a documentary on fatherhood, and at thirty Ada saw that her female friends were being gobbled alive by motherhood and wouldn't emerge for another two decades, should she join them, adopt, foster? The answer was no, of course not, because since being told by a doctor she would never bear children (briskly, as one might tell a teenager to hold cutlery properly), Ada had become used to the idea, and the only life she could now envisage for herself was of one without children, one of absolute autonomy. So she and Michael had held firm, become godparents once or twice over the years, hosted nieces and nephews when they visited Oxford for open days, sent birthday cards when Ada thought to check her diary. Being child-free had served Michael's career well: leaving the country for research trips was a decision lightly taken, and Ada, too, had liked it; it felt moral, if not downright radical. But she'd noticed over the years that other people found her childlessness hard to swallow – should they show this barren woman empathy and ask her what had 'gone wrong', or should they thrust the gory details of their own child-rearing experiences at her, to make her believe she'd dodged a bullet?

Presently, confronted with what could easily be a request for a cheap babysitter, Ada decided to risk it. 'Would be happy to help,' she texted back. Camille sent over her address; she lived on a street Ada didn't know in Rose Hill. For a second she considered asking Camille to come to her instead: Rose Hill was known for its council estates and deprivation, the sort of place that was mentioned when talk turned to Oxford's gentrification – as a counterargument.

The children turned out to be charming. Mame, the three-year-old, was formidably cute, and began hanging onto Ada's calf the moment she walked into the flat. There were also two boys that introduced themselves with uncanny composure, saying their names were Milton and Daniel, and that they liked fridge magnets.

Camille asked Ada a few sharp questions about who she was, where she lived, why she was selling her time, but she soon decided to trust her and softened. Ada found herself wondering what had happened to the children's father – presumably he was off the scene; locked up or something, a tale as old as time.

'Their dad's on a business trip, due back this evening,' Camille said as she buttoned her coat.

'Wonderful,' Ada said quickly. 'Have you warned him that I'm here?'

'Yep, he thinks it's mad.' Camille beamed, kissed her children goodbye and explained to them what was going to happen. She gave Ada a copy of *The Twits* and left, promising to return soon with food for the rest of the week.

The moment their mother was out of the door the children clambered onto the sofa. Ada began to read aloud. Every so often, the weirdness of the situation made her smile broadly – how very odd, that she'd orchestrated her life in such a way as to be now in a flat in Rose Hill, reading to children that were not her own. Milton was fairly literate and Ada persuaded him to perform the snippets of Roald Dahl dialogue, putting on a woman's voice for Mrs Twit and an ogre voice for Mr Twit. Soon the child was acting out the characters' mischief-making in the middle of the living room, until both he and Daniel were laughing helplessly, rolling their little bodies around on the floor. Mame got the giggles too, though Ada wasn't convinced she knew what was happening.

'Now you'll have to play with us,' Daniel instructed Ada once they'd finished reading.

'Er, alright,' Ada said. 'But you know I'm ancient and creaky and haven't played in – oh, decades.'

Daniel stared at her. 'It's eeeeeasy,' he sighed. He explained that he and his brother were involved in a top-secret mission to recapture the castle they had grown up in, now unjustly occupied by dead soldiers brought back to life by aliens. Mame played the helpless babe whose role in combat was correspondingly minimal; he and his brother took care of all that, as the game's rebel princes. Ada, if she liked, could be their squire or litter-picker.

The mission got under way. Soon Ada was clambering around with the boys, shouting things like, 'Watch out – archers!' as Mame sat in the corner with toy trucks, ignoring the silliness. Ada's back donged every so often with pain and she felt oafish and lumbering in comparison to these lithe child soldiers, but she was happy too, and increasingly committed to driving the zombies out of the keep.

Just as the mission was nearing completion Camille returned to the flat with her partner in tow. He was a bespectacled mixed-race man with a quiet manner; Milton and Daniel forgot their game and threw themselves onto him. Camille thanked Ada warmly for her help, gave her some money and asked how it had gone.

'Great!' shouted Milton.

'She's a big Twit,' shrieked Mame, throwing her arms around like a rag doll. Ada frowned indulgently, assured

Camille it had gone well and said goodbye to the children. She felt like Nanny McPhee.

Outside night had fallen. Ada's body was broken; she felt she had run five miles. There were teenagers on the estate staircase, all in sportswear, their trainers moony white in the light of a strip bulb above. Two hours earlier Ada might have been intimidated to see them; now she noted their cautious eyes and tentativeness, the dimples that made and unmade themselves in their cheeks as they spoke and smiled.

'Good evening,' she said graciously as she walked down the steps.

The teenagers greeted her back quietly, moving out of the way to let her descend the stairs. Wrapping her arms around herself to stave off the cold, Ada walked back home.

By the middle of March, Ada almost had more Rent-a-Gran clients than she knew what to do with. There was a snowy-tongued man of ninety who paid Ada to talk to him about his youth; Dom, the boy with ADHD she played Battleships with; a rather unpleasant professor from Oxford Brookes who asked Ada to read his academic papers to ensure they made sense to the 'average dipshit' (a word she had to look up on Google); twins who wanted to be taught to knit (Ada spent the day before the lesson learning to knit herself). There was also Alice the nineteen-year-old whose mother, Florence, hired Ada to teach her how to drive. Alice, Florence said, had been learning for a year and kept crashing into trees; no trained instructor in the vicinity seemed to be able to help her. Any day now she'd mow down a pedestrian. Drastic measures were called for. They could practise around the estate. Ada assumed it would be the sort of estate Camille lived in but when she arrived at the address, deep in the Buckinghamshire hills, she realised it was a Mr Darcy-type affair with a mile-long drive and scurrying staff. There was a field behind the stone house, dotted with alpacas and beech trees. Alice was a lovely girl, rowdy and compassionate, a truly hopeless driver, and Ada spent an agreeable two hours twice a week thonking around in the passenger seat, wishing she had an emergency brake, as alpacas dodged the car wearily, used to nearly being killed.

Before Ada knew it, the day she'd been dreading toppled onto her: the second anniversary of Michael's death. She awoke feeling wary. She was sleeping in the middle of the bed as she had for weeks now but she'd shifted to the left in the night. She looked for a long time at the space his body used to fill and reflected on how bewildering life's sudden confiscations were, how smoothly cruel.

The sky was a flavourless grey. In the house opposite she could see the pink-haired young woman who had once knocked on her door looking out of the window as though she too had just awoken. Ada raised a hand to wave at her neighbour, assuming the young woman wouldn't notice. But she waved back.

The problem today wasn't so much that Ada believed anniversary milestones meant anything, more that she feared she had been granted a tacit licence to wallow and might run off with the privilege. She already thought of Michael daily, hourly, but today could set into motion a different order of thinking. It was odd, rather as if she was frightened of herself, but she'd learned since he'd died that grief had a way of splitting you from the self you thought you were, and cleaving you too from the person you wanted to be. Sewing those people back together to form a coherent whole was difficult.

She made herself breakfast in the way that Michael would have done. She sat outside in the garden as they used to. She read as much of the paper as she could endure; the referendum campaign was clattering on, becoming more farcical with each passing day. She had a cry. It was the first in a couple of months and it felt luxurious; afterwards she was cocooned in a warm sticky tiredness she associated with being very small.

Above all, she tried not to confront the truth of her situation; that for all her Rent-a-Gran mania, for all the quantity of people in her life now, she'd been happier two years ago when her days were spent doing nothing much at all with Michael, pottering, eating, making variations of jokes they'd made for decades. She missed him abjectly.

When it was too cold to stay outside, Ada returned to the living room. The room struck her abruptly as intolerable, its layout and very purpose violently banal. Even Primo Levi's wire owl seemed idiotic; she had to stop herself from lobbing the tangled creature out of the window. She contented herself instead with turning the framed picture of her and Michael around, so she wasn't tormented by their myopic cheer. Everything in the house seemed pernicious, everything wan and trivial. She didn't want this life or any pallid alternative; she didn't want to live. She lay on the floor for a long time, listening to sounds from the street outside.

Eventually she stirred. She was living, she reminded herself; she was putting one day in front of the next. She stretched and washed her face, then checked her emails in the study, filtering out the usual requests for sex or interviews. That left one email from a man called Peter. He said he was an Oxford local, thirty-two and about to marry his partner of five years, Yannis. He'd heard about Ada on the Oxford grapevine and wanted to ask whether she might consider attending his wedding. His parents were 'insistent Anglicans' who didn't approve of the marriage, or indeed of Peter's preference for men over women. They weren't planning on attending the ceremony. Nor were his grandparents. He wanted someone old and dignified to be by his side on the day. Yannis had practically cleared Greece out of its elderly, he had so many relatives coming – could they meet to discuss?

Ada was perturbed by the enquiry. Not so long ago, the idea of gay men marrying had struck her as niche and laughable; she remembered arguing with Michael about it before the vote. 'But why must they marry?' she'd asked him. 'Why can't they get a civil ceremony thingy?'

'Because they want to and they're just like us!' he'd roared, thumping the table.

She imagined this man, Peter, squaring up to what he'd hoped would be the most joyful day of his life, a momentous occasion for his whole family, only now he was having to face it alone. 'Would be delighted to meet,' she typed back. 'Perhaps your fiancé and you could come for coffee this afternoon.'

A few hours later, the two men arrived. Ada was dazed by their glamour: they were hunks, the pair of them. Peter was blonde with long-lashed navy eyes, Yannis tall and well-carved. She had never, to her knowledge, had homosexuals in the house and she felt suddenly

embarrassed about it, as if the very walls would divulge
her secret.

Yannis and Peter walked hand-in-hand into the kitchen.
Ada had made them a pistachio and orange blossom cake
from a recipe given to her by one of the Iffley shopkeepers.
The men looked surprised at her choice of cake, as though
they would have expected her to wheel out a Victoria
sponge. When she explained why she'd started going to
the shop rather than the supermarket, Peter and Yannis
exchanged a look. They were stirred by her isolation. Ada
saw her life configure itself into the shape they must see
it in; she felt briefly moved, the way that catching herself
in the mirror after Michael had died used to make her
cry because she saw how alone she looked, and how well
her reflection teed up with reality.

'Are you looking forward to decades of marriage then?'
she asked.

'Absolutely not!' they cried at the same time, then
grinned. Ada grinned too, giving herself over to their
charm and good humour. Their love for one another was
natural and nonchalant, a luminous thing that made Ada
feel weak by the strength of it. Soon they were making
her laugh, telling her stories about how they'd got together
(a phone app called Grindr – Peter had been looking
for sex, Yannis for conversation to improve his English).
Drunk on their attention, Ada suggested a tour of the
house. Peter and Yannis leapt to their feet and followed
her around, complimenting everything, suggesting this
and that, noticing things that Ada didn't know she still
owned. They asked in the bedroom if she had a partner
and she felt her whole being pause. She said that she was

widowed. The men nodded. She added, because she trusted them, and because they were in love, that it was two years to the day since Michael had died. They nodded again. She was grateful they didn't ask more. As they went back downstairs Peter laid his hands on Ada's shoulders lightly; it should have been mawkish and forward but somehow it wasn't. The pair of them left in the early evening after they'd shared a bottle of wine, and once the men had gone Ada sat contentedly in the sitting room, feeling the house thrum with pleasure.

Yannis dropped off a wedding invitation the following day. He was on a run and said between gasps on the doorstep that his family knew about the plan, and were looking forward to welcoming Ada into the fold.

'I can't wait,' Ada said.

She returned to the kitchen, delighted. She was finishing off a poem she'd started the previous night. For weeks now she'd been writing poems unlike any she'd composed before – rhyming still, but not as predictable or sewn up as her normal ones; many about Michael but others about her childhood, a subject she'd barely touched on in previous collections, and her own mother, who had died fifteen years ago. She was sending her work to James almost daily and had never known her agent to be so enthused; there was talk of a reading in London sometime in the summer, and poetry publishers were apparently already sniffing round.

The rest of the week passed in a swirl of client appointments. Ada began to restrict herself to one a day so as not to tire herself out. On Tuesday, a John from Milton Keynes asked her to help clear out his dead grandmother's belongings. On Thursday she met a couple in Pizza Express.

They were divorcing and didn't want to pay for a lawyer; would Ada sit with them as they discussed who got what? It was enthralling: by the time the dough balls arrived the woman, Samantha, was weeping and her ex, Chris, was swivelling his head around to see if anybody in the restaurant had noticed. Ada did what she could for them and came away with an amplified understanding of the small brutalities men and women could do to one another when they were hurt and disappointed with the gifts their lives had bestowed.

Before she knew it Saturday arrived, and with it the pressure to look presentable. The fiancés were getting ready separately, Yannis with his family, Peter with friends in a suite at the Hotel du Vin. Ada got there at 8 a.m. sharp. She'd dug out her foulest carpet bag and filled it with grannyish items: hairspray, flapjacks, safety pins, pound cake, blister plasters, a thumbed copy of *Riders*, a pristine copy of the Gospels, gin and champagne.

Ada had a bewildering morning. She had never got the hang of pampering, the act or the submission to it, but she was thrust into hours of hardcore 'self-care', as Peter called it. She ran him a bath and sat in the room next door, saying soothing grandmotherly things whenever he seemed to need it. She scrutinised his morning suit. She devised a way of softening a rather solid face mask that Peter said he wanted for his 'T-zone' – by sitting for ten minutes with the packet clamped between her thighs as she sucked mints. She was even persuaded to put on a face mask herself and inspected her skin afterwards: nothing was different.

'You must lead quite the life,' Peter said as he polished his shoes. 'Are you finding this odd?'

'A little,' she said. 'Are you?'

'A little.'

Ada wanted to ask if she was being the grandmother Peter wanted her to be. If she was in any way plugging a gap. 'You're doing brilliantly,' she said instead.

'Thanks,' Peter said. Then, quietly, 'I wish my parents were here.' He looked painfully handsome in his pale suit, with a white rose pinned to the lapel. Ada told him so. He blinked hard, his eyes shining.

'D'you know, even I didn't think homosexual people should marry until recently,' Ada said, her voice gentle. 'I don't have conviction as an excuse. Just – laziness, crusty thinking.'

Peter looked at her.

'People change,' Ada said. 'Even old people. Your parents may come round.'

She sat next to him on the sofa and covered his hand with her own. His skin was soft, the nails glossy from the buffing he'd given them earlier. He squeezed Ada's fingers, then wiped his eyes.

Throughout the day she did her best to be there for both Peter and Yannis – she sang the hymns with gusto; she made sure all the speech givers were not dying of nerves, she entertained children abandoned by their drunk parents.

'And what about you?' Peter asked at one point. It must have been after the reception dinner; he was tipsy.

'What about me what?' Ada said. She too was a little boozed.

'Well, don't you want to fall in love again?'

Ada thought. She had considered the question since Michael's death, of course, but being asked to articulate a settled position was another matter. There was also something in the phrasing of Peter's question that made her feel defensive – 'don't you' – as if her behaviour suggested for all the world that she'd given up.

'I'd love to love again,' she said. 'Only I don't imagine it would be easy. It might not be fair on the person – I'd be drawing a comparison between them and Michael, probably forever.'

'You don't know that. Maybe it just needs to happen to you and then you'll see.'

'I suppose,' she smiled. 'You want your rent-a-gran to find a rent-a-grandad.'

Peter looked serious, in a sloshed way. 'I think it's a shame when people give up on love,' he said. 'But to be honest I don't really know anything about this stuff. I don't know what that is like to go through.'

To Ada's amazement there was, in fact, an implication of romantic interest from a fellow guest – one of Yannis's great-uncles, Alek. He was a nice man, dressed in a grey suit, with a lustrous moustache that reminded Ada of Stalin. She was bemused to find herself attracted to him, pleased when she made him laugh. After dessert they made their way to the disco to watch Yannis and Peter dance. They were too settled in their bodies and personalities to feel uncomfortable. A barrage of belters thrashed by, then a slowish song came on; Ada didn't know who it was by but she liked the sound – a conked-out female voice and not much else, maybe some saxophone plumes here and there. There were orange and red lights roving around the dancefloor but they slowed their orbit, and the disco ball too began rotating less frenetically. Alek asked if she would like to dance. Ada said she would, remembering when she'd been asked the same question decades ago, long before she and Michael had got together. She'd gone to a charity ball in her village and a boy called Alexander had tapped her shoulder. She couldn't hear his voice over the band but she read the question on his face and said yes. They spent ten minutes together, their bodies pressed into one another, swaying and rotating. Ada's nose was deep in his soft, boy-smelling hair. His ear was impossibly delicate, the rim barely curved. His palm was pressed against her coccyx. She could feel the heat of it through the material of her skirt, and his erection against her hip. It didn't disgust her as she expected it to. She never saw him again; for years she wondered what his voice had sounded like when he'd asked her to dance, and if his life was going the right way for him, wherever he'd gone.

'I'm not very rhythmic,' she said.

Alek smiled. They held one another, shuffling in loose loops like they were in a care home. Ada liked it at first, the rebellion of it: they were the only couple moving in a pair, and easily the oldest people on the dancefloor. Then she began noticing her feet didn't know where to step, and her arms looked oddly angled. Alek's face was disarmingly close to hers; she'd never intended for it to get so near, she could see every white hair sprouting from his eyebrows. She considered his body discreetly; really he was very attractive for his age, well-composed and solid. But she couldn't kick the certainty that he wasn't right, somehow, and that she didn't want his arms encircling her or his cheekbone within licking distance. She had no compulsion to familiarise herself with a new set of legs, a new penis, new toes and moles and scars, a new life biography, books and films and music to discuss a second

156

time or admit she knew nothing about. Abruptly she was back in the kitchen in Swinburne Road, and it was Michael whose hand was on her lower back, his warm stomach ballooning into hers as it did increasingly as they aged and changed shapes, and she almost cried out with the pain of it, of him not being with her now and the bitterness of the fact that she'd wanted the same thing for more than two years now, without it coming true.

She closed her eyes. She waited for it to pass. Such moments of crystalline recall were becoming rarer and more shocking, and when they occurred Ada suffered and held them to her like a dark gift.

The song began to fade out. Alek looked into Ada's eyes. She couldn't read his expression, she didn't know him well enough to interpret what she saw there, if he thought they'd just had a great erotic connection or was disappointed they hadn't. Shards of a new song began to pierce the old one. The kids around them erupted, it was some nineties track they liked. Ada thanked Alek for the dance and went off to the bar to get a glass of water.

At midnight she found her bag and left. The day seemed to have lasted a week. It had been her most draining Rent-a-Gran session to date, partly because she'd been on her feet for much of it but also because it had filled her with a dry sort of lust: Peter and Yannis were just getting going, they had years ahead of them; they would go through so many evolutions. She was envious and she couldn't help but sense the precariousness of it all too; as if the most precious clay bowl had been fired and lacquered and placed on a narrow shelf where footsteps nearby might shake it off at any moment.

Chapter Sixteen

Eliza was preparing to leave the house when she got a text. It was two weeks since she'd been to Carlisle and she'd not spoken to her parents since. People never texted her these days and she tapped her phone blithely, assuming it would be some automated message reminding her about an approaching appointment.

It was Nick the developer.

'Renovating ur room next so get ready to leave the house pls, tks.'

Eliza stared at the message. Stress scrunched up her chest.

With trembling fingers she asked by return text how long she had. She'd never signed any sort of contract, in theory Nick could kick her out within the hour. The developer read the message but didn't reply, or answer Eliza's ensuing texts and calls over the following few days. She began living in a febrile state of readiness, her clothes packed away by the door, her books in boxes.

She told George about what had happened and he dragged her down to London for the day to distract her, there was some big exhibition he wanted to see. He was a history of art student and evangelical about the power of paintings to balm the soul. Eliza was sceptical but she didn't want to work, so she took the coach down. The gallery was full of people, the well-spoken elderly affluent, mostly, and George went into a sort of trance, standing for minutes in front of the canvases, incapable of hearing anything. Eliza tried to imitate him. The centrepiece of the exhibition was a Van Gogh that rarely travelled: one of his sunflower pictures. Eliza stood in front of it for a long time, along with other people, willing the painting to do something to her. It was so familiar it might as well be a signpost or a food label. She gave up and went to the gift shop. George found her there an hour later reading a comic book. His eyes were gleaming. He felt renewed by what he'd seen. She said she'd loved the art, that she'd only been in the shop for a minute or so.

The next day Baleotti began setting up a series of formal meetings in college to discuss her 'well-being'. Even the word made her jumpy. She'd barely been seen in the department and had not showed up to a single meeting all term; he wrote that he was worried about her, copying the head of graduate pastoral care into the email. She couldn't quell the suspicion that it was futile carrying on with her thesis; that she was polishing yet another pebble to be chucked into the vast academic quarry. She tried refreshing her relationship with Levi – reading his books again, reminding herself of the traumas he'd lived through, looking at videos of him, all in an attempt to shock herself into connection again – but nothing cut through; he seemed remote and improbable, a small Italian man who had lived decades ago through events Eliza couldn't imagine very easily.

She whittled down to her last fifty quid and began to feel

landlocked by her not-quite-poverty. At Oxford students were discouraged from geting a job in term time; she could ask for emergency financial aid from college but she didn't want to make them think she was completely losing the plot. She devised more and more ingenious ways to spend zero money until it became a goal in its own right; there were a number of big cafés in the centre that had such a churn of tourists that the waiters never noticed if she sat at a table to finish leftovers, and in the evenings, she could eat for free at Oxford's endless talks and lectures; you just had to read the college noticeboards carefully and sign up to the right Facebook events. The university's Christians were a particularly reliable source of nourishment: they had a hotline you could text if you wanted a cheese toastie delivered to you in college. Eliza did this several times. All she had to do when the food arrived was endure the attempted conversion by whichever Christian had brought it to her, then gently shoo them away so she could eat in peace.

On her college's recommendation she started seeing a therapist. She didn't know whether it would help but she wanted to look back and know that she'd behaved sensibly. It turned out to be more of an interesting experience than a restorative one. The therapist was a woman called Candida who wore Joules-type outfits; her voice packed in so much empathy it was oppressive. Mostly Eliza filled in mental health questionnaires or talked about the past, which Eliza found depressing because some of her past was depressing. Candida encouraged her to articulate the feeling she had these days that she was living wrapped in cling film, nothing piercing through; she had no preference for where she was or what she was doing. Everything felt similar, like she'd already searched on Google Images what the different phases of her life would look like and now she knew, so there wasn't much joy to be had in living them out.

Sometimes they sat in silence. Candida liked to say that she was a great believer in silence. In these pauses Eliza would do things like mentally list fruit in order of preference and wonder how places like Venezuela and Senegal were getting on; she'd not heard what was happening in those countries in a while. She suspected she wasn't using the silences productively and when she voiced that concern Candida insisted that she was, and that anyway their sessions weren't about 'using' time for this or that purpose; time was not a commodity. OK, Eliza would reply. She'd never been sure what a commodity was.

She started attending daily services in the New College chapel. She wished she and Rich had gone in during their tour of the university; he would have been blown away by its grandeur, the carved wood and stone, the stained-glass window even Eliza could see was exquisite. The choir sang well and Eliza liked it most when they sat down after performing; the choristers would catch one another's eyes like they had noticed something funny. Eliza didn't feel excluded by these glances but amused, as if she knew the singers well and knew what they were joking about. She enjoyed the readings too; it was comforting to be told things like 'the meek shall inherit the earth', even though she didn't believe a word of it: just being told that sort of thing was nice. She tried her best to have a momentous religious experience by staring at the crucifix above the altar, but nothing perforated her carapace; she was a solid atheist and may as well have tried to convince herself of the existence of nymphs.

Chapter Seventeen

In the days after the wedding, Ada continued to rent herself out to the people who got in touch, but it was with increasing reluctance. She didn't need the money, though she was making it in fistfuls. She was tired of filtering out smutty messages from desolate men who should know better. She was bored of travelling all over Oxfordshire. Her favourite regulars began not to need her: Alice gave up driving after she nearly reversed over a small child and Henry got a job in a TV studio in Birmingham. The business was making Ada feel increasingly flimsy and unreal, like she was a pop-up card: diverting for a bit but then sort of extraneous and disposable. Many clients wanted to use Rent-a-Gran because they were simply curious to see how it worked; a few just wanted to be able to cash in a banterous anecdote later – 'And so I hired a grandmother!' Some were after the power trip of paying a woman to be with them for whatever non-sexual reason they could confect. Not reliably non-sexual, in any case: she got a shock one day when a forty-year-old solicitor summoned Ada to his house in Abingdon to get her to make him a cake, only when she arrived and began setting out the ingredients, he came into the kitchen wearing a dressing gown, which he opened.

His erection was maroon and vast, quivering like a dog at dinnertime as they both stared at it, and it ran through Ada's mind that she might be raped and murdered. The possibility didn't scare her, precisely; it intrigued her, though she decided she'd prefer that were not the outcome of the afternoon and told the solicitor that she was here to make a cake, and that he was making things difficult.

'Oh,' he said. 'Right.'

'I'm terribly sorry,' Ada said.

'Not to worry.'

The solicitor went upstairs and put some clothes on. Ada began mashing caster sugar into a bowl of butter. An hour later, the cake was finished and she left.

She had started Rent-a-Gran to create a bustling social life; to combat, she supposed, her loneliness. Against the odds, the business was flourishing and she could see that she'd acquired a bustling social life – but she could also see that her loneliness remained, the ghost at the feast. In fact, flitting in and out of people's lives, witnessing and strengthening the bonds that tied families together, made Ada acutely alert to the contours of her own isolation: she was the one who needed a hireable bloody grandmother, she was the person that needed visiting and coddling and looking out for. The whole situation was perverse. Clients paid her to help them so they seldom asked her about herself: you'd not demand the life story of your therapist or waiter. Yet the more people she met that didn't think to engage with her as an equal, the more she felt her impulse to talk about herself kick in. It was as if she needed to hear herself tell her own stories or they wouldn't feel real, her past would melt away like ice cubes in water. She wrote and wrote, sending reams of poems to James in London, who eventually telephoned to say there was enough material for a collection and that he was setting up a series of readings heralding her triumphant return to form. 'These are brilliant poems,' he told her. 'The best you've written.' That, at least, was something.

One morning Camille, mother of Milton and the others, called to ask if she would help out her friend Cathy. Ada agreed. Cathy lived in Rose Hill too, she was a hospital secretary with four kids under eight. Almost the minute Ada arrived, Cathy announced that she was leaving to run some errands. She was a skeletal woman with circles around her eyes. When their mother was gone the children went nuts, declaring they were leaving, all four of them, to have chicken nuggets at McDonald's. The oldest found a way to open the front door and for ten horrible minutes they escaped the maisonette and went charging off into the surrounding streets, except for the one-year-old, Cora, who was dumped by her brother in a pot plant near the front door, and left to gurgle forlornly.

With difficulty Ada herded them all back into the house. She wanted to read to them but there were no books around; then one of them found a copy of *Horrid Henry* in his satchel and she settled them down to listen. Ada asked the oldest one, Hara, to turn the pages. After half an hour he reached for the paper edge in a particular way and his sleeve rode up. She saw something odd.

The skin on his narrow wrist was liver-red. She caught his hand softly and pulled the sleeve back. His whole arm was bruised. The patches were different colours and sizes; some looked like birthmarks, they were so dark against the milk of his skin.

For a moment Ada's body went still. She asked Hara gently to show her his other arm and he held it out; that arm too had a few marks, blues and lavenders and uneasy storm greens. Before long Ada learned that the other children had bruises, even the littlest, Cora, who smiled and clapped as Ada checked her back, her arms, her chubby legs, feeling nauseous and appalled, so angry she could barely see.

'Do you know how you all got these bruises?' she asked Hara. Her voice sounded thin, scraped.

He shook his head. His eyes were huge. He kept pulling his sleeves down to his fingertips. None of the others said a word when she asked them in turn. Ingrid, who was four, was staring at the television as if it were showing her favourite programme.

'Have you been told not to talk about your bruises?' Ada asked the room.

Silence. The book slid to the floor. Ada couldn't get a word out of any of them and felt a kind of darkness swelling within her, pushing out her chest, reaching right down to her pelvic bone until she wanted to curl up in the corner among the toys and DVDs. Before she could devise anything approaching an action plan, Cathy returned. Ada was shaking, she thought she might faint. She asked to talk to Cathy in the kitchen. She felt completely out of her depth, like she'd tripped into an alternative life as a social worker, only she wasn't qualified and might make everything worse.

'The kids are bashed up,' she said, once she'd closed the door behind them.

There was a pause.

'They play rough,' Cathy said.

She spoke robotically. Her eyes were light blue, like swimming pools. Ada could see the bone-pallor of the woman's knuckles as she clutched the table edge.

Ada replied levelly that it was more than that; there were fingermarks in the bruising, patterns that were not the normal assortment of kiddie scrapes. Was there a man on the scene? Who was responsible here? Cathy smoothed her jeans and asked Ada to get out of the house. Ada didn't move. Cathy said it again. Ada stood up, dizzied by a sense of unreality, and walked into the living room to collect her things. Cathy followed her, tried to give her a twenty-quid note. Ada didn't take it. Cathy returned to the kitchen. The children watched Ada soundlessly. Her coat buttons felt flimsy, like the thread keeping them on was down to its last follicles. She ruffled Hara's hair as she walked to the front door. The boy flinched at her touch, his mouth pulling back into a grimace of fear, like Ada might do worse. She didn't want him to see the expression on her face so she hurried out as quickly as she could.

At home, she sat in the living room with a lamp on by her shoulder. She couldn't write or eat. She kept going to the kitchen to make some tea, then would forget her cup was there, and have to pour the tepid liquid down the sink.

Chapter Eighteen

One evening after supper with Judy in college, a message flashed up on Eliza's Facebook. She was lying on her bed with her laptop open. She clicked on the message idly. It was from Ruby. She saw enough of the message to know it started off with something like, 'Heyyyyy what are you up to . . .'

She careered to her feet and opened one of the bedroom windows, desperate for air. Her heart was bounding crazily and she felt unsteady; later she remembered the physicality of the reaction with slight embarrassment, like she'd been sick after a sip of wine. The timing of the message was shit; she'd been thinking of Ruby more and more over the past few weeks, reading the last messages they'd exchanged, poring over birthday cards and letters, playing voicemails she still had of hers saved on her phone. It was a form of self-harm and she knew it, but she wanted to do it so badly she didn't stop herself, like how when she really wanted to scratch a mosquito bite she always let herself do it, even if it was going to make it itch more later. She'd been dreaming of Ruby too, vivid dreams full of sex and conversation, and when she awoke she'd rebuke her subconscious for its treachery – her daylight self had worked hard to move on from the relationship and yet here was an insubordinate faction within her that seemed determined to drag her into the mire again. Why couldn't the different parts of her work as a team? Why did one have to undermine the other?

She returned to the bed and flipped the laptop open. She tapped Command-T, filling up the other tabs with websites like *The New Yorker* and Reddit in case she needed a quick getaway. She opened the message.

'Heyyyyy what are you up to?' it began. 'Been ages. Hope you're good . . . I've been missing you a load and ran into one of your St Antonia's friends (lol) who told me you're at Oxford now, well done babe. I'm living in Marlow at the mo, not doing much, lmk if you want lunch.' It finished with a love heart emoji, not the red heart but the orange one that carried fewer romantic connotations. Eliza read the message over and over. She found it hard to identify with the tone; it was so prosaic and chatty, almost as if the last time they'd seen one another Ruby hadn't just banged some guy downstairs in the home she and Eliza had been sharing for months. She knew vaguely that it was a pernicious message but she couldn't see where that was actually evident in the text; maybe it was in the word 'babe', which they used to call one another affectionately, or perhaps it was in Ruby's decision not to acknowledge the fucked-up terms on which they'd parted.

Whatever. Eliza stood up. She tied her hair into a bun. She tried to feel normal. She put on a podcast about abuse in the Catholic Church and picked up odd bits of clothing. She drank a glass of water. She bit her nails, stripping the loose tassels of skin away until the tips of her fingers were neon pink. There was a feeling in her torso like heartache, not the rabid desperation she'd been trammelled by in the hours following her and Ruby's break-up but a deeper, bodily sadness that had come in the weeks after. It was strange feeling it again, like how until you vomited, you never knew quite what it was like to do it, and then suddenly you were vomiting and you thought, 'Oh yes, this is what vomiting feels like'. Eliza had tried to quash her heartache, yet here it was again. Emotions she thought she'd long since eliminated had actually been crouching in her the whole time, biding their time, strengthening. She'd not been as thorough in her purge as she'd thought.

Too soon the bedroom was spotless. There were no more clothes to be folded away and she'd even cleaned the mini-fridge. She had not absorbed a word of the podcast or the one after. She curled up on the bed, her arms crossed over her breasts, looking through the things she'd unearthed in her tidy-up – a five-pound note in a jeans pocket, a stamped loyalty card from Sylvie's, the Rent-a-Gran advertisement that the lady opposite had given her when she'd been campaigning with Paola. Eliza unfolded the piece of paper and reread it. Without Paola here to laugh about it, there was something sad about the jauntiness of the words. Some quiet despair pulsed out: 'Hire me, and we could spend the day baking Eccles Cakes that taste like the good old days,' it read. 'Need company? I'm an accomplished conversation-alist . . . with 60-plus years' experience!'

Eliza decided, on a whim, to investigate. She sprang to her feet and pulled her hair out of her bun, then tied it up again. She couldn't stay in her bedroom with Ruby's message cramped in her computer, a lurking scorpion, she had to do something, anything would be better than remaining in her current stasis. She put on some shoes and went downstairs, the ad folded tight in her hand.

It was cold out. Eliza went to the house with the yellow door. She stood for some time in front of the knocker, a little scared. There was a matte patch on the door as if someone had thudded their forehead on it while the paint was still wet. A doorbell, too. She peered through the letterbox. All she could see was a wall of shiny black brush, the kind that people got installed when they didn't want thieves or neighbours nosing into their hallway. Then, abruptly, without thinking it through or knowing what she'd say if she got a reaction, Eliza rang the bell.

She heard movement inside the house and stepped back. She wanted to run off but some instinct for civility kept her rooted to the spot. The door opened.

A woman was standing in the hallway, her body encircled by soft light coming from a lamp further inside. Paintings lined the walls. It looked so homely and warm that Eliza's breath caught in her throat.

'Hello?' the lady said. Eliza was sure it was the same person she'd met with Paola. She was smiling, wearing a kind of blousy Victorian nightie and crocs, but she didn't look like she'd gone to bed yet.

'Um, hi,' Eliza said. She didn't know what to say next so she just told the woman her name and showed her the advert. She felt suddenly ashamed to be there, mortified she so needed company that she'd been driven to this.

'Ah,' the woman said.

There was a question in her tone but her eyes were on Eliza's face and they seemed to take in her whole being. Then she said the words that made Eliza want to press her palms against her chest, to keep something inside from beaming out.

'Why don't you come in from the chill?'

Eliza said she would love to. She wanted to cry. She stepped into the house. The woman nodded as if them seeing one another was a prearranged thing. It would have been unsettling if it hadn't felt so natural. They walked to the kitchen.

'You like Lapsang Souchong,' Ada said as she led Eliza through. It wasn't a question, not quite. 'So do I. Let's have a pot of tea.'

Chapter Nineteen

They spent their first evening together in the kitchen. Ada put on an old Tom Waits album and steered Eliza into the winged wooden chair that used to be Michael's. It was padded out with ragged cushions and the boiled sweets he used to stow in the folds; sometimes even now they fell to the ground, landing with a cellophane crackle on the floor.

Ada liked how differently Eliza filled the chair. She was one third Michael's size, dressed in a pair of ripped jeans, trainers and a grey T-shirt. Her legs were pulled up with her, the pink hair she said needed redyeing in a spiky bun on top of her head. Ada knew that she was the young woman she'd seen standing in the middle of Swinburne Road waiting for lightning to strike her, until a car drove up and took her away.

They didn't talk much as Ada prepared the tea, both grateful for the roar of the kettle; its elimination of the possibility of conversation. Ada saw that Eliza, for whatever reason, was near depletion – even her head was tipped forward like her neck was weakening from the weight of her skull. Her cheekbones were severe and her skin had a strange translucency.

Eliza, for her part, didn't have the energy to decide who Ada actually was, whether this was some bourgeois kidnapping situation she'd walked herself into or if every-thing was actually fine. She still had the Rent-a-Gran advert in her hands and she was vaguely aware that every minute she spent in the house might be totted up and charged for later down the line, but she could not rouse herself to care. Ada exuded a warmth and inclusivity that she could feel thawing her bones. Just being in her pres-ence for now was enough.

In time the water in the kettle stilled itself. Ada went to it. Tea leaves, scrunched black like punctuation. Teapot, water.

'Do you want sugar?'

'No.'

'Did you want milk?'

'Yes.'

'I'm sorry, I added some to your cup without asking.'

'I wanted it anyway, thank you.'

They blew on their tea together at the kitchen table. Ada saw that Eliza was cold, the hairs on her narrow white forearms were standing up, so she found her an old yellow cashmere blanket and wrapped it over her shoulders. They both thought at the same moment that the tea tasted of old rifles. Once Ada had served them both a second cup, they began to talk. Eliza explained that she'd kept the Rent-a-Gran advert after they met briefly when she'd been canvassing for the Remain campaign. She hadn't been sure whether the advert was for real. Ada said it was 'for real' and that she thought she'd seen Eliza drinking Lapsang Souchong once at Sylvie's café on Iffley Road.

'Oh yeah? I don't remember that,' Eliza said. 'But Lapsang is what I get there.'

'I was going to come up to you and say I liked it too but I didn't, in the end,' Ada said. 'I don't know why.'

'I don't remember that at all. I'm sorry.'

'Maybe it's for the best. I might have come off a bit strong. I wanted to charge over and let you know you were on to a good brew. You may have been alarmed.'

'I'd have agreed. Lapsang's the best.'

Ada smiled. 'My grandmother introduced me to it,' she said.

'Same here,' Eliza said.

She told Ada that she'd seen her a few times at night, her silhouette motionless in a room upstairs. It had given her the heebie-jeebies, a bit. 'Unless that was someone else who lives in this house,' she added, unsure if it was a question.

'I live alone now,' Ada said. 'It must have been me.'

Eliza registered the word 'now' and hoped it didn't imply what she sensed it did. 'It was actually quite freaky,' she said. 'Seeing you look out on to the street, without opening the curtains to actually see it.'

'Yes, I can see that might have looked rather dramatic. I'm a bad sleeper. Standing helps.'

'I stay up too late.'

They looked at one another, pleased at the idea they were both awake in the night on opposite sides of the street. They began to talk about how they'd ended up on Swinburne Road in the first place. In Ada's case the tale involved a whole lot, a sizeable portion of her life story really, because it was to do with Michael and their old

existence in Manchester. Eliza understood that Michael
had worked at the university and passed away; precisely
when was unclear, she didn't want to ask too many questions if it was a sensitive subject. She was moved by the
way in which Ada spoke of her husband. Most of the time
it was in a matter-of-fact tone, the way very old people
mentioned relatives who'd died decades ago, but occasionally, something jammed Ada's instinct for concision
and slowed her down. She would linger on the step of
whatever memory she was recounting, relive it as she was
describing it. She eventually revealed that he had died in
this very room, in fact on the chair Eliza was sitting on.

Eliza looked down at the cushions, startled, realising
at the same moment that it would be rude to leap out of
the seat as if it were haunted. Ada burst into laughter at
the conflicted look on her face. Eliza laughed too, guiltily
then properly, because she could imagine the expression
on her face and she knew it must have been funny, and
anyway, there was something amusing about someone
just dying at a kitchen table, and they both knew it and
wanted to laugh about it.

In time they quietened. Ada found some digestives and
fanned them out on a plate. She still hadn't asked why
Eliza had decided to come over and she knew she wouldn't,
not yet; she didn't want Eliza to feel uncomfortable about
her need for conversation, for human contact. Eliza took
a biscuit at once, realising she was ravenous; she'd only
had chips with Judy in the college canteen earlier because
they cost less than a quid. She dipped the digestive into
her tea, keeping half the biscuit submerged until it was
quivering, about to break off.

'I came downstairs and everything was exactly as it should be, apart from him,' Ada said.

Eliza looked up. She put the biscuit in her mouth. It softened on her tongue.

'He had his forehead on the table.' It was the first time Ada had described finding him to anyone.

Eliza said nothing. She couldn't imagine being with someone for as long as long marriages seemed to last. She didn't know what it must feel like for that person to suddenly be taken from you.

'Odd how these things play out,' Ada said.

Eliza reached for Ada's hand. She didn't intend to hold it, that would be too much, but she wanted Ada to know that if she needed to hold a hand, she could: there was one right there.

'I'm very sorry,' she said.

Ada smiled tightly and stood up. 'Ho-hum,' she replied. 'So you're a student at Oxford – undergraduate or graduate? I'm afraid I can't tell.'

'Grad student,' she said. 'I'm in the Italian department.'

'Oh really? My husband worked there.'

'Did he?'

'Yes, Michael Robertson. He did twentieth-century stuff.'

Eliza almost dropped the remainder of her biscuit. 'Michael Robertson?' she repeated.

Ada nodded. Eliza said she knew exactly who her husband was; he was one of the reasons she'd wanted to come to Oxford in the first place, he'd been brilliant, the leading light in the department, most of her thinking about Primo Levi was based on ideas he'd had and laid out in articles that sounded fresh even now, fifteen years after some of them were published.

Ada smiled at Eliza's fervour, all millennial awkwardness cast aside. She'd encountered many of Michael's youthful acolytes over the decades but none, she thought, since his funeral. As she watched Eliza enthuse, Ada felt her body pulse with longing, with a sadness so primitive it seemed to pull at her from within. Michael had always had a way of putting people at ease, making them forget themselves and the ludicrous codes they tangled themselves within, and here he was, doing it from beyond the grave, connecting Ada to this young woman. Ada thought she saw who Eliza really was, now that she was speaking on impulse, from a place of real conviction.

'I'm sorry,' Eliza said suddenly.

She stopped talking. She realised she'd been banging on, barely giving Ada time to speak, taking her nods as fuel for more soliloquising. She saw too that Ada's eyes were vivid and shining, her right hand drawn to her neck, the long, pale fingers pulling at the loose skin of her throat.

'I shouldn't have jumped on you like that, gone on about— I'm sorry,' Eliza said.

Ada cleared her throat. 'It's fine,' she said, and she thumped her chest to give her voice more welly. 'It's jolly nice to hear about him, to be frank. I forget that his scholarship remains. Of course I know that there are students still taking his books out of libraries and so on but one only knows that in theory, one never gets to see their faces or hear what they think.'

Eliza nodded.

'It would have been nice,' Ada sighed, 'for him to have been here when you knocked.'

Eliza nodded. She helped herself to more tea, still embarrassed that she'd shown such fervent interest: had Ada endured a lifetime of being sidelined, of smiling woodenly as other women went mad for her husband, raved about his genius? She feared she wasn't being a very good feminist, sidestepping the woman before her for the memory of her dead male partner.

Ada patted Eliza's hand, seeing she was discomfited. They looked at one another for a moment, Eliza trying not to think about what Ada's husband must have been like, and whether there was a library upstairs full of the books he'd read and written. Ada saw more, as she looked into Eliza's face, guessed what she was thinking, what she was trying not to say.

At midnight Eliza became conscious that she had imposed on this woman's hospitality for hours now. She stretched and said that she'd better make the long journey home. She was hyper-aware as she put her cup in the dishwasher that Ada might want money.

'How much do I owe you?' she made herself ask, screwing up her face at the awkwardness of the question, watching her hands slide her teaspoon into the dishwasher grate.

Ada looked blank for a second, then shook her head.

'Oh, you're not paying me for an evening of chit-chat,' she said. 'Do be sensible. I'd have told you if I were going to charge.'

Eliza tried not to let her relief show. 'We haven't even spoken about your business,' she said. 'I'd love to hear about it.'

'Another time,' Ada said.

'That would be great.'

They had a brief, comfortable squabble about who should wash the teapot, then Eliza washed it and they walked to the front door. Ada pointed to the patch of matte yellow paint; if you looked closely, you could see Michael's palm lines.

'It looks like those groovy waves you get on maps of mountains, to show how steep the terrain is,' Eliza said.

'So it does,' Ada said, smiling. She'd not thought of that before; Eliza was perfectly right. They examined the patch of paint for a second longer, then Eliza turned to cross the road. She wanted to give Ada a hug or something but she wasn't sure of the etiquette. Ada chivvied her away.

'Come back tomorrow,' she said as Eliza reached the pavement. 'If the urge grips you.'

Eliza called something affirmative back. From the other side of the street she gave her neighbour a wave. Ada waved back. She looked small, framed in the amber light of the hallway.

Chapter Twenty

Eliza awoke the following morning with the sumptuous sensation that her sleep had been so rich and deep she had not dreamed at all.

She luxuriated in the feeling for a while, stretching out in her bed, scrunching her toes like pretty girls did in films. She allowed her mind to piece itself together gradually, wondering vaguely if she was thirsty and if so, whether she should trouble herself to reach for the glass of water on the desk.

She got to her feet and opened the curtains. It was a sparkling spring day and the sight of the house opposite triggered recollections of the night before. She almost gasped at the feeling of being so abruptly heaped upon. The idea that she'd marched across to that zingy yellow door yesterday and rung the bell, been invited in and made friends with the woman who lived there, was strange to her now, as if she'd not seen a relative in decades and was being told by them about something outlandish that she'd done when she was very young, that she couldn't imagine ever doing, even as a tiny infant.

With the memories of Ada came the recollection of the thing that had driven Eliza across the road in the first place: Ruby's message and the interior slide that had provoked, the return of a self she'd thought gone for good. She wished that she had deleted the message before she'd read it. She wished she was resilient enough, had sufficiently developed instincts for self-preservation, not to care that Ruby seemed to care for her still. It was lame to be so impacted by a message from an ex: it was textbook, run of the mill. Eliza had become one of those women now, one of those trashed hearts. She brushed her teeth crossly and packed her laptop into her bag, wondering if it would rain today and whether she should take a waterproof coat to the library. As she left she tried not to look at the house opposite but as she was unlocking her bike, the sitting room curtain split and Eliza saw Ada gesturing at her from a sofa inside.

For a second Eliza decided to pretend not to see her. She couldn't quite believe how late she'd stayed. It wasn't dissimilar from waking up next to someone you'd had drunk sex with and you weren't sure, observing them the following morning, how much of your true self you'd exposed in the night, how much you'd been able to hold back. Ada had even made Eliza a pot of her favourite tea, for heaven's sake. She'd been hideously kind. Eliza must have come across as a maniac in need of emergency soothing.

She doubled down on her resolution to go into town without engaging with the house opposite and crammed her helmet onto her head. But Ada continued to wave. There was something so optimistic about the gesture, something so open and killable, that Eliza realised she would never forgive herself for not responding. She waved back at Ada and mouthed 'Good morning'.

Ada beckoned to Eliza to come over. Eliza found herself nodding and crossing the street and suddenly the front door was open and Ada was right there in her crocs and nightdress. Eliza blinked disconcertedly.

'The road smells of biscuits!' Ada cried.

'Er, does it?' Eliza asked.

'Yes!'

Eliza sniffed. It was true, the road smelled of biscuits.

'Why?' she asked.

'No idea,' Ada said.

Eliza felt herself grin. It was nice, actually, to see this eccentric woman again, though Eliza felt hyper-visible and abashed too. They chatted for a bit, Eliza standing gauchely by the bins with her bike lock in her hand, trying to beat back her urge to go. Ada asked if she'd had breakfast. Eliza said that she'd not, wondering whether Ada was known to the police for luring grads into her house and, what, dismembering them or brainwashing them or something. Maybe she was a Scientologist.

'I was about to make porridge,' Ada said.

'That sounds great,' Eliza said. She really liked porridge, so it wasn't a lie.

The house seemed different in daylight. The look of it chased off any concerns Eliza had about it belonging to a psychopath; it was quite evidently the home of a bookish widow who lived alone. There were cards everywhere, on mantelpieces and stools and side tables; Eliza thought initially Ada must have had a birthday but then she realised that they were sympathy cards bearing daffodils and condolence slogans in slanty silver writing. Eliza racked her brains to remember if Ada had told her when her husband had died; perhaps it had been a few weeks ago.

'I ought to pack these away, really,' Ada said, seeing Eliza take in the cards. 'He died two years ago.'

Eliza swallowed. She wanted to hug her. They went into the kitchen, Eliza keeping an eye out for cats: it felt like the sort of house where at dusk, a mob of strays would turn up at the back door, to scratch and yowl until they were pacified with hot kippers.

'There are five secrets to good porridge,' Ada chattered as she turned on the hob.

'Oh yeah?' Eliza asked.

'Whole milk, one. Proper oats, two – solid ones with shape and a Scottish sort of attitude. Three: toast the oats in the pan first. Four: add a decent pinch of Maldon sea salt midway through the process. And it's a good idea to splash in a bit of double cream. Right at the end when the oats have thickened up.'

'How much cream?'

'Oh, a tablespoon or two. Then you should leave the porridge to collect its thoughts.'

Eliza laughed. 'How long does that take?'

'Fifteen minutes. At least.'

When it was ready Eliza recounted how she and her father had it in Carlisle: with toasted hazelnuts and a great heap of muscovado sugar. Ada dug out some nuts and said she'd have the same on hers. They browned the nuts in a pan. The kitchen warmed with the smell of them. They decided to eat outside, on fold-up chairs under the cherry tree. A red kite was hovering not far off, so still it looked hung from the sky. They didn't talk much, just clinked their spoons in their bowls and said things like how nice the porridge was, because it was; it was delicious.

*

Eliza ended up spending the whole day there. She worked in the kitchen as Ada pottered around her, making tea, looking for this or that poetry collection, tidying and humming. Eliza could sense how happy this woman was to have her in the house. She needed to go to the modern languages library to collect a book she'd ordered but she couldn't bring herself to leave. Besides, it was surprisingly soothing to work with Ada bustling around.

At two they had soup for lunch, which Ada extracted from a couple of tins written all over in Arabic. Neither of them knew what the soup would be, and they still weren't sure after they'd finished it, but it was hot and smoky, so they continued eating anyway with some pita bread Ada heated in the oven. As they ate Ada told Eliza about her business, how she'd set it up, how lately she'd realised it wasn't quite the rescue rope she'd hoped it might be.

'Can't you just stop giving the sessions?' Eliza asked. 'If you're not enjoying them anymore?'

Ada considered. 'I suppose I feel a sense of duty to continue with it all,' she said.

'Why?'

'Oh, not sure really. It took a while to get a decent number of customers, and it seemed such a silly idea that now I feel I rather owe it to myself to go on with it. Maybe that sounds mad.'

'I don't think it sounds mad but I don't think that makes total sense either. The business was about making you happy, wasn't it?'

'Yes, I suppose so.'

'And now it's not doing that. So pause it for a bit.'

'I could try.'

As Ada imagined herself simply not replying to the requests being emailed and texted to her multiple times a day, she felt an abrupt rush of relief. She'd not noticed that the prospect of endless Rent-a-Gran engagements was making her feel put-upon, even slightly nervy. It was clarifying talking it through with this intelligent young woman. Eliza listened with a kind of absorbed sobriety, but when Ada said something that amused her she shrugged off her natural gravity and gave a great shout of laughter. Eliza was especially gripped by the tale of two warring sisters Ada had helped a couple of weeks ago, who had paid her to adjudicate the tussle they were having over their dead mother's collection of ivory hairbrushes. And when Ada told Eliza about the solicitor who'd dropped his dressing gown to reveal his penis, Eliza giggled until she nearly cried, saying again and again, 'But why did you stay to finish the cake?'

After lunch they went to the sitting room. Eliza was fascinated by Rent-a-Gran and all the curious situations Ada had thrown herself into; it was invigorating, it made her want to take control of her life, act to change things rather than feel the weight of them on her. Before either of them expected it, the sun began to set. The sky over Swinburne Road dimmed. Soon it was feathered with long, low licks of orange and lilac. Ada embroidered: having taught the twins to knit, she'd remembered how much she loved needlework, and was reimmersing herself in all that again. A year ago she would have felt self-conscious about acting so stereotypically her age; now she didn't mind. Rent-a-Gran had done that at least: made her realise how crossable the supposed generational lines were, how ludicrous it was to invest in fixed ideas of elderliness. She thought of her mother as she sewed. The most vivid memories Ada had of Jane were of her sitting on her tartan armchair in Christow, needle in hand, a pile of fabric and the black Jack Russell they had then on her lap.

Eliza stopped reading after a bit and stretched languidly. She began looking at the little bowls and paintings and shells dotted around the room between the cards; every item seemed to have a story of its own, to have soaked up a memory. Every so often Ada looked up from her armchair, explaining why there was a large jar of thimbles by the window, which Italian beach the glossy white pebbles came from. Eliza was about to sit back on the sofa and continue reading her book when her eye snagged on something on one of the little tables in the corner.

There was an object on it. She hadn't noticed it before. It was no bigger than a man's hand, in front of a picture frame that had been turned around so Eliza couldn't see what the photograph was of.

She walked to the table, her heart crisping up. She kneeled down to look at the object more closely. A mesh of reddish wire. A shape emerging from the tangle: an owl. A small beak and a stout body. Wire wings closed on its back, tufty ears that flicked upwards, like it was listening attentively.

It was a lovely thing. Eliza looked at it for a long time, feeling her body flush with joy. She knew who must have made the sculpture and she could barely believe what she was seeing, or that she was seeing it here, in a house she'd lived opposite for months without ever suspecting it contained such a treasure. Certainly she couldn't touch the owl, it was too precious, so she just looked and looked as Ada watched her from her armchair, knowing Eliza was moved and allowing her to be so, unimpeded by a rustle in the room or an explanation.

'This figurine,' Eliza said at last. She coughed to clear her throat; she could feel tears in her eyes but knew they were the sort not to fall. 'Who made it?'

Ada stood up. She picked up the owl fondly. It looked light in her hands, delicate and alive. 'A writer my husband loved,' she said. She didn't want to say more, not now at least.

Eliza nodded, feeling as if a shawl of sunlight had been wrapped around her arms, around her chest.

'Would you like to hold it?'

Eliza nodded. She put out her hands. Ada placed the copper-wire sculpture on her flat palms, where the owl seemed to look up at Eliza with a lively sort of curiosity, unless it was irony.

'Primo Levi made it?' Eliza asked, though she knew the answer.

'That's right,' Ada replied.

For a second she wanted to stop there, to say nothing else. The thought of the missing owl was still too disheartening for Ada to contemplate for long; a greyness would gather in her like dust in a barn whenever she dwelled upon the fact that the second little fellow had been abandoned, probably somewhere in Manchester, and that Michael had died not knowing what had happened to it. It was ridiculous, of course, it was yawningly sentimental and Ada rebuked herself regularly for feeling so stricken – the wire sculptures were objects, not people or pets – but she could only hold onto that conviction for so long before a great peal of sadness at the missing owl would ring out in her heart.

Looking at Eliza now strengthened her resolve.

'There were two,' she said.

Her voice was quiet. There was just that in the room, and the clicking of the clock.

Eliza waited for Ada to continue. She could sense that if she spoke too soon or with too much vigour, Ada might never go on.

'Michael bought a pair originally,' Ada said. 'Two figurines: one for me, one for him. Their wings interlocked. They were made for one another, to be beside one another.'

'Where did he get them?'

'Turin. I was with him when we bought them. You might be aware how rare they are, I don't know. We were close to a friend of the Levi family who would only sell to someone who'd really take care of them. Who'd cherish them, I suppose.'

'I thought they must have come directly from Italy. I didn't even know you could buy Levi's wire sculptures, they're not mentioned often in the scholarship about him.'

'I don't think one can just buy them, or not easily at any rate. When Michael got them it was probably the happiest moment of his life. He used to joke it pipped our wedding day.'

Eliza smiled. 'I'd have been happy too.'

Ada picked up the picture frame behind where the sculpture normally sat. For some time now the photo had been facing the wall so that she didn't have to see it. She showed the picture to Eliza.

'This was us a few hours after Michael bought the owls,' she said. 'It was taken in the Alps, on a path that Levi apparently liked. You know he was a keen mountaineer.'

Eliza nodded and stared at the image. Michael and Ada were in purple caps on a scrubby path, with a big rock in the background. Eliza could just make out the copper owls in their hands. Michael looked fat and jolly; the only thing that hinted that he was an academic was a book sticking out of his coat pocket – and with a rush Eliza remembered how Primo Levi's own father used to have his jackets specially tailored, so that his pockets were deep enough to keep novels in. She looked at Michael's outfit – his coat pockets seemed to have been cut for purpose too. Ada, meanwhile, was fresh and joyful, her hair in a shining bob under a cap, graceful somehow in her stocky walking outfit.

'It's a great picture,' Eliza said.

'Yes. It was a wonderful holiday, maybe our best. I wore my hair shorter then.'

'Usually it's the other way around. Older women seem to feel they should have short hair. I've always found it strange.'

'Quite. Well, that's why I grew mine long.'

'It's nice to see what Michael looked like. I don't think I ever knew, even though I've read so many of his books.'

'He got rather fatter towards the end.'

They both laughed.

'I don't think you should have the photo facing the wall,' Eliza said.

'No, that's probably right.'

'Why did you turn it around?'

'Oh, melodrama, you know. I was feeling sorry for myself.'

'Well, maybe you should keep it facing the room.'

'Yes. I dare say you're right.'

Ada put the frame back down, the other way around now so that the picture faced the sitting room. They admired the new arrangement for a bit, then Ada explained how the second owl had gone missing. Her voice was weaker than usual, her mouth stiffer and smaller, but she wanted Eliza to know so she pushed on.

'The other owl might, you know, be living the high life with another couple,' Eliza suggested gently.

Ada rolled her eyes. 'I think not,' she said. 'I imagine in the move things weren't packed up properly and the owl was left on our driveway until the binmen came.'

'Maybe it was taken to China or something,' Eliza said. 'And now it's getting stuck into the culture. Learning the lingo, bedding down with the locals.'

Ada smiled, shrugging.

'Was the other owl in a box or anything?' Eliza asked.

'When we unpacked here we found this owl in his little container, so I assume the other one was tucked away too. It's a black velvet box, the jeweller's sort.'

'I know the kind.'

There was a silence.

'We searched,' Ada said. It felt important that Eliza should know. 'I can't tell you how hard we searched.'

'I'm sure.'

'Yes. Well. Much worse things have been lost, of course. One shouldn't moan.'

They looked at one another, both a little watery, then Ada returned to her armchair and Eliza to the sofa, where she began reading again. The clock continued to flick sound into the room. Every so often, the quiet was shuffled by the sound of people on the pavement coming back from work, or car doors closing. After a while Ada came over to sit next to Eliza on the sofa. In a break in Eliza's reading she glanced over Ada's shoulder and saw what she was embroidering on a piece of white cloth – two owls sewn in gold thread in a tree, and in silver thread around them: the moon tossing its silk among the branches.

Chapter Twenty-One

Eliza wasn't quite sure why the discovery of the copper-wire sculpture in Ada's house changed her attitude to her doctorate, but it did. 'It was like he'd just left the room,' she said to Ada a few days later, trying to put her finger on what had shifted. 'Like Primo Levi had twisted the owl out of some spare wire he had lying around, and popped out just before I came in.'

For the first time in months she felt that current of connection again. Not a sensation of knowing someone, as Levi was too much of a riddle for that, but something closer to the feeling of being known by someone. She remembered playing at her grandad's as a child before he died, when the gentle old man would keep an eye on Eliza contentedly, twinkling from his rocking chair as she gallivanted, and she felt protected and cherished in the circle of his semi-attention. This feeling now was rather like that, like Levi was a benevolent relative she felt understood by, loved by. Ideas that she'd been struggling for months to scoop from the slough of her mind came to her willingly, whole and clean and radiant. Academia no longer seemed quite as pointless. She turned up one evening to a literature salon organised by fellow grads in the Italian department and felt the eyes of the other students fall on her, surprised she'd come. Baleotti was in the corner and raised his walking stick at her when she came in. The salon happened every week; it was a sort of book club, all you had to do to take part was read a contemporary Italian short story assigned by the organisers and arrive willing to discuss it. That was manageable.

She went and met with the college and department to assure them she was on the right track. 'It's weird,' she explained to Ada. 'I genuinely want to spend my time on my work right now.' She reread *The Periodic Table*, Levi's memoir about his eccentric relatives, and finished it in a day; she moved on immediately to *The Drowned and the Saved*, and was floored once more by its unruffled fury, its wisdom, by the spare grace of its prose. She whipped through the little poems Levi had written, so many of them featuring animals he must have seen on his walks in the Alps, and at last she could picture the man moving, speaking, being. Before seeing the owl, his writing had felt listless to Eliza, flattened by how many times she'd read it; now the letters of every sentence dusted themselves off and stood tall.

Without either of them proposing it or noticing it, Eliza began going to Ada's every day for breakfast. It was strange for Eliza to suddenly be spending so much time in Michael Robertson's house, to have taken such a personal route to the scholar's work. As time passed Eliza asked Ada more questions about her own work, too, about her poetry and methods of writing. She read Ada's collections – there weren't that many so it didn't take long – and she liked them more with every revisit: there was something solid about Ada's poetry, something consoling and permanent.

'It's not wank, that's one of the things I like about it,' she mused one Friday, looking up from *Measure*, which she was halfway through.

Ada gave a sort of squawk. It was hard to tell if she was flattered or offended. 'Thank you, Eliza,' she said dryly. Then she softened. 'Actually that means rather a lot.'

So many years had passed now since her heyday that Ada dropped the pretence she'd maintained for decades and began talking openly to Eliza about how disappointed she was that she'd not made more of her career – as a writer or as anything else.

'It's not that I wish I'd been Ted Hughes or whoever,' she specified. 'It's more that – well, the cliché is true – one only lives once. I feel I rather squandered my opportunities.'

'What do you mean?'

'I didn't do enough. My sixteen-year-old self would have been disappointed, I should think. She was hungry for the world, for success and experience and renown. In some ways I followed the conventional route for women of my generation: I had a disappointing series of jobs, then got married and did nothing much at all.'

Eliza frowned. They were in the garden: the weather was getting warmer every day. When it wasn't raining they took their breakfast outside, ate with woolly hats on if they had to.

'I don't like the idea of you measuring your output in such a bald way,' Eliza said. 'I'm sure other poets have produced more in the past few decades, who cares? There's always someone doing better, doing more. As soon as you start thinking about life in quantities – numbers of readers, numbers of collections – you get in the mud, I reckon.'

Ada chuckled at Eliza's attempt at wisdom. But it was a warm laugh, that recognised the truth of her wisdom nonetheless.

'I dare say you're right,' she said. 'I've read endlessly about how you millennials are all about quality in life, not quantity. Experiences, not possessions. Avocados, not mortgages. It's probably because you can't afford anything.'

Eliza scowled.

'I've had a nice time, in any case,' Ada said. 'I was very lucky in my marriage. And some of my poems have meant something to some people. That's something.'

They scraped out their bowls, as a soft breeze tousled the growing cherry leaves above.

Most days, Eliza arrived at the house at nine, unless she had something to do in town. While Ada made the porridge, Eliza prepared a cafetière of strong coffee to take out with them, with some milk she picked up from the doorstep and heated in the microwave. She didn't know it, but the cafetière hadn't been used since Michael died. The first time Eliza pulled it out of the cupboard and set it on a counter, mission in mind, Ada saw the little glass jug and felt stricken, clobbered. She had to sit down. For a moment she could see Michael galumphing around the kitchen in his ludicrous Irish socks, singing thunderously and scattering coffee everywhere as he made breakfast to take upstairs to her. Then she returned to the present, and it was Eliza who was busy pouring water into the kettle;

she hadn't noticed Ada having to take a seat or the grief that had slipped between her ribs. Ada was glad.

Outside, they read the newspaper that Ada had sent to the house every day. Eliza had never had a paper delivered before and it felt alien and luxurious to read the news in such a considered, elective way. Normally she just went onto the BBC or the *Guardian* website as soon as she woke up, swiped and tapped until she felt orientated in the world. They developed an unspoken system: Eliza went for the culture reviews first, while Ada studied the news and the columns, tutting or nodding or rolling her eyes, then they swapped sections and bullied one another into reading the business and foreign pages. Sometimes they read aloud sentences that were funny, or book reviews that were particularly catty.

Occasionally they spoke of Michael. Ada was surprised to discover that she liked talking about him. The fact that Eliza hadn't known him was liberating: Ada could describe the man he had been to her. With old friends of theirs, she always had to hold up what she remembered of him against their memories, which seemed to vie for primacy.

One morning Ada persuaded Eliza to show her around her house on the other side of the street. The renovation works had been going on for so long now that Ada wanted to see what the builders were up to.

'Honestly, there's nothing to see,' Eliza said, over and over. 'It's grim, you won't like it.'

'I'm a nosy old woman,' Ada retorted.

'There's no point,' Eliza replied. 'Anyway, any day now I'll have to move, the developer told me he wants to do up my room soon.'

'Let me snoop!' Ada insisted, trying not to think about Eliza moving out.

Her face drained the moment she stepped inside the building. She began coughing daintily, clamping the silk scarf she was wearing to her mouth. Eliza watched her, trying not to laugh: her distaste was palpable. Ada didn't say much that was overtly critical but she couldn't keep from arching her eyebrows at every heap of plaster or rotting floorboard. She noticed things that Eliza had endured for a long time and didn't even see anymore: the damp, the cold, the maddening tap-tap of dripping water, the nails sticking out of walls like torture hooks.

Ada was mollified when Eliza showed her where she slept: the room was basic, certainly, but just about liveable. Then Eliza announced the grand tour was done and Ada's face darkened.

'But you don't have a kitchen!' she cried. The Rubicon had been crossed.

'I eat perfectly adequately using my toaster and mini-fridge,' Eliza said primly.

'It's the size of a shoebox!'

'You do know that the stomach itself is only as big as a make-up bag?'

'Oh do be sensible.'

Ada took thereafter to inviting Eliza round for dinner every night as well. It amused Eliza to learn that thanks to her neighbour's friendship with the local shopkeepers, she was dining as if she'd been raised in the Middle East, except that everything was a little off-centre. They had roast chicken smeared with date paste, pita bread stuffed with harissa and Cheddar, samosas dipped in oyster sauce.

It wasn't disgusting per se but it wasn't altogether nice either, and one evening Eliza asked tremulously if she might be charged with the cooking from now on, to which Ada consented eagerly.

'As you may have noticed,' she said, 'there are hundreds of cookbooks in the house.'

Eliza nodded. An entire wall in the kitchen was devoted to bookshelves. 'Are they yours?' she asked.

'Michael's,' Ada replied. 'He used to say he was going to become a great cook in his retirement. He spent an awful amount of money buying the recipe books. I doubt many have even been opened.'

'I'd love to use them,' Eliza said. 'Would that bother you?'

'No, darling, no,' Ada said. She patted Eliza's hand. 'It would be lovely. Frankly I'm sick of cooking, I've done it for fifty years.'

For the first time in Eliza's life she began to take an interest in food. It was a pleasure to potter about after a day of studying with the back doors open and the World Service on half-volume, the garden breeze meandering through the kitchen as if it were a forest clearing. There were so many spices, so many pots and whisks and pepper grinders, that it was a joy to peruse the recipes, knowing she had all the tools they could possibly demand, and that if not, there were enough things around to improvise. It was vastly different to cooking in Carlisle, where Eliza's goal was always to get the food on the table quickly, producing as little mess as possible as they didn't have a dishwasher. Eliza never had to worry about the cost of the ingredients either because Ada bought everything, intuiting that Eliza was broke and couldn't have afforded to get all the things she wanted to.

Mostly, they ate in front of the small television in the sitting room. Eliza managed to rig the screen up to her computer and when there was nothing on they watched pirated box sets that Eliza could find in about a minute of internet browsing. Ada liked watching her do it: she was amazed by how resourceful Eliza was, the tricks she knew to get the content she wanted. They started off with *Spaced*, Eliza's favourite comedy, then they moved on to *Green Wing*. There was so much intimacy and innuendo in these programmes that initially both Eliza and Ada felt uncomfortable, hyper-aware of the age gap ballooning between them and unsure whether to acknowledge in their body language that they were even aware that sex existed. But soon enough they learned to make jokes to smooth it over, or watch the rutting as if nothing of interest were happening in front of them.

'I don't know why these shows all feel the need to use words like "twat" and "fuck" so incessantly,' Ada mused one evening.

Eliza grinned.

'No really,' Ada said, looking at her severely. 'There's no need. Do you find swearing funny?'

Eliza considered. 'Sometimes, I really do,' she said.

Ada rolled her eyes. 'Barmy,' she said in an undertone. Their eyes met. They began to laugh.

A few evenings later, as April was tipping into May, Ada made Eliza watch *Airplane!*, outraged she'd not seen it before. Eliza was reluctant because the film looked sort of dumb from the picture on the DVD case, but within ten minutes she was giggling so much her stomach hurt and she worried she might burst her intestine or something. Ada laughed too, mostly at Eliza's loss of control, and a little shyly after the film ended she went up to Michael's study to fetch his guitar. She knew how to play the song sung by the nun on the plane to the sick child in the film. Eliza was amazed and stretched out on the sofa at once, pretending to be the boy whose life support machine kept being flicked off, while Ada sang loudly and badly to an invisible audience of passengers.

Eventually, grinning and happy, Eliza declared that she should go back home. Ada put the guitar away, sad that Eliza had to leave; it was getting harder every night to say goodbye to her. They walked to the front door together.

'Have you heard from that wretched developer?' Ada asked.

'No,' Eliza sighed.

'What a horrid man, to keep you hanging in the balance.'

Eliza nodded. The evening was cooler than it had been in weeks, the half-moon blue-white in the clear charcoal sky. Back in her bedroom on the other side of the street, Eliza watched the golden living room lights on the ground floor of the house opposite turn off, lamp by lamp, then the upstairs rooms light up as Ada prepared to go to bed. There was comfort in knowing that she was right there, that Eliza would see her again for breakfast in a few hours, that neither of them would face the following day alone.

Chapter Twenty-Two

A week later, as Ada and Eliza sat with a lamb and apricot tagine Eliza had made for them on trays on their laps – they were watching *Come Dine with Me* – Ada posed the question she'd been burning to ask for days now.

'And are you a lesbian?'

Eliza spluttered and began to snigger.

'Well, you've not mentioned a man,' Ada said briskly.

Eliza explained that she was actually bisexual.

Ada sat up straight. She laid her spoon next to her plate and turned the television down, greatly interested.

'Isn't that terribly exhausting?' she asked. 'Doesn't it mean you take a shine to – well, everyone?'

'No!' Eliza yelped. She clarified. Ada listened, captivated.

'And are you a trans as well?' she asked.

'Nope,' Eliza said.

'I thought you might be because I so seldom see you in dresses. And your hair, of course.'

'It's true that I wear quite androgynous clothing and have short pink hair.'

'But that's just because it's fashionable?'

'Yes, sort of. I don't feel like myself if I look too "girly".'

'I know the feeling. But you're not, um, burning to become a chap?'

Eliza smiled. 'No. I mean, everything's on a spectrum, but broadly I identify as a woman, and I'm happy being one for the foreseeable future.'

Ada considered. 'D'you think I'm on a spectrum too?' she asked.

'Well, yes, personally.'

'News to me. I just thought I was a woman who was attracted to men and that was pretty much it.'

Eliza laughed. 'Fair enough. Maybe you're at one end of the spectrum.'

'Some spectrum.'

'Have you really never felt a thing for a woman? Even when you were younger?'

Ada blushed. Eliza watched her placidly. Ada tried to pull herself together. 'I had snogs with girls when I was a teenager,' she said. 'But those were just for practice, you know, to make sure I was good enough when the boys wanted a go.'

'That's so tragic!'

Ada blinked. 'Why?' she asked.

'I don't like the idea of you thinking you needed to reach a certain level of kissing competency before you released yourself on men.'

Ada rolled her eyes. 'Darling, by the time I kissed a boy I was frightfully glad I'd already had a warm-up with my girlfriends. Can you imagine? I would have slobbered all over the poor child, he would have been traumatised.'

'But all those times you were kissing your female friends, you didn't feel a thing?'

'I'm afraid not,' Ada said. She looked at Eliza search-ingly, wondering if she'd caused offence. 'Do you mind me asking you these personal things? Are you, um, "triggered"?'

'No!' Eliza cried.

'I feel like one can't ask anything these days. Especially of the young, you're all so anxious. One can get accused of bigotry in three seconds flat.'

'I don't think you're a bigot.'

'Nor do I.'

'You're the pioneering female founder of Oxford's hottest start-up.'

'Well quite.'

They returned to *Come Dine with Me*. The dinner party was a fiasco: the cocktails were too weak and the pie was burnt. In an advert break Eliza went to the kitchen to bring dessert through. Ada turned off the television.

'And do you have a boyfriend or girlfriend at the moment?' she asked as they tucked in.

'No,' said Eliza flatly. She wasn't sure why, but she added that she'd heard from her last girlfriend recently and that it had rather thrown her off-kilter.

It had been weeks since she'd received the Facebook message from Ruby. Eliza must have composed a dozen replies; she'd even started a depressing document with all her possible answers on it so that when she found the wherewithal to actually deal with the message, she'd have a selection of carefully crafted ripostes to choose from. Then all her work had come undone a few days ago, when she was rereading the message in the library and she tapped her phone screen by accident, sending a big blue thumbs-up through to Ruby. That was it; it couldn't be deleted or undone. All was lost. One second later, a little icon on the app showed that Ruby had seen the thumbs-up. Three dots started to shimmy on Eliza's phone, indicating Ruby was composing a reply. Eliza thought she might be having a heart attack. She put her phone under the cushion she was sitting on and didn't look at it for an hour, doubling up every ten minutes or so with embarrassment.

When she looked at her phone again, mortified still, she saw that Ruby hadn't written anything. She must have typed out a reply then deleted it. They were both playing games. Eliza quickly tapped out, 'Sorry haha didn't mean to send you that thumbs-up, but nice to hear from you, I'll reply soon,' and pressed send. She didn't know whether to add an x at the end and very nearly tapped the blue thumbs-up button again, which may actually have killed her. She found an emoji of a surfer and threw that in instead, hoping Ruby would be wrong-footed by its inclusion and think it louche and enigmatic.

Eliza didn't explain all that to Ada, but she did begin to talk about the relationship itself – how it had started, what sort of person Ruby was, what sort of person Eliza had been and become when they were together. With anyone else the conversation would have been uncomfortable: other people seemed to get over their exes in a matter of weeks and she felt a degree of shame if she brought up Ruby with them now, like she was harping on about some prehistoric slight.

Ada didn't crowd her with suggestions or verdicts. There were no winking urges to 'get back on the market', no baying even for Ruby's blood. She listened calmly, even when Eliza told her about how controlling Ruby had become when they lived together, how she'd demanded to know at the end of each day who Eliza had spoken to, even if it was just to Rich. Ada didn't seem to pity or revile Eliza for the fact that she was still feeling the aftershocks of a break-up that was well over a year ago and which had also, confusingly, generated a gorgeous, almost orgasmic, sense of freedom. She didn't find it odd that Eliza was both glad to be rid of Ruby and ravenous for her attention even now. Something in Ada's way of responding made Eliza trust that she knew these things were complicated; that she'd learned over the decades that people could be ruthless to one another and lovely in the same afternoon; that you could pluck what you thought was the plumpest blackberry on the bush, and still find yourself chewing a beetle.

'She wasn't very kind to me, but I'm not sure I would have been receptive to kindness,' Eliza said. 'I was younger than my age. I was overwhelmed by university. I hadn't spoken to my mother in three years and I was a mess. Ruby zapped me at just the wrong moment.'

'You deserve kindness, my love,' Ada replied. Not with force or sugar, just so. Like it was true.

Eliza got up and began walking around the sitting room, looking at the hanging pictures, the little ornaments and shells.

'I've never loved anyone more,' she said. 'I probably still love her now. It's humiliating. It was as if all the time before we met, I was living in a sort of fug, you know that feeling when you've taken a sleeping pill and you're drowsy the next day. But she made me feel – I don't know, like I was experiencing things sharply for the first time. I'd found the vein or something. Even in her worst moments. I'm not sure I could resist her if she asked for me back, even though I know she's basically shit.'

'Yes, well, first love tends to kick us furthest,' Ada said from her armchair, in her plain, clipped way.

Eliza nodded. She'd heard variations of this idea for so long it felt like a fact as immovable as geology. But she'd learned there was a river running between the two: between knowing your love mutilations would heal, and them actually healing.

'What saddens me,' Ada said, more softly, 'is that this young lady's way of loving you doesn't strike me as loving at all.'

'Yeah,' Eliza said. She knew Ada was right. She wished her knowledge could translate into some emotional change within her, some renunciation.

The following morning, a Sunday, Eliza arrived at the front door to announce that they were going on an expedition to the centre of town. It was straightforward weather, neither hot nor cold, the sky a scramble of blue and white.

'We've not even had breakfast yet,' Ada said, alarmed.

She seldom went to town these days; if she had a Rent-a-Gran appointment she avoided going through the centre: all those tourists and chain restaurants and bicycles.

'We'll have food there,' Eliza said. 'Come on.'

Ada felt harassed. Really she needed a good two hours before she left the house. Then she told herself to buck up. Maybe she and Eliza needed to go somewhere new together; it might be prudent to check whether their friendship existed outside of Swinburne Road, whether in a new environment all the ease in their rapport would seize up. Ada went upstairs, pulled on a pair of grey flannel trousers and a stripy T-shirt, and hurried back down. Eliza was waiting by the door.

As they were preparing to leave, the landline rang. Eliza scowled. Ada rolled her eyes at her impatience and went into the living room to take the call. It was probably Eve, she thought; they'd not spoken in a few weeks.

It wasn't Eve. It was James, her agent.

'Ada!' he boomed.

Ada mouthed who it was at Eliza and motioned that she'd be one minute.

'I'm on my way out, James, is it urgent?'

'It is!' he cried. He sounded twenty years younger. He suddenly laughed joyfully. Ada was so taken by surprise that she held the phone receiver away from her ear, staring at it. James wasn't the laughing type.

'Well, what's the matter?' she asked, when she judged he'd probably stopped.

'We have a deal!'

'What for?'

'For your next collection. And they want three new books from you, not just the one!'

Ada sat down. When she heard which publisher it was, she put her hand to her mouth, and when she heard how much they were offering, she actually gasped. She'd known James had been getting lots of interest from publishers but there turned out to have been something of a scrum between four of them. Eliza was in the sitting room too, listening to everything James was saying: Ada had beckoned her over to press her ear to the phone, she wanted Eliza to hear it all.

'So the upshot of it is, we need some bloody champagne,' James concluded. Ada wasn't sure she could speak.

'Right,' she croaked.

They talked a little more about next steps, then put the phone down. Ada looked shocked still.

'I just didn't think my poems would find readers again,' she said.

Eliza gave her a hug. Ada noticed she smelled faintly of lemons. It was a light, curling fragrance that made her feel calmer. Her eyes fell on the copper-wire owl next to her armchair. It was strange to realise that just this minute, with Eliza holding her hands and brimming with pride, there was no one else she'd rather be sharing the room with.

They stopped by Sylvie's for breakfast. Kate was at the till and exclaimed when she saw them together. 'I thought you said you didn't have children!' she said to Ada.

Ada and Eliza grinned, feeling their chests fan with pleasure.

'Don't insult me,' Ada said. 'She's far too old to be a daughter of mine.'

They all laughed, that satisfied British chuckle at a joke that wasn't very funny but which filled a gap nicely enough. After granola and a pot of Lapsang Souchong, Ada and Eliza set off again. Ada presumed that Eliza must have a plan, an idea about where they were heading to. 'Oh no, I don't,' Eliza said when this became clear. 'I thought we should just – you know, venture off.'

Ada rolled her eyes. Really, it was so typical of the younger generation, she thought, to baldly launch an assault without any real strategising.

'I'll take it from here,' she said.

Eliza tried not to smirk at Ada's huffy tone. They walked up Iffley Road for twenty minutes and over the broad

stone bridge into the centre of town. Eliza was conscious
of having to pace a little slower so as not to lope ahead;
Ada meanwhile forced herself to keep up a quick march,
she didn't want to be an albatross around the younger
woman's neck. As they passed the Botanic Garden, Eliza
commented idly that she'd never been. Ada was shocked.

'We will have to correct that,' she said.

The centre of town was busy, prams and cyclists and
tourists and coaches, everyone crossing in front of one
another and blocking each other's way. Eliza watched
Ada become more and more agitated by the crowds. It
was rare that she felt their age gap keenly, but doing so
now she wanted to whip out a megaphone and demand
that anyone in Ada's path vacate it.

Ada could sense Eliza fretting about her. She narrowed
her eyes and tried to envisage the crammed city centre
as some form of obstacle course to be negotiated with
elegance and speed. They reached the University Church
of St Mary the Virgin with no major incidents. Eliza had
walked past it many times but never thought to go in, as
with most of the famous buildings in Oxford.

'The church has been here for a thousand years,' Ada
said. 'And we're going to climb the tower.'

'Ooh,' Eliza replied, grinning. 'I do love a tower.'

'Good. Michael and I went up it a week or so after
we moved in. I remember it having cracking views of the
Radcliffe Camera. Will this do as an outing?'

'Very much so, thanks Ade.'

There wasn't anyone around. Immediately as they walked
inside the church they met the cloistral scent of books and
ancient stone. The heavy door was unlocked but when they

got to the bottom of the staircase leading up to the tower, they saw that the attraction was closed until 11.45. It wasn't yet ten. Ada was terribly disappointed, and annoyed with herself too: she usually thought to·check such things, she hadn't been meticulous before they left the house.

There was a warden who seemed to be in charge of selling tickets to the tower. He was sitting at a desk a few metres from the tower entrance, watching them. 'Perhaps you could get a coffee while you wait for 11.45 to come round?' he suggested.

Ada and Eliza nodded doubtfully. The warden got up from his desk and walked away. Ada looked at Eliza despondently.

'We've already had bloody breakfast,' she said.

'Don't be defeatist,' Eliza replied. 'We'll just go up the tower anyway.'

Ada looked round, scandalised and nodding fervently. The warden was nowhere to be seen. They stepped over the red velvet rope cordoning off the tower and set off up the staircase as quietly as they could. Ada was quivery with a sense of her own rebelliousness; she felt as if she'd drunk five espressos on the trot and chased them down with a couple of cigarettes.

The steps were shiny with age. The soft pat of their shoes on the grey stone sounded ancient, like they could have been in any century over the past two millennia. Eliza didn't find the climb tiring but did get a little dizzy; Ada had to pause every so often to press a palm against the stone and calm her heartbeat. The air in the staircase was cool and smelled of caves. The two women spoke only in the quietest of whispers as they knew anything louder would spiral down to the warden, who may have returned to his desk.

At the top of the tower they burst out onto a stunning view, the city a tawny etching of itself. It was a windy day now and the clouds were stripping themselves into dove-grey lines. Oxford looked perfect, the cylindrical Camera below so handsome it almost hurt to look at it. The chilly air pushed itself into their lungs. They felt exhilarated and young. Eliza threw open her arms like Rose on the bow of the *Titanic*; Ada got the reference at once and laughed. She walked around the top of the tower, measuring the view, identifying buildings she recognised, feeling happier than she had in months, if not years. Her book deal. Her city. Her friend, just there. Eliza took a photo of Ada on her phone then insisted they take a selfie – Ada's first ever. She was appalled by the picture – 'I look like an ostrich' – but she failed to persuade Eliza to delete it. They walked back down the tower, elated and chatting freely now they'd got what they'd come for. At the bottom, the warden was waiting for them like a disappointed headmaster.

He was a large man, with black eyebrows and a head of white hair pulled into a ratty ponytail. 'I did rather think,' he said testily, 'that I told you two the tower wasn't open yet.'

Ada was jangly with adrenaline. A plan sauntered into her head and she decided on a whim to deploy it.

She made herself look up vacantly at the ceiling, then at her shoes. She let her jaw hang loose and her eyes bulge. As Eliza and the warden watched her, mystified, she squatted on the floor for a moment then got up and went over to the man's desk. She stroked the wood tenderly and laid a cheek on his mousepad. Then she picked up a postcard from the rack by the desk and made to slip it under her top. Eliza, understanding what was going on, went over and pulled the postcard out of her hand gently.

'She gets confused,' Eliza told the warden piously. 'When you left, she started making a fuss about us not going up the tower. I'm sorry but I just had to take her up there.'

The warden looked annoyed still, but alarmed by Ada's peculiar behaviour.

'It wasn't safe,' he muttered. 'Not safe at all.'

Eliza offered to pay for their visit but the man shook his head, his eyes glued on Ada, who was now sticking all her fingers in her mouth one by one.

They left the church. As they closed the heavy doors behind them they heard an organ strike up, arpeggios sounding deep within.

'That was very bad of you,' Eliza said.

'Your fault we went up the tower,' Ada replied.

Her whole body was zinging with the sense that she'd done wrong, she'd lied, she'd misled a stranger, she'd trespassed, she'd enjoyed it all. Something in her expression made Eliza laugh. Ada joined in, first softly then riotously, and suddenly the bells started to ring, the city's churches calling to one another, all around them calling and inside them too, it seemed, and they found some steps to sit on by the Camera and they listened.

Chapter Twenty-Three

Returning to Swinburne Road after their visit to the tower, Eliza and Ada had their first argument.

Ada insisted they should visit the Botanic Garden, given Eliza had never been. Eliza wasn't keen: she knew the plants would remind her of Rich, and she wanted her good mood to persist. But Ada seemed so keen to go in that she agreed, saying nothing of her reservations: she'd not spoken to Ada much about her family situation, she wasn't sure she was ready for that yet, and Ada, detecting some sensitivity there, hadn't persisted in asking questions.

By the time they got their tickets it was early lunchtime and quite fraught, lots of young families and couples crowding out the greenery. As Ada and Eliza left the Walled Garden and headed towards some greenhouses, Ada mentioned that she'd been having a recurring dream. It was so disturbing she was having trouble falling asleep, for fear of slipping into it again.

'What's the dream?' Eliza asked, concerned.

She'd never known Ada to have trouble sleeping; they were different in that way, normally Ada was the one to console Eliza when she'd had a bad night.

'It's actually a Rent-a-Gran visit I did weeks ago,' Ada said. 'The session I did the afternoon before I met you. It was in Rose Hill. I was babysitting for a woman called Cathy.' She recounted discovering that the children she was looking after were covered in bruises, even the youngest one, who was barely out of babyhood. She must still be shaken up about it because she kept dreaming of them all, their milky skin blotched and mottled, particularly Hara, who in these nightmares would begin rolling up his sleeves to show Ada his bruises, only he'd find for some reason that he couldn't, he couldn't show her a thing, the sleeve got stuck or his fingers were too weak to roll the material.

'What did the police say?' Eliza asked.

'About what?' Ada said.

'About the kids being bruised.'

Ada looked at her blankly. They were in the Cloud Forest Glasshouse, the greenish air warm and damp and dense. Ada felt something drip onto her hand and looked up: there was a giant fern hung over her head that was weeping water.

She replied that she hadn't gone to the police. She hadn't done anything or told anyone about what she'd noticed on the children's bodies. She didn't want to interfere, she didn't know what she'd tell the police anyway; it wasn't her business.

Eliza looked at her aghast.

'They're being fucking abused,' she said. 'Of course you should have gone to the police. You should still go to the police.'

'I'm not a social worker, Eliza,' Ada retorted. 'It's not my role to— to— to butt in and—'

'Help?' Eliza demanded. 'To stop kids from being battered?'

She tried to contain her fury. She couldn't actually believe that Ada had just walked away from the house, left those children with their mother without lifting a finger for them.

'Jesus, Ada, you read the news, this kind of thing happens all the time – kids start being beaten up by their parents and end up being actually killed by them, and people can't be bothered to act on their suspicions! I cannot believe you didn't report it, you're meant to be an adult!'

Ada felt flustered and defensive. She'd thought about going to the police but picturing the trip had blocked her impulse to go ahead with it – what would she do, sweep into the local station and say she'd seen some bruises in Rose Hill and that the authorities should probably know about it? The idea seemed absurd. She tried articulating that to Eliza, who just got angrier, until they were both almost shouting at one another as the fern above drenched their clothes, flattening their hair to their foreheads.

Soon there seemed nothing else to add. Eliza said that she needed to go to the library. She was livid and upset, but also ashamed that she was being so nakedly critical of a woman who'd been so kind to her, who was on the cusp of elderliness. It felt slightly criminal, like knocking a walking stick out from an old man crossing a road.

Ada, meanwhile, felt attacked. And misunderstood. But she saw she was probably in the wrong and saw too that Eliza was trying not to be angry and wanted to be alone, so she told her in a cheery voice to have a good time at the library. 'Work hard – but not too hard.' She added lightly that she hoped to see her for dinner later. Eliza didn't say anything in reply. Her mouth was a mauve line, she was pale. She swung her backpack on and turned around.

As Eliza left the glasshouse, Ada stood rooted to the spot, watching the young woman leave. Humiliation pulsed through her like sour blood; the feeling that she'd behaved poorly tussling with a truculence and a defiance she couldn't suppress either. On the way home she stopped in her tracks and doubled back. She would visit the police station, as Eliza wanted.

Eliza didn't turn up that evening for dinner. Ada ate alone, feeling awful. Sometimes she opened the sitting room curtain a little to see if Eliza had returned yet: she hadn't. Just as Ada was about to go to bed she noticed a light turn on in the house opposite. Ada went to sleep feeling a little better after that, resigned to the fact that she'd have to go over and talk to Eliza tomorrow.

But the next day Eliza arrived at the usual time to have breakfast. Her mouth was tight, like she'd been worrying about coming over for a long time before she gathered the strength to. The moment Eliza was inside the house Ada told her what she'd done after their argument in the Botanic Garden: gone to the police and explained what she'd seen.

'What did they say?' Eliza asked, relieved.

They walked into the kitchen. 'Not much,' Ada said. 'I had the impression they knew about the family who lives there already. Maybe the social services are involved. Anyway, it's done now.'

Eliza nodded and sat in Michael's old chair. 'I'm sorry I was cross,' she said.

'No, no,' Ada said. 'You were right. It was silly of me not to report what I saw. I should have gone to the police the moment I left.'

'Well, yes, I think so, but it wasn't very nice of me to just pile on top of you.'

'I deserved it.'

They looked at one another for a moment. 'Do you still think I'm a dreadful person for not having tried to help those kids right away?' Ada asked, her voice small.

'Of course not,' Eliza replied at once.

She took Ada's hands instinctively and squeezed them. Ada smiled tremulously.

'Right,' Eliza said. 'Let's make this porridge then.'

Ada nodded, more business-like. 'Yup,' she said. 'You toast the oats. I'll handle the nuts.'

That afternoon, Eliza settled in the sitting room to continue reading *The Truce*, the novel Levi had written about returning to Italy after his internment in Poland. His characters seemed more real to Eliza now than people she actually knew, and certainly more likely to be her family members than Rich and Flora, to whom she'd not spoken since she went to Carlisle.

Rich was telephoning her daily; she wasn't picking up. Flora was sending her emails as often; in fact Eliza had to fight not to be stirred by the messages, which were full of apologies and affection. It was disconcerting: Flora really did seem to have been softened by pregnancy and was telling Eliza things about herself that neither of them had ever thought to discuss. She didn't seem to be deterred by Eliza's radio silence, and kept writing to her anyway. Eliza couldn't sort her feelings out and didn't see why she should try to, until it looked like both her parents were getting seriously worried and were about to contact the university to check up on her, so she sent Rich a line or two saying she was fine, that she was getting on with her work. She was no longer angry with her parents – that had been wrung out over the last few weeks – but what had taken anger's place was something less honourable: envy. Rich and Flora were beginning a new family in Cumbria without her. Their domestic fairy tale was beginning, if belatedly. Her miserly prophecies that it would go catastrophically could prove untrue: it might go well; they might at long last be happy and Eliza would be excluded from it all, a living reminder of past mistakes.

She began to speak to Ada about it a little. Usually the subject came up when they were in the garden – it was early May and Eliza had suggested that they plant some beetroot in an old ceramic flowerbed at the end of the garden; once they'd spruced it up they had seen there was room inside for plenty more vegetables. They drove out to a garden centre and spent an hour buying seeds and plants. Eliza couldn't help but think of her father as she worked the soil – the sight alone of her blackened fingernails reminded her of him, of his empathy when she'd come back from Bath post-Ruby, dragging her melancholy like a boulder. Rich had done all he could to lighten the load of her own company.

Ada listened more than she advised. She observed and

compiled information. She thought. When Eliza begged her to voice her opinions – should she go up and see Flora again, for instance – Ada advocated the path that looked the most generous, the most likely to lead to all the slushy things: trust, compassion, tranquil afternoons in good company. Eliza listened to her advice but knew she couldn't bring herself to go back up north yet. The injury was still too fresh.

Just before lunch one Wednesday, as Eliza was nearing the end of *The Truce*, she decided she needed some fresh air.

'We're sowing snap peas,' she told Ada, who was repotting a basil plant in the kitchen.

'Righto,' Ada smiled.

The work made Eliza miss Rich more than she could say. Ada seemed to sense she was thinking of him.

'I so regret that I didn't spend more time with my parents,' Ada told her as they took the little seeds one by one and pressed them into the earth, each one an inch deep. 'You take your eye off them and parents weaken, and then they go.'

'Did your parents live near here?' Eliza asked.

'Not at all. They were in a village near Exeter. They were happy there and stayed put while Michael and I moved around the country with our work. I didn't really see them more than twice a year until a few months before my father died. Then I went to live with them with my sister Eve, to help out as they were getting so frail. When Dad passed away Mum followed right after, she didn't want to carry on.'

'Were you close to them?'

'I don't really know. I hope they thought so.'

'Do you miss them?'

'Yes. Well. I won't think of them for ten days on the trot, then I'll miss one of them unbearably. That's the way of things.'

'Did they like your husband?'

'Oh, they adored him. Didn't like him at first, mind you, thought he was a bit brash, but they came round. When he died, I expected my grief for Michael to eclipse my grief for them. It didn't happen that way.'

'No?'

'Losing him sort of clarified what I'd lost in losing them. If that makes sense. Suddenly I realised that these three great columns fundamental to my identity and happiness were nowhere at all. All those memories, I was the only store of them suddenly. I felt dreadfully alone. I keep forgetting, you see. I had a much keener sense once Michael was gone of how much I'd loved all three of them, how wonderful they'd been.'

Eliza was moved. She clapped her hands together softly to shake the earth off, and picked up her phone to WhatsApp her father.

'Missing you,' she typed. It was true. 'Hope Flora doing well,' she added. She scanned herself anxiously to check if that was true too; whether she was being genuine or just saying what she ought to. Yes, she realised, she really did hope her mother was alright.

Before she had the time to consider adding more, Rich replied.

'Thanksssssss!!!!!' he wrote jubilantly. 'Miss u2!!'

It was their first exchange in weeks. Eliza smiled and chucked her phone onto the lawn behind her. The sun had been warming the grass all morning. She returned to the flowerbed and sank her fingers into the earth. It was cool and damp. Ada straightened up and announced she was fixing them both a pisco sour. She disappeared into the house. Not long after, Eliza joined her and they drank the cocktails in the sitting room, eating almonds from a bowl on the coffee table, some Mahler playing quietly on Ada's CD player.

Chapter Twenty-Four

About a month before the Brexit referendum Eliza heard from Ruby again. Her message had the same disarmingly chatty tone as the first.

'I'll be in Oxford with friends' for the night of the referendum. Would be great to catch up – just thought I'd tell you I'm planning on being in your ends on the night of doom! Xxx'

It was weird; Eliza had so far reneged on her promise to reply to Ruby's original Facebook message because she'd spoken to Ada about it, who'd advised not engaging further. There was an opportunity here, Ada had pointed out, for Eliza to act in a way that would preserve the fragile happiness she was building up. She should do all she could to protect it. But now Ruby was in touch again. The moment she read the message Eliza wanted to write back, demand to know why Ruby was planning on coming to Oxford. It spooked her out to know she had friends in the city. Who? Why did they like her? Did they know Eliza, were they feeding information back to Ruby about her? But she stopped herself from replying, thinking partly of the slow, ruminative way in which

Ada would digest the news that Eliza had intentionally opened herself up to harm.

Instead she contented herself with reading the message every hour or so, then swiping up to close down the app. Every time she did so she put her phone away with resolution, almost with nostalgia, sure that this would be the last time. She told herself that over time the spirit of the message would deaden, that she would stop caring about it or wanting to read it. None of those things happened. Not replying was difficult.

A few days later the developer Nick who owned the house Eliza was living in turned up with a couple of builders in tow wearing high-vis jackets. The men didn't knock on the front door, they just walked in, and Eliza only became aware there were people in the house when she took off her headphones and heard voices right outside her bedroom. She opened the door holding a fork for a weapon, terrified.

'Oh,' she said.

The men seemed surprised to find Eliza still living there, though as she told them, Nick hadn't responded to any of her calls or texts so she'd not known when to leave.

'Sorry,' Nick said breezily, entering her bedroom and looking around. 'Well we're starting work on this part of the house tomorrow, so you'd better go.'

Eliza looked at him. 'You need me out of here by tomorrow?' she said.

'Yeah, if that's OK. In the morning if poss. Got to start the electrics.'

The two builders came into the bedroom too. They had the grace to look slightly uncomfortable at its obvious state of inhabitation. But Nick took in Eliza's boxes of belongings, the bare desk, the mini-fridge unplugged and ready to go by the door. 'I see you've packed already,' he pointed out. 'How's this, I'll give you your rent back for the month to sweeten your departure.' He got out his wallet and gave Eliza a wad of cash.

'Thanks,' Eliza heard herself say robotically, taking the money.

The men started talking logistics. One of the builders got onto Eliza's bed to measure something on the ceiling; he was wearing big camel boots and left dusty white footprints on the tarpaulin. Meanwhile the other builder tapped at the bedroom wall to see if it was load-bearing, as Nick inspected the mould florets by the door. Eliza watched all these things from the corner. She would never have expected to feel proprietorial about her crappy little bedroom, with its dirt and dust and scummy windows, but she suddenly did. She chewed her fingers raw until the builders had done their assessments and left, then she pulled back the tarpaulin cover and got into the bedsheets, trying to decide what to do.

At lunchtime, with no firm resolutions made, she went over to Ada's. They hadn't had breakfast together, as Ada had risen first thing to edit some poems she was hoping would form the backbone of her next collection.

'I'm being evicted,' Eliza said in a rush, the moment Ada opened the door.

She actually laughed at the phrase, it sounded so absurd coming from her mouth. Ada stared over Eliza's shoulder at the house behind, with the manner of one looking for billowing flames.

'Bastards!' she breathed.

'Yup,' Eliza said. Her elation at the novelty of the situation drained away, leaving something duller, like dread.

'Oh, my darling,' Ada murmured, hugging her. 'Come in and we'll see what can be done.'

They went to the kitchen. Eliza could smell baking bread. Ada's poems were spread all over the table, some annotated, a few crossed out. Ada pulled a loaf of soda bread out of the oven and began to clear up for lunch. Eliza found some chicken soup she'd made a few days ago and heated it in a pan.

'Did your editing go well?' Eliza asked.

'Quite, quite.'

'I'm looking forward to reading the poems.'

'So am I.'

Was it a joke? Eliza didn't think so. Ada's mind was obviously elsewhere: she looked nervy, Eliza thought, she kept looking at Eliza penetratingly then glancing away or poofing her hair airily.

Eliza poured the soup into their bowls and they sat down.

'I imagine you won't want to,' Ada began. She stopped and tried again. 'I imagine the very notion will fill you with repulsion and make you want to run screaming for the hills . . .'

Eliza smiled. It was unlike Ada to be bashful. 'Go on,' she said.

'But, well dear, why not move in with me?'

There was a silence as Eliza processed the offer.

Ada felt too self-conscious to look directly into Eliza's eyes; she was certain the young woman would reject her, find her suggestion abhorrent, so she slurped her soup noisily and looked out at the garden. There was a ladybird clicking against the glass pane of the door.

'Move in here?' Eliza said.

'Yes,' Ada replied, still riveted by the garden.

Eliza realised Ada was being serious: she wanted them to live together. A cramped sort of joy began to flower within her, like when you heard the opening of a song you loved but had forgotten existed.

'God, Ada, that would be great!' she said.

Ada looked at her sharply. 'Really?'

'Yes. Definitely.' Eliza frowned. 'But you're not just offering out of guilt?'

'No! I have no reason to feel guilt. I know your generation believes mine owes you one, but I'm not dogged by such a concern.'

'You know you don't have to offer?'

'I'm aware, thank you.'

'You already buy nearly all my food, there's no need to do this too.'

'You do the cooking. Me buying the groceries is only fair,' Ada said. She paused, resting her spoon for a moment. 'I'd love you to come live here,' she said softly. 'I imagine we'd rub along well.'

Eliza grinned. 'I mean I basically live here already.'

'I'd noticed.'

'Living with people is a nightmare, you might start to hate me.'

Ada laughed. 'How odd at my age to be considering taking on a housemate,' she sang.

'Have you had one before? Other than Michael?'

226

'Oh, yes. At university, obviously, then Michael and I used to have lodgers when we first bought decades ago, to help pay the mortgage. There were some real oddballs.'

Eliza still felt hesitant; she wanted to move in but didn't want Ada to feel pressured into doing something she didn't want to.

'Let's give it a trial run,' she suggested. 'Reassess in a couple of weeks. If you feel crowded by me or whatever, that's fine, I'll be able to find another place.'

Ada couldn't imagine it not going well but she agreed to a trial run anyway, sensing it would make Eliza feel more at ease.

'And I'll pay rent,' Eliza added.

'Oh goodness, not a chance,' Ada said.

They argued about it, Ada's eyes progressively narrowing until she looked like a hawk. Eliza saw she wasn't going to win. She gave in, pledging to take charge of the cleaning, the shopping and the cooking in exchange.

'You can have the guest bedroom,' Ada said. 'It'll need a tidy-up as it's full of stuff but I think it'll work.'

'I don't have many things,' Eliza said. 'The guest room sounds perfect. Thank you.'

They looked at one another for a moment, feeling beloved. Then Ada pulled a hunk of fragrant bread loose and began to butter it lasciviously. Eliza stirred her soup, prospecting for chunks of chicken. They said nothing much more until one of them remembered they'd watched the same television programme last night, and they slid into an easy conversation about that, and about whether they should watch the next episode.

*

Eliza moved into Ada's house that very afternoon. She didn't have much choice: Nick texted to say that the builders needed her out of her room by eight the following day. She'd been planning on seeing Judy for a coffee, who offered instead to come round and help move her belongings across the street.

It was odd packing everything up and transporting it to so nearby a destination. Ada had been told firmly that she wasn't allowed to do any heavy lifting and so, somewhat relieved, she retreated to the study to catch up on Rent-a-Gran emails. She was still hiring herself out to people in the area but had cut back significantly on the number of sessions she was doing: now she went out once a week or so, only if she felt she was really needed.

Eventually Ada came downstairs to see how the move was coming along. Judy and Eliza had done the laborious bits now and were having a cigarette in the garden. The clouds thinned as they sat chatting, until they could see a wash of blue beneath the grey. Ada found them one of Michael's old ashtrays and made them all a pot of Lapsang tea; she was thrilled to meet one of Eliza's friends. Judy in turn was star-struck, for news that a rentable grandmother was plying her trade in Oxford had whipped around town the moment Ada had advertised the business months ago. Few people had actually seen the entrepreneur in question, but here she was in the flesh, and happy to be quizzed about her work.

Things with Judy were going well. She and Sam were going to spend the summer in Jamaica. She had decided

English Literature wasn't for her; she was dropping out to start law school in London in the autumn. She seemed to approve of Eliza's decision to live with her neighbour, and if she found the age gap bizarre she didn't say so. She laughed when Ada told her that Eliza had frogmarched her a few days ago to the opticians to get her eyes tested – Ada hadn't been since she was twenty-one, and it turned out she needed glasses urgently. Eliza and Judy had a good afternoon together, both reflecting in the pauses between speech that they'd miss one another next year. It was pleasant to think about; it made Eliza feel she'd not so messed up the start of her DPhil that she had no real friends to show for it. They hung around in the garden all afternoon, the sunlight waxing and waning, Ada meandering onto the lawn every so often to hoik out a weed. Eventually Eliza realised that she'd better start sorting her room out and Judy left, carrying a Tupperware box of flapjacks that Ada made her take home for sustenance.

Eliza's new bedroom wasn't vast but it had a large clean window overlooking the garden. It was, as Ada had warned, full of belongings, and a significant number of moths that fluttered out at unexpected moments. Eliza didn't mind. She enjoyed cleaning, and the room slowly became habitable. She put on some music as she tidied and hoovered, glad that Ada was on hand to tell her where the things that had filled the space should be stored now. Midway through Eliza's clear-out she went down to the kitchen to make Ada and her some dinner.

'Are you sure the room's alright?' Ada asked. They were eating a spinach and filo tart.

'It's perfect,' Eliza said.

'Watch out for the moths. They've been in there so long they're probably flesh-eating.'

'I'll keep a close eye.'

They watched the news then peeled off to bed. Eliza didn't have a curtain yet but she didn't care: if she turned off her lamp she could see the moon from her bed and the massed blue-black of the neighbours' poplar tree. It took her some time to relax, as her body was zinging with the feeling of being somewhere so new, yet eventually she slept, waking the following morning long after the sun had risen to the sound of Ada downstairs making coffee, and outside, of two birds chirruping and chittering to one another on the roof tiles.

Chapter Twenty-Five

When Ada awoke, she was convinced there were strange men in the house.

She lay in bed for a minute, her body stiff with fear, because from the sound of them they were upstairs, somewhere really quite nearby. She forced herself to get out of bed and hobbled stiffly to the door. The men were in the bathroom.

'Hello?' Ada called. Her voice was thin.

The bathroom door flew open. It was Eliza. She was listening to something on her phone as she washed her face. She smiled and said something along the lines of 'good morning'. There was a chair on the landing that Ada sat on blearily.

'I thought there were men in the house,' she said.

'We wish,' Eliza said, grinning.

Ada laughed weakly.

Over the following days she discovered that Eliza was utterly incapable of doing anything manual or administrative without the accompaniment of a podcast. Ada had heard of podcasts, of course, but she'd never quite grasped what they were; Eliza explained that they were simply radio programmes that one could listen to at the time of one's choosing.

Eliza too began to see patterns in her new housemate's habits: Ada's mania for fresh sponges, her obsession with Tupperware, her creaturely fear of leaving the stove or gas on overnight. Both had to adjust to living with someone else – at first Ada decided she should probably get dressed before she came down in the morning, but then she abandoned the idea, it was so much cosier to loaf about in one's nightdress.

Eliza was soon more settled into her new home than she'd ever been on the other side of the street. Ada's house was spacious for two and it helped that they were both private people, disinclined to make noise or need regular injections of conversation. They adjusted to one another, made small accommodations. Once they had found a rhythm of sorts, they began to draw untold comfort from the knowledge that they were in close proximity to a person they greatly liked; it had a rooting effect, like knowing your fridge was full of good food or your radiators churning out heat.

Finding many of the books she needed in Michael's study, Eliza motored on with her thesis. The conference Baleotti had wanted her to assist with had been and gone but he was setting up an outreach programme to encourage students from supposedly 'unconventional backgrounds' to apply to Oxford. Eliza agreed to help, pledging to develop the part of the programme boosting applications from deprived sixth-formers in the north-west of England. At the beginning of June she went to dinner at Baleotti's house, the first in months. Cosima, his wife, joined them. They spoke Italian as they used to. Over tiramisu on their terrace, Eliza finally worked up the courage to apologise for her flakiness so far that academic year. She'd not dared to yet – apologies so often amounted to a confession of guilt – but she was glad she did: saying sorry made her feel footloose and liberated. In for a penny, she thought, and tried to describe the trouble she'd had clicking into her Levi research, as well as her doubts about the doctorate itself. Baleotti nodded gravely at this.

'Misgivings about the doctorate are a completely natural thing,' he said. 'I dropped out myself, of course.'

Eliza was stunned. She'd assumed Baleotti had always known he would be an academic, he was one of those professors that it was impossible to imagine doing any other job.

'*È vero*, it's true,' Cosima said, smiling at Eliza's surprise. 'We were studying in *Sicilia* at the time, I was finishing up my doctorate, he was starting his. He was struck down by all these sweet existential woes . . .' She mimed clutching her head miserably. Eliza laughed: Italians could be so direct.

'So what did you do after? Why did you drop out?' she asked.

'I became a baker,' Baleotti said, nodding in response to Eliza's surprised expression. 'Which was tough for someone with polio, I'd not repeat it. And then I decided that I would best serve the world by doing what I loved. What I enjoyed. What I was good at. I wouldn't have the stamina to do anything less. That meant going back to the academy.'

'But do you still question what you're doing now?'

'All the time,' Baleotti said. 'How could I not? These films . . . These books, these operas I've been giving you. I'm spectating, not creating. I'm a parasite. I'm not brave, I'm not taking any risks.'

The early summer sky above them was dimming to saffron. *'Non sono un leone,'* Baleotti said to his wife.

Cosima ruffled his hair lovingly. 'You are a lion,' she said.

Eliza smiled at the wryness of her tone. Baleotti added that he often feared he was misusing his time, that his career was self-indulgent, vain, rarefied, a retreat into imaginary worlds. It became obvious to Eliza that he would always have responded to her concerns as compassionately as he was now. She wished they'd spoken about it all earlier. They talked for a long time, dipping their teaspoons into the mulch of their dessert. Eliza had a gift for academia, Baleotti said through a mouthful of cream; she had the right sort of mind. She wasn't doing harm by exploring Levi's literature, quite the opposite; and there was every chance she would start teaching undergrads at the university soon, which would increase her sense of worth. There was good to be done at Oxford, though it didn't always seem that way. Stick it out for a bit, he exhorted, then reassess. His words tangled in Eliza's hair, in her chest, and she found from then on she cared less about the fact that her thesis wasn't likely to change much on a macrocosmic level: so what? She wanted to do meaningful work, she wanted to make some sort of impact over the course of her life and she still wasn't sure the way to do it would be to remain a scholar, but for now a DPhil wasn't harming anyone. For God's sake, it would do.

Two weeks after Eliza moved in, Ada had her first poetry reading in years. James, her agent, set it up to mark the upcoming publication of her new collection. Ada was disconcerted one morning when Eliza showed her the page for the event on Facebook: people had actually clicked in advance to indicate that they were attending, as though it was something worth going to.

The reading was hosted by one of the Oxford colleges. It turned out to be in an uninspiring seminar room that appalled Ada the moment she walked in.

'Talk about dingy,' she stage-whispered to Eliza, when they arrived an hour early to scope out the premises.

'You'll be great,' Eliza told her. 'Anyway,' she added, twinkling, 'a poor workwoman blames her tools.'

Ada scowled. 'I dare say it doesn't matter if the room feels like a bunker,' she mused. 'No one'll turn up apart from you.'

'I'm not coming, I'm just dropping you off. I've got a hot date.'

'Of course you don't.'

'I'm sure plenty of people will come.'

'You'd better clap bloody hard if they don't.'

'I will.'

'You aren't really going on a date, are you?'

'Nope. I'll be here. And if it's just me, good, because I won't be distracted from your poetry by other people's rustlings.'

Ada smiled. She was nervous but looked fantastic. She'd spent the morning reading her work aloud in the garden to the cherry tree, which waved its young leaves at her languidly, unimpressed by the poetry. The last time she had performed in front of an audience felt like decades ago; Michael had been alive, she'd been – to all intents and purposes – a different person with a radically different life. She was frightened that she had lost the trick of it, that she'd get up on the stage and find she couldn't do it anymore, that in the intervening time some poltergeist had stolen from her the ability to read what she'd written, in front of people who wanted to hear it.

Eliza had asked to dress her for the occasion. Ada, too wired to put up much of a resistance, had allowed herself to be styled. She was wearing a grey T-shirt tucked into a black midi skirt, with leopard print boots that Eliza had bought from an antique dealer in Venice; the two women had the same sized feet. Eliza had even applied a sheen of rust-coloured eyeshadow and some lipstick to her friend's face, though Ada insisted that her hair be piled on top of her head in its usual unruly way. Looking so good might normally have made her uneasy but somehow with Eliza there, she felt nothing more extreme than the occasional shimmy of self-love as she caught her reflection in the mirror.

James pitched up to the reading twenty minutes before it was due to start. He'd come from Paddington with Harriet, the editor who had bought the rights to Ada's forthcoming collection. Eliza had heard a good deal about James, and she watched him curiously from the sidelines. She decided he was a towering red trouser, but broadly harmless and obviously fond of Ada. Altogether Eliza was far more impressed by Harriet: a large black woman in her thirties with dreadlocks she tied up with other dreadlocks and a great laugh like pots clattering to the floor. She was wearing a suit so colourful and patterned it resembled one of those psychedelic optical illusions. Eliza took to her at once; in fact she was initially too awed by

Harriet's palpable intellect and sense of fun to say much to her. Yet soon she forgot to be daunted and sat next to Harriet on the front row, chatting to her about her and Ada's living situation, until the crowd that had blown in from outdoors fell silent to listen.

Ada walked onto the stage, accompanied by a professor from the English department. She smoothed her skirt and waited on the left as the professor introduced her, looming over the lectern to declare sonorously that they were all fortunate to be in the presence of 'one of the age's greatest transcribers of human emotion'. At this point Ada caught Eliza's eye wickedly. The man stopped talking. After throwing one smouldering look at the audience, as if to remind them that they were about to receive great poetry from on high, he let Ada assume her place at the lectern.

A great sudden swoop of horror passed through her, and she cleared her throat to check if her voice would produce anything approaching sound. The spotlight was hot on her skin. The ovals of people's faces were in rows in front of her like so many eggs in a carton. She thought of how desperately she didn't want to speak or be listened to. Then she began. The first sentence she said was a mess, a cobbled thank you to the audience for showing up. The second sentence was slightly more coherent. Slowly, as everything became easier, she remembered what giving readings was like: really rather nice, because everyone looked at you admiringly and laughed at your jokes.

'I've been going in all sorts of unexpected directions with my poetry in recent months,' she told the audience. 'Just as I thought my pen nib was drying up and that I'd

better give up all this rubbish, things in my life reconfig-
ured themselves a bit. My husband died, for one thing. I
started a rather peculiar business, for another. It's been a
tough couple of years and for many months after Michael
died I couldn't write a word. I've never believed the idea
that happiness writes white. Especially at first, grief wrote
white for me. But as I say. Things shifted. I have also
made a precious new friendship; a not inconsiderable
achievement at my age. There aren't enough poems about
women loving one another, especially across generational
divides. Some of these poems try to address that lack.'

Eliza glowed. Her throat felt quite tight. She knotted
her hands together on her lap.

Ada looked at her for a second from the lectern, her
eyes bright and steady with affection. Harriet, sitting on
Eliza's left, gave Eliza a low thumbs-up.

Ada took a sip of water and began to wind through her
poems. She was a good reader: leisurely but not funereal, and
she didn't assume the otherworldly manner so many poets
seemed to think they needed to adopt to seem like heavy-
weights. Ada picked some poems that were about Michael
and one or two that were about Eliza, but many more were
about things that simply interested her these days: Holly
Willoughby, persimmons, the beautiful world of crap telly.
Some poems rhymed, some didn't. Before every one she said
a few words about how she'd come to write it. The room
wasn't heaving but there were only a handful of empty chairs.
People seemed to smile at the right moments and look glum
when she hoped they would. Ada knew that it was going
well, that the poems were landing as none of hers ever had
before, except perhaps ones from her first collection, *Measure*,

published all those years ago. After an hour she found herself getting bored of the sound of her own voice. She skipped the poem she'd written about the widow she'd seen in the cemetery who had been doing such a good job at mourning, and finished on a funny one about arthritis.

Everyone clapped; more loudly and appreciatively, Ada couldn't help but notice, than they were perhaps duty-bound to do. In fact people looked rather devastated that Ada had finished. But perhaps it was pity or revulsion; perhaps it had been dreadful after all. She felt tired out. She walked off the stage and flumped next to Eliza on the front row, as the organiser of the reading said words of thanks. Then everyone clapped again, less loudly this time, and people began checking their phones. But many more came up to Ada to congratulate her and enthuse about 'the work'; so many that she had to stand up and play the poet. She realised the people around her were being genuine, they were actually moved, her words really had pierced them in some small way. She was overwhelmed – and queasy, suddenly, with longing for Michael; he had always taken such delight in her success. He would have lovingly watched her be loved by these strangers, and then the pair of them would have gone home together on the bus, talking about the poems and how well Harriet had edited them, chuckling about the pompous professor who'd introduced Ada at the start of the reading.

Everyone that wanted to talk to Ada had done so. She looked quite pale, Eliza thought. They hugged.

'I loved the poems,' Eliza said into her soft grey hair.

'Thank you,' Ada replied. Eliza smelled of lemons, as always. 'Thank you.'

Eliza could tell that Ada wasn't just thanking her for the compliment, and Ada knew Eliza knew. They broke apart, knowing their voices were too weak in their throats to bear more words just yet.

The room emptied. The four of them were left standing in a loose circle: Harriet, Ada, Eliza and James, proud of how the reading had gone, wondering what to do now.

'I think it's dinnertime,' James declared. 'On me.'

They took a taxi to a Thai restaurant in Cowley and ploughed through great piles of papaya matchsticks and fish cooked in leaves; it was the best meal any of them had eaten in months. James turned out to be quite the one for a mid-dinner toast and he raised his glass to Ada and her 'punchy new poems' so frequently they got a bit sick of knowingly clinking their champagne flutes. They drank too much. They felt like they were at the beginning of something important. After the meal was over Ada, Eliza and Harriet walked back to Swinburne Road, James having decided to make a drunken dash for the last train to London.

'Fantastic!' he bellowed at Ada as he pushed himself into a taxi. 'You brilliant transcriber of emotion! You Dante, you Wordsworth, you Emily Dickinson!' She rolled her eyes, waved him off.

Eliza wasn't sure, the following morning, quite at what time she, Ada and Harriet had gone to bed. She knew that a sizeable portion of the night had been spent showing Ada how Tinder worked. Ada was mesmerised and found it astounding that she could flick through eligible men in the vicinity from her seat on the sofa.

'It's like *Who's Who!*' she kept saying.

'Not entirely,' Eliza laughed.

A Tinder date had sent her an unsolicited picture of his penis just a couple of days ago, she added. She'd never read *Who's Who* but she didn't think that was the kind of content it included. Ada was appalled to hear about the photo and insisted on seeing evidence. Eliza demurred but finally gave in. She double-tapped the picture so that it filled her phone screen.

'CHRIST!' Ada shrieked. Then, 'Zoom in, zoom in.'

Harriet and Eliza grew feeble from giggling as Ada ogled the penis, magnifying every inch; she could not get over how bulbous it looked, how ready for action, how the chap, bless his heart, had obviously tried to find a good angle for the camera. When Harriet and Eliza offered to make Ada her own Tinder profile ('we can set the age bracket – bag you a thirty-year-old!') she actually screamed. Eliza pointed out that they could lure men in by catfishing the picture of the elderly model Ada had used on her Rent-a-Gran advert. Once she'd learned what catfishing was, Ada realised she was being teased and she laughed guiltily. They opened a bottle of vodka and drank the spirit on ice, shaken up with clementine juice, maple syrup and egg whites. At some point they rushed into the garden to start painting the old bench under the cherry tree using a tin of paint Ada fetched from under the stairs. The night was still. The moon was loosing its milk onto the lawn. No lights in the other houses were on, they might have been the only people awake in England. Ada kept saying she'd been meaning to do the bench 'for years'. To her surprise the paint was half liquid still, like it had last been used a few days ago.

Eliza wasn't sure if Ada was happy or sad; she had tears in her eyes as she stirred the paint to release the smell of it, but that might have been the chill in the air. A fox joined them for a moment; they all watched the animal, its fur rusty grey in the moonlight, then it melted into a hedge. For a while the three of them made passable progress, but painting a bench turned out to be fiddly when you were boozed and it was 2 a.m. and too dark to see your hands well, so at Ada's insistence they trooped back to the kitchen for whisky and a game of cards.

The next morning Ada awoke in a fug of pain. Her skull felt several sizes too small, her mouth dry and rancid. She looked at the alarm clock she kept on her bedside table and sighed: it must have stopped working at midnight; she'd need to root out some new batteries. She sat up, noticed that the light filtering through the curtains was different today: whiter, more settled. She checked her watch and gave a start: it really was bloody noon, she had slept until midday; the clock on her bedside table was right.

For a minute she simply marvelled. She'd not awoken past nine in thirty years and would never have dreamed herself capable. She was pleased and tried to spring out of bed puckishly to greet the afternoon. Then her head began to pound. A brass band seemed to be getting going somewhere deep in her cranium. She opened the curtains an inch. Sunlight jabbed her, two forks to the eyes. She groaned. Covered her face with her hands. Groped her way back to bed.

A couple of hours later, unable to sleep, she gathered the strength to pad downstairs in her nightdress. Her body must have been put in a tumble dryer by accident, that was all. Eliza was sitting in her usual chair in the kitchen with a book open on the table.

'I've got an apocalyptic hangover,' Ada whispered as she entered the room.

Eliza grinned. 'Me too!'

Ada stared crossly at her happy smiling face. Then she remembered that being well over twice Eliza's age, she probably had at least twice the hangover: such things had only become a problem for Ada when she reached her thirties.

At least Harriet was having a grim time too. 'What fresh hell is this,' she gargled from the sitting room. They all began to laugh feebly. Harriet had ended up sleeping on the sofa in her suit; she'd woken at ten, drooling on her wrist having missed a breakfast meeting in Holborn.

'Alcohol is a wicked thing,' Ada said.

'Agreed,' Eliza sang.

The kitchen was gleaming; all the flotsam from last night spirited away.

'Thanks for tidying up,' Ada croaked.

'Welcome,' Eliza said.

Ada saw hazily that Eliza was taking notes on a book written by Michael, a critical overview of Italian novels from the seventies. She felt her torso sort of solidify for a moment; like Michael was standing right behind her if only she would twist around and look. Then the sensation loosened and she found she could think again. Oh yes. That book. She and Michael had talked a good deal about it while he was writing it; it was odd and not unpleasant to see it being used in his kitchen all these years later.

'Enjoying it?' Ada asked.

'Very much,' Eliza said.

'He wrote a lot of it in Turin. He liked that book, he was happy whenever he was working on it.'

'It shows in the writing. It's full of life. And humour. I didn't know academic writing could be so funny.'

'Good. Yes. He was a witty man.'

Eliza stood up and poured Ada a glass of orange juice. She steered her to a chair, sat her down and popped out a couple of Ibuprofen, instructing her to swallow them immediately.

'If I must,' Ada said. She knocked the pills back and closed her eyes. 'I'm never drinking again,' she murmured.

'Seconded,' called Harriet from the sitting room.

'You'll live,' Eliza told them both.

Ada could hear her smiling. As she opened her eyes Eliza set down a bowl of porridge, covered in toasted nuts and muscovado sugar. Eliza sat opposite, nursing a cup of hot milky coffee, and declared she wasn't budging until Ada had got some food down her. Ada ate obediently and flicked through the paper, noticing that even her fingers were throbbing. At some point Harriet came into the kitchen and ate some porridge, still in her mad colourful suit. The afternoon slurred into a sort of pyjama party, only one interrupted by regular expressions of extreme pain and regret. None of them were in the mood for sophisticated conversation so they parsed indolently through what had happened the night before, their voices deeper and more rutted than normal, their laughter quiet and frequent, as light rain began to fall outside, polishing the grass and speckling the half-yellow bench with moisture.

Chapter Twenty-Six

The country was being asked to decide whether to remain within or leave the EU. The day of the vote broke without colour. Eliza had stayed up for much of the night watching a storm toss itself onto her window, the house rattling in the wind. She hadn't replied to Ruby's message yet and it was taking every iota of self-control she had not to. Her days with Ada and in the library were peaceful, but late at night something would stir within her, an energy would thrum through her limbs and she'd be able to think of nothing but Ruby, her scorched blonde hair, the caramel smell of her, the slow way she took Eliza's body into her mouth.

Eliza awoke early. Her body was taut with anticipation at the vote, like she'd been watching a trashy TV series for months and was on the last episode: how would it go, would the plot twist that Twitter foretold come to pass, which characters would be killed off? A sense of trepidation at the possible consequences of the day pulsed through her too – but its beat was less sugary, easier to ignore, and anyway, there was nothing she could do now to change the course of things; they would go the way they must.

'We're going to leave,' Ada declared over breakfast.

She had slept through the storm. Eliza objected, pointing to the modest lead Remain was showing in the polls. 'Also everyone's been saying for months that we'll become even more broke if we do leave,' she added, 'so maybe voters will take that on board.'

'I don't want to lord it over you with my very great age,' Ada replied, 'but allow me to do so for an instant.'

Eliza smirked. 'Go for it.'

'Britain's had a hot and cold relationship with Europe since before you were born. We've never quite clicked with the EU, partly because of our experiences in the war, and I wouldn't be surprised if today brought that uneasiness out.'

'Hmmmm.'

'People care about immigration, you can wish they don't my darling but I'm afraid they jolly well do. Everyone is still shell-shocked by the financial crisis. Austerity's shaken the can even more. Things haven't got much better, especially not for people your age, not that you seem keen to act on it.'

Eliza glared. Ada smiled naughtily and continued. 'There's nothing the British like to do more than jab authority figures in the eyes and we've been given a gold-plated opportunity to do so.'

'Well I hope we resist the urge.'

'I'm inclined to agree. But I don't know how it'll all turn out. No one knows. Maybe it'll be clear in twenty years.'

Eliza considered. 'I don't want to wait twenty years,' she said.

'Understandable. Whichever outcome we get, things are going to become very boring indeed. The Brexiteers will never shut up if we remain. They'll want a second vote sharpish. And it'll be a tremendous faff if we do decide to leave.'

Eliza could agree with that at least. They made bets and stuck them on the fridge with a magnet: Ada predicted a 53–47 result, giving Leave the win, and Eliza predicted Remain would nab it by 51 to 49.

Then Ada left Swinburne Road to spend the morning with a Rent-a-Gran client: an elderly woman from Bicester who had been lumbered with so many grandchildren to look after when her son went to work that she wanted 'another gran on hand' to support her.

Eliza had too much nervous energy to sit around the house so she decided to walk to the centre of town. The atmosphere was uncanny, like a coronation or something was happening, the streets emptier than usual, conversation constricted to one topic. It became a day of running into people – Eliza spotted Paola going into Mansfield College surrounded by pro-EU campaigners, and Sam made Eliza jump by tapping her shoulder while she was picking up her post in the porters' lodge. She even bumped into Nat, the undergrad she'd kissed in her first term. They were in a deli near Merton when they noticed one another. Eliza was relieved to discover that Nat wasn't the sort of person to get off with someone then pretend not to recognise them in daylight; she cried 'Eliza!' and hugged her. They talked about the only subject conceivable, then by some miracle they shook it off and talked of other things. It was lovely seeing Nat again, Eliza thought as they chatted. It felt easy. Nat made her laugh, telling Eliza what had happened with all the anti-examination activism she'd been involved with, recounting how the academic year had gone for her. She looked really nice, her light brown skin firm and rounded and luminous, like she used moisturiser and ate pomegranates regularly.

'It would be great to see you for, like, a drink or something,' Nat said once she had collected her baguette from the guy behind the counter. She didn't sound edgy or anything, she sounded like she meant it, like she would love to see Eliza for a drink.

Eliza shimmered. 'Same here,' she said.

Nat nodded cheerfully.

'I'm sorry I didn't text you or anything,' Eliza said abruptly. 'After we met. I know this sounds shit but I didn't really know what to do, what the protocol was, so I put it off and then it seemed too weird and late to act.'

'No worries,' Nat said. Her nails were painted silver again. She smiled warmly. 'Let's make it work this time.'

Eliza nodded. Nat put her baguette in her backpack and kissed Eliza on the cheek, then left.

Eliza basked in the feeling of being liked for a while, then ordered a panini. As she waited for it she watched the high street tick by; she couldn't help but infer a greater sense of purpose to the way people were striding, a solemnity to their conversations that was palpable even from behind glass. She felt for the first time in her life that history was being made and she was a conscious witness to it, a participant even; she'd only been young when the World Trade Center had come down and that had felt like watching an apocalypse film, nothing like this. A voice called out her order. She was about to turn to the counter to pick up the panini when she saw something outside that made her stop.

She went rigid.

She turned around slowly to face the window. Horror moved through her like inching floodwater.

She forgot, as she watched Ruby walk past on the pavement outside, laughing and throwing back her head, that she had a body, she forgot she had a name and an interior life all of her own. She could do nothing but stare at the portion of street Ruby was walking through and suddenly had passed through, as if the air were swaying with the heat of her still, as if every cat in Oxford was arching its back in fear.

'Aubergine panini,' a voice called again. 'Panini . . .'

Then: 'This yours, love?'

Eliza jumped.

She turned around. She took the panini.

She saw that three of her fingers were doing that thing where they seemed to lose their blood and become the fingers of a dead person. She brought them close to her eyes. They were waxy and yellow. She probably hadn't seen Ruby at all, she told herself; that person that had just gone past might easily have been someone else. It wasn't the first time Eliza had mistakenly 'seen' her ex-girlfriend: for a while after they had broken up it had been bleakly comical how frequently Ruby's features colonised the faces of innocent passers-by, who would stand there frightened as Eliza stared at them until she realised who they were definitely not and looked away, embarrassed.

But there was no pretending in this case. Eliza knew Ruby had walked past as surely as she could feel the clothes on her body and the panini in her hand, and anyway, Ruby had said she'd come to Oxford today; here she fucking was.

Eliza left the deli. She ate the panini on the street and threw it up in a Costa bathroom. She walked to Exeter College, looking around her all the time, trying not to linger on what had meandered through her mind in the deli: that Ruby was still palpably the woman Eliza wanted to be with for all her cruelties, that no one else could make her feel as intensely, as quickly, as fulsomely. She realised she was standing in an ivy-hung quad somewhere in Exeter; she remembered that George, her and Judy's friend, texted her that morning to say he was working there for the day. She must have decided to go to the college to study alongside him. She asked a student for directions to the library. When George came out to let her in (you had to have an Exeter card to enter) he asked something like, 'Are you OK?' Eliza rebuffed the question convincingly enough to be left alone with her laptop and books. She had an afternoon that felt like a night of no sleep, every hour the witching hour, every minute unwanted and punishing. She skimmed her books and touched her phone fitfully, refreshing the BBC news page again and again to avoid confronting her own creaturely fear. She spent a long time on Instagram wondering if Ruby would upload a dreaming spires-type photo as Eliza monitored her page. She knew she should return to Swinburne Road, seek refuge in Ada; she knew she should ring Ellie or Jess and get their advice; she could even telephone Rich, distract herself with all the latest from Carlisle – Flora was getting really big now – but she could only spectate as she failed to act, like her limbs were the limbs she had in dreams, irresponsive, mired in air too dense to move through.

And now she watched herself write Ruby a message on Facebook. She wasn't sure what she was typing, it was along the lines of, 'Just saw you walk past me in Oxford, would be great to catch up while you're in town.' She didn't check the contents of the message before she sent it, she just let it wing away from her like prayer. She telephoned Ada's mobile as she had promised to earlier; they arranged to meet at six at a primary school where a polling booth had been set up. George was nowhere to be seen.

'Are you ready to vote?' Eliza said on the phone.

'Raring,' Ada said.

'OK.'

Ada thought there was something odd in Eliza's voice. 'Are you alright?' she asked.

'I'm alright.'

Ada wasn't convinced but she was walking to her car as they spoke and was distracted by the beauty of the afternoon – sunlight lancing and scattering as the clouds conjoined and loosened, the early summer trees swaying like hips, everything radiantly young.

Half an hour later she and Eliza met up at the school and voted. There were lots of people in and around the polling booth, everything everywhere felt coiled, alert. Afterwards they walked back home.

Eliza didn't mention who she'd seen in town; she knew Ada would counsel a course of inaction that Eliza didn't feel mentally equipped to heed. Ada knew something serious was disturbing Eliza but whatever it was seemed too locked within her to be investigated now, so she left her in peace.

At home, they parted for a couple of hours. Eliza went to her room and Ada installed herself at the kitchen table, working. A fortnight ago Eliza had given her a collection by the Canadian writer Anne Carson, and it had pierced Ada deeply; she wanted to write a poem like 'The Glass Essay' and was trying to establish what form hers should take.

Night began to dab the sky teal. Eliza came downstairs. Her face was haggard. Ada asked her what was wrong. Eliza said she was sad, and that she wasn't feeling very talkative today if that was OK. Ada understood both those things. She poured two tins of macaroni cheese into a pan and heated it up for them. They ate the food with buttered toast in front of the TV.

Soon it was 9 p.m. One more hour of voting to go. Eliza knew a few people going to a referendum party in Jericho but she wasn't even slightly tempted to join them. Boris Johnson put out a statement that trumpeted, 'Don't lose this chance to make today our Independence Day!!!' Robert Peston was on the TV eating M&Ms at a big desk.

10 p.m. Hedge fund exit polls were murmuring that Remain had clinched it. There were people at Glastonbury dressed as poll boxes and EU countries. It looked like a fun time, it looked like a party. All around the world, men in financial markets were staring at screens, their skin grey. In Peterborough a man was arrested for a stabbing. Eliza found the news comforting, like it was any other day in Britain, not this day.

11 p.m. Tory MPs were circulating a letter urging David Cameron to stay on whatever the result. Ada fixed a couple of gin and tonics and brought them through from the kitchen. She and Eliza sipped the sour drinks quickly, to the skitter of the news channels. Ada began eating ginger nut biscuits, one after the other without noticing. Eliza just

watched the TV and the mouths of the people onscreen, making shapes and rushing out sound. She wondered if Ruby was watching this channel too. Sometimes the presenters' bodies raised an arm to point at a detail on a graphic. Their hands kept joining and parting to emphasise all the important points they were making.

Gibraltar declared its result – Remain, overwhelmingly. Ada made them another gin and tonic, she added cucumber this time. Eliza wondered which way Ada had voted and decided she didn't want to know. Ada wondered if she had voted the right way; in the booth at the last moment she'd changed her mind.

Midnight. Eliza hadn't made some grand decision to stay up late but sleep wasn't conceivable now. She was thinking of Ruby, her burnt blonde hair, how it got lighter in summer. The moles she had on her back.

Newcastle declared. Remain but narrowly. The pound plummeted. Eliza's Twitter began to ticker its alarm. Orkney announced. Remain too.

'Well, my dear,' Ada said, yawning and getting to her feet. 'It looks like you won't be disappointed.'

She said goodnight. Eliza said that she hoped she slept well. She watched Ada climb the stairs, her movements stiff as she'd been sitting for so long. Eliza wanted for a second to stop Ada from going to bed so they could talk; she imagined how freeing it would be to cast off the monkish reserve she'd maintained all night, how liberating to just tell Ada she'd seen Ruby on the high street and the bad things she wanted to do with that information now. Ada would want to know, she would want to protect Eliza from herself. But Eliza couldn't find her voice, and in any case she didn't really want to, so the older woman went upstairs without returning to talk to the younger one on the sofa, who was watching her lean on the banister, grip, heave up. There were more sounds from upstairs for a few minutes as Ada moved around her bedroom and bathroom, then silence.

Eliza turned back to the television. She felt like her brain had been put in the freezer some time ago and was now in a state of semi-thaw. Ruby's name was marching through her mind, Ru-by, Ru-by, on and on like a great army going to war.

Sunderland declared. Leavey as you like, someone on Twitter crowed. Massive turnout we're all screwed, someone else screeched. Eliza swiped up on her phone to shut the app down. She opened her laptop and checked Facebook. Ruby had replied. Cold tinkled down Eliza's neck like refrigerated syrup.

'Ahhhh you shoulda said Hi!' the message read. 'Where are you now? I'm watching the ref at a friend's but she's thinking of going to bed and I'm too pumped to sleep.'

Eliza looked at the screen for a bit.

'I'm in Iffley,' she typed back.

Ruby: Same wtf! Where?!

Eliza: Swinburne Road

Ruby: Don't know it

Eliza: No one does

Ruby: Oh lol you literally are almost next to me, just googlemapped and I'm on Freelands Road

Eliza: Yeah I know Freelands

Ruby: OK cool well . . . I mean . . . you up for me coming over?

Ruby: Completely get it if not

Ruby: Been missing you tbh and would love to see you

Ruby: We can obv talk about all the crap I did, I really want to

Ruby: Whatever, lemme know

Chapter Twenty-Seven

Eliza didn't know what to do about Ruby so she just watched the television.

UKIPers were cheering up. Helen Lewis said that she was 'laughing through the horror'. Liz Kendall was denying that the vote was a wake-up call, saying some people had actually been 'awake for a long time'. Eliza agreed, she felt she'd been awake forever. She downloaded an app on her phone so she could watch the pound ski downwards. She wondered if she should go to a cashpoint and take out what little money she had, stash it under a mattress or whatever. The national papers were doing live blogs and she flicked from tab to tab on her laptop; everyone was saying the same sort of thing, like, 'This is a great shock' and 'History is being unmade before our eyes'. Eliza listened to them impassively. If this was what history felt like, history felt like nothing much at all, it felt like disappointment.

She could see she was reading the news now through Ruby's eyes, trying to imagine how she'd be interpreting what seemed to be happening, what she might think the fallout from all this change would be. To distract herself she sent messages to Rich in Carlisle but then he went to sleep. Flora was still up though, and she and Eliza began WhatsApping one another as more results rolled in; it heightened Eliza's sense of unreality, as if all the rules of daytime had laid down their arms and given way to a new order, in which Eliza spoke to her mother about politics.

Swindon declared. Leave. Eliza poured herself another gin and tonic. Ruby liked them, she had hers with slices of clementine. The ice made musical notes as it tinkled against the glass. Eliza supposed she was drunk now, her limbs felt more loosely screwed on.

Glasgow declared. The city went remain but it was a low turnout. 'Fuuudge,' breathed Stephen Bush.

1 a.m. Eliza felt drunk now, she couldn't find the concentration to focus her eyes on anything. She wanted to lie down on the floor but she knew the booze would go to her head, make her feel worse. She replied to Ruby, told her she was welcome to come over if she wanted. She tossed the phone away from her and went to the kitchen to open the garden door. She stood barefoot outside on the black lawn. The grass was soaking. The night was cool. A light breeze was running its fingers through the branches of the cherry tree, flicking the leaves up and around. The moon wasn't full but it looked like it had been recently, with grey blots on its face like cataracts. Eliza breathed in deeply, wishing she had some cigarettes, and went back into the sitting room.

Oxford declared. Remain as expected though the turnout again wasn't great. Eliza rolled her eyes and went to the bathroom. Dread at what she might do and feel if Ruby arrived at the house began to shoulder aside her numbness. She looked at herself in the mirror as she peed, the two spider plants framing her body. Her face looked sort of fastened onto her head. She was wearing a black T-shirt tucked into black jeans, she thought she looked quite like a heroin addict. Her mascara was flaking in little hyphens under her eyes; she tried to scratch the flecks off but they clung to the skin.

She returned to the television. South Tyneside declared, another Labour stronghold. Leave. She stretched out on the floor. She sensed it would be therapeutic for her to scream or something but no part of her knew how to instigate that and it would be ridiculous to do so anyway while Ada was asleep upstairs. Everything felt artificial, theoretical, from the crystallising Brexit vote to the fact that Ruby was presumably walking to Swinburne Road now and would knock on the yellow door quietly, as Eliza had instructed her to.

2 a.m. Eliza was still lying on the floor in the sitting room when she heard someone at the front door. It was exactly the sort of noise you'd expect to hear in the night when you started awake after a nightmare; a muted tap-tap that was only just too audible to be ignored. She sat up. Her body was crisp with fear. She'd had too much to drink; there was nothing she could do now but ride it out. She got to her feet woozily. There was a big rectangular mirror in the hallway; she turned on the light and checked her reflection. She took her pink hair out of its ponytail, applied a smile, plucked at her T-shirt so it fell nicer on her torso and rubbed her face to make herself look fresh and rosy. She unlatched the door.

Ruby was standing on the step. It was so weird. They stared at one another, maybe for ten seconds.

Eliza hadn't seen Ruby in almost two years. She was wearing dark lipstick and a green silk dress that fell below her knees, with a leather jacket and Doc Martens. Eliza's heart felt swollen, it was surely bulging her T-shirt out; she wanted to press her palms to her chest, push it back into place. Ruby had worn the same shoes to work the day they'd broken up in Bath, when she'd brought that randomer back to their house, had sex with him downstairs as Eliza listened on the landing, holding her own neck with her hands. Over the past few months imagining Ruby's face had become difficult; Eliza could only picture her for a second before she slid away, but now Ruby was right here, her features solid and verifiable; it was satisfying to see them in their familiar configuration again. They didn't disappear, they seemed obvious, inevitable, like they'd lodge in Eliza's memory for good this time.

'Hi,' Ruby said.

Her hair was longer, Eliza noticed; it was down to her shoulders, the colour of heated honey. Last time they'd seen one another it had come up to her ears. She was beautiful, her skin bone-white in the moonlight.

Eliza said hi back, then something like, 'Come in, come in.' Ruby stepped into the house. Eliza tried to shut the front door softly behind her, holding the latch to make sure it didn't make a noise. She was too drunk to pull it off and the door closed with the same metallic shudder it always made. The hallway was narrow. Ruby's body was close. She was tall, way taller than Eliza, and she moved in a way that made people ask her if she'd done ballet. Eliza could smell her perfume, she could see her long ivory neck in the hall mirror. The detachment she'd felt since seeing Ruby walk past the deli that morning was buried now; Eliza felt only a slow drubbing longing, like wanting someone dead to be alive once more, or wishing you were at the start of your twenties again. She could tell that Ruby hadn't changed. She was still unkind. Eliza had known it the moment she'd opened the door and Ruby's darkened lips had split, almost smiling, parting in a way that made Eliza know in her bones that she would hurt her again. And yet Eliza wanted her.

They went into the sitting room. Ruby had brought along a bottle of champagne, half of it finished. Some of the bubbles might be gone, she said. Eliza really didn't want anything more to drink but Ruby kind of insisted, said that they'd not seen one another in ages so they should 'mark the moment', and that anyway they'd need Dutch courage to get through the rest of the night's Brexit coverage. They watched the television and talked about what they saw on it. Any other subject for now was too big. Another slab of results came in – Lincoln, Ribble Valley, Hertsmere all voted to leave; Liverpool went remain. Eliza went to the kitchen to find a couple of glasses. She felt alone and aged. She drank a glass of tap water from the fridge, relishing the coldness of it, she'd not known she was so thirsty, the liquid tasted sugary it was so welcome. She could not believe she had summoned Ruby here, to Ada's home; there was no part of her that did not feel guilty at the breach of trust. Ada wouldn't want Ruby to be in her house after all she'd heard about her. Eliza had to do anything, say anything, to get her out. She had sullied something precious, something unspoken but important; now everything was jeopardised.

She returned to the sitting room with the glasses. Ruby had taken her boots off and was sitting on Ada's armchair. There was no way she could know whose chair it was but Eliza bristled anyway. Ruby had also adjusted the lighting, maybe turned a few lamps off. The room looked sultrier. She asked if she could have a ginger nut biscuit, there were still a few in the packet by the armchair. Yes, Eliza said, wanting to shout no. Then she saw that Ruby had something on her lap. It was Primo Levi's sculpture, the owl. It was just sitting on her thighs, on its side.

Eliza put the glasses on the table where the copper-wire figurine usually perched. She could feel herself shaking, her wrists especially. The picture of Ada and her husband looked oddly stripped without the owl in front of it; the happiness they radiated phoney somehow.

'Did you get the owl from here?' Eliza asked, pointing at the table. She wanted her voice to sound nonchalant; she wasn't sure if it did. She was frightened Ruby would crush the copper-wire figurine out of spite, or run off with it and Eliza would be unable to get it back.

Ruby looked confused, then realised Eliza was talking about the owl on her lap.

'Oh,' she said. 'I just picked it up, it's such a dainty thing.'

'Mmm,' Eliza said.

She went over to Ruby and made to pick the owl up from her lap, in a casual way that wouldn't elicit suspicion. Ruby caught her arm, which made Eliza jump, but she wasn't trying to stop her from taking the owl back, she was just holding her arm in a simulation of tenderness, which was almost worse. The moment Ruby touched her

Eliza remembered all the other times Ruby had gripped her in this way – lightly enough, with confected care, but always in a way that made you know she'd only let go when she felt like it.

'I'm sorry if you think I didn't treat you well when we were together,' Ruby said.

Her eyes looked greener than they normally did, and cold. There was a question in her voice.

'I just wanted to say,' she continued, 'I don't want you to remember me in a bad light. It's so easy for things to fix in the past in a way that's not useful.'

Eliza looked at her arm.

'Useful for who?' she asked.

Ruby said nothing. Eliza thought about what Ruby had said, the emotional stinginess of it.

Ruby kept hold of her wrist. Her other hand started scratching Eliza's arm softly. It felt nice, up and down. Eliza cleared her throat, flexed her fingers a bit. Ruby released her. Eliza went to the little table to pour them some champagne. They drank and talked some more. It was easier for Eliza not to look at Ruby so she sat at her feet on the floor, facing the television. Ruby played with her hair, massaged her scalp with her fingers, her nails were long so it felt good. She spoke about herself, mostly, what she'd been up to, how she felt about the vote, how often she'd thought of Eliza and hoped she was 'flourishing'.

'I realised a couple of months ago that I'm not as happy as I was when I was with you,' she said abruptly. 'I used to be more content when you were around.'

Eliza considered this admission silently. Were she feeling stronger she might have experienced a sense of triumph: it was rare for Ruby to say she lacked anything. As it was, she could not feel vindicated. Ruby didn't ask if Eliza was feeling more content alone, she seemed to assume that Eliza must miss her, must want to return to what they had. She clearly wanted to rewrite their relationship, to reupholster it as a normal romance that had ended conventionally, without one of them being appallingly hurt. Eliza listened half insatiably, half with a cool interest in how Ruby was carrying out her intentions. She knew it would be the last time she saw Ruby, this night; she could not have this woman in her life now. She had learned to live without her and she would, she must, do so again. Yet part of her wanted this last night together not to end, so she sat against Ruby's legs as the TV presenters soldiered on and Ruby ran her fingers through Eliza's hair and talked about how Eliza was important to her, how she'd sometimes regretted being 'a bit controlling' when they lived together, how maybe she shouldn't have monitored Eliza's movements, read her emails, supervised her phone calls, but that all that stuff came from a place of care.

Eliza watched the shapes on the television bloom and wither. The pound had fallen further, she wondered if that would impact her life in any way. She thought of Nat, actually quite a lot, and of how if she emerged from this unending night she'd like to see her for the drink Nat had suggested. She thought of Ada, and of the bench they'd been meaning to finish in the garden, only they were running out of paint and needed to go to the shop to buy more.

*

Upstairs, Ada's sleep was thinning. She could hear talking on the ground floor but assumed it was the television. She was dreaming of something silly, that she was making a panna cotta only it kept flopping out of the bowl and squelching away from her, like a runaway flubber. She sat up, looked at her alarm clock and sighed. It was 4.15. The referendum was presumably decided, then. She made to turn on the World Service to hear the latest, then chose not to; she'd find out later, hearing which way the vote had swung would do nothing to change the course of things now.

She switched on the lamp and closed her eyes for a while to adjust to the brightness of the room. She was too awake to attempt sleep again just yet, too tired to read. She listened for movement downstairs, heard none and wondered if Eliza had fallen asleep in front of the news. She might need tucking up, or even waking depending on what position she was sleeping in.

Ada put on her slippers and dressing gown. As she walked downstairs, the open door of the sitting room made her stop and clutch the banister in surprise. There was a young woman she had never seen before sitting in the armchair opposite the fireplace. Eliza was at her feet. The television was on, though they weren't paying much attention to it; they were talking in low voices that Ada knew she would be able to overhear if she stepped closer.

Ada didn't want to embarrass Eliza or interrupt some flowering romance, so she moved down the stairs as silently as she could, curious and mesmerised; it was such an intimate scene. The young woman was doing most of the talking, as Eliza stared ahead. There was a bottle of champagne on the side table though their glasses were empty. Ada wondered who the stranger was: she was pretty, to be sure, though something about the way she was talking, so confidently and fluently with her small white teeth catching the light, filled Ada with mistrust. Both of them were too absorbed in their conversation to look at the dark staircase or notice the woman in a dressing gown on the bottom step, hearing every word.

Eliza was feeling reckless. Being with Ruby after all these months was like holding the wire of an electric fence; the current wasn't on constantly but it pulsed in waves so the longer you held it the greater your chance of being ripped up by an electric shock. They had finished the champagne and she was trying to keep her eyes focused on the framed photo of Ada and Michael on the table; it had a fortifying effect. She wished more than anything that she'd not allowed Ruby to come here; she'd already suggested they go to Ruby's friend's house but Ruby had said she wanted to stay for a while longer. Eliza was fighting to keep the details of her new life to herself, though a guerrilla faction within her wanted to surrender them completely, to tell Ruby everything that had happened to her since Bath, give herself back to her until she felt gutted and bare.

'These are great digs,' Ruby said.

'Thanks,' Eliza said.

'Who do you live with?' Ruby asked.

'Ah, nobody you know,' Eliza said. Hopefully that would quell the topic.

'No seriously, who?'

'Nobody important.'

Ruby began massaging Eliza's shoulders, her neck. She had strong, thin fingers.

'I've missed you,' she murmured. She'd said that a bit. Eliza wished she hadn't enjoyed her saying so, but she had every time. She thought Ruby was telling the truth.

'I used to make you so joyful,' Ruby continued.

Eliza twisted around, looked at Ruby's face. It was impossible to read. Eliza thought she had never known anyone so vicious. Her lipstick had dried out: Eliza could see loose flakes of wine-red skin in front of teeth that looked whiter than Eliza remembered, maybe Ruby had had them bleached. Levi's copper-wire owl was still on her lap, witnessing their intimacy. Eliza wanted to snatch it back, to tell Ruby to get out. She felt weighted down, mired in her, she felt that time would not pass and that she'd remain at this woman's feet until she sickened or grew old.

On the staircase, with a blow that felt bodily, Ada saw that the young woman on the armchair had Michael's copper-wire owl on her legs, and that Eliza must be able to see it was there, only she wasn't trying to return it to the table, to keep it safe. She wanted to go in and introduce herself, put the figure back in its place, but there was something so private about the conversation she was overhearing that she couldn't bring herself to interrupt. Perhaps Eliza would be uncomfortable if she appeared: maybe this young woman knew nothing about who Eliza was living with, and would revile the loneliness that had driven both of them into one another's company.

'How long have you been living here?' Ruby asked lightly.

'Not long,' Eliza said. Her eyes were on the television now, the map of the country was coloured in splodges according to which areas had voted which way. She didn't want to talk about her living situation but Ruby had always been able to sense when they were on to a subject Eliza didn't like; she enjoyed drawing such conversations out.

'You said you live with an older woman – are you together?' Ruby probed.

'God no,' Eliza said. 'It's nothing like that.'

'How old is she?' Ruby asked, her eyes narrowing.

'I don't know,' Eliza said. She knew. A desperation to zip the conversation closed was scrabbling at her chest. 'But she's properly old, I mean she's got grey hair and stuff,' she said in a rush.

Ada blinked.

Ruby raised her eyebrows.

'Jesus,' she said. 'What do you talk about?'

'Er, nothing.'

'You don't talk?'

'We don't talk much, no.'

'How did you come to live with her?'

'She offered me a room.'

'Why d'you say yes? You must have had other options.'

'She wasn't asking for rent.'

Ruby considered. 'You're not paying any rent at all? Well played.'

'Yeah,' Eliza said tonelessly.

'Don't you feel you've stepped backwards a bit? Moved in with a grandmother?'

Eliza screwed up her face. A few more sentences and Ruby's curiosity would be sated. Say anything, she willed herself, do anything to get it finished with, then take her out of the house and tell her you never want to see her again.

'The woman took a liking to me,' she said. 'I dunno, she's a loner. It's quite sad. I'm saving up so I can move out. Her husband died and she really isn't over it. She thinks we're super-close and she wanted me to live with her. Obviously I said yes. I'm skint, whatever, it made sense, it's not been too bad anyway. I'm not gonna stay here for long.'

Ada listened. She became aware of the heart that was beating in her chest. She felt skinny and insubstantial. Her face slowly crumpled. She turned on the spot, moving as quietly as she could, and went back up the stairs to her room. She got into bed on the left side. She curled up. At some point she heard the front door close and two voices on the street talking as they walked away from the house. She got out of bed, opened the curtains to watch Eliza leave her.

Dawn was breaking, the sky washed with rose. Eliza and the woman were walking up Swinburne Road. They were the only two living beings among the cars and brightening trees. Ada looked at their bodies until they vanished from view. Then she went back to bed and closed her eyes until seven, when she rose properly, went to the kitchen in the empty house, made coffee, watched the news and put the dishwasher on. She tried to edit but no better words came to her, and the poems seemed dull, flat things, tangles of intellectuality that wouldn't help anyone or be useful for anything. At ten she texted Eliza to say that their living arrangement wasn't quite working out for her, and that she was going to go to her sister's in Brighton; that if it didn't bother Eliza too much it would be greatly appreciated if she could move her things to another house, and that she was sorry for the abruptness of her decision but it just seemed easier to get it done quickly. She'd left two hundred quid on the sideboard in the kitchen to pay for removal men.

Some time passed, then Eliza called her, and called her and called her. Ada didn't pick up though she watched her phone vibrate on the table, a beetle in a glass. Eliza texted to ask if she was joking. Ada replied saying she wasn't. Eliza texted to say she was coming back home right now to talk about it. Ada replied asking her not to, then instructed her not to enter her house until noon, by which time she'd be on her way to Brighton. She wanted to tell Eliza to leave the house keys behind too but she couldn't bring herself to. Ada added, because she didn't want to hurt Eliza by letting her know what she'd overheard in the night, that she was finding it too difficult to live with someone after having lived with Michael, that she was mourning him and wanted solitude, that it wasn't Eliza's fault: she was too young to understand, too unattached to anyone, too unloved by anyone, to know what loss was really like. After that Eliza stopped replying.

Ada put some clothes in the carpet bag she'd taken to Peter and Yannis's wedding and called her sister to tell her she was coming. Eve sounded bemused but perfectly willing to have her. She was accompanying Tom on a school trip and kids were making a racket in the background. Ada had to hold the phone a few inches away from her ear so the noise didn't deafen her.

Before she left Swinburne Road she went into Eliza's bedroom and lay on her bed. It smelled of Eliza; it smelled of lemons. Her pyjamas were rolled neatly under the pillow. The books on her desk overlooking the cherry tree were all Michael's. Ada wept until her stomach ached, until her eyes felt small and chlorinated. Eventually a taxi beeped outside. She sat up, smoothed the duvet, smoothed her face, brought one of Eliza's dirty mugs downstairs and saw that Eliza had put Levi's copper-wire owl back in its place in front of the picture of Ada and Michael. There was that at least.

Chapter Twenty-Eight

The day after the referendum was one of the strangest of Eliza's life. Just after dawn she walked with Ruby to Freelands Road. The June morning was stunning, the sky ploughed up by great tracks of ice-cream pink, the birds chatty and visible. There was something comforting about the parked cars along streets Eliza knew so well, all those closed curtains, the sleeping bodies in implied proximity. She felt cocooned and surer than ever that she would not see Ruby again after this morning, that she was coming to the conclusion of something, a period in her life that had been instructive but had its end point, like everything else. She wanted to rush the drama to its close but she knew she shouldn't, it needed to come to a finish naturally.

Ruby talked; Eliza tuned in and out. She knew she would love Ruby for a long time yet but she now knew also – and the knowledge felt quietly pivotal – that she could love other people more, and be loved better.

They reached Freelands Road. It was fully light now, a beautiful morning. Ruby said she was staying with a friend, Angela, who lived in the top-floor flat. When they unlocked the door Eliza barely had time to register the drab living room before she was struck by fatigue; she asked if Angela would mind if she had a nap on the sofa. Ruby said she wouldn't. Eliza curled up and Ruby kneeled by her body, throwing a blanket over her. She tucked a strand of hair behind Eliza's ear, leaned in to kiss her. Eliza closed her eyes, pretended she was more drunk than she was and turned away. After a while she heard Ruby stand up and pad out of the room.

When Eliza awoke the flat was silent. There were little bags of coke on the coffee table that she'd not noticed when they'd come in earlier, and a few magazines. She poured herself a glass of water in the kitchen, listening to the sound of a television on in the flat below; it sounded like a news programme. She was shattered but it was the sort of tiredness that felt more like clarity, like she was thinking with a concision she'd been lacking for months now, if not years.

Ruby came into the kitchen. She was in a silk slip, a white one, with lace at the top covering her creamy breasts. Eliza could see the familiar clusters of deep brown moles on her shoulder, the long flat plane of her collarbones. She was surprised to feel nothing as they looked at one another. Then Eliza poured Ruby a glass of water. She took it wordlessly and drank it down in one.

'I'm going home now,' Eliza said.

There was a silence.

'Where?' Ruby asked. 'What home?'

'Back to Swinburne Road.'

Ruby tipped her chin up. 'Come on,' she said. 'We both know you're going to stay here with me.'

'No,' Eliza said. 'I don't want to spend any more time with you.'

Her voice was steady. The tap was dripping silver into the sink. Tap-tap.

Ruby watched Eliza for a minute before replying.

'Well fuck off then,' she said, wiping her mouth.

Eliza smiled.

'Thank you,' she said.

She picked up her coat and her phone. Ruby was motionless, watching every move. Eliza plumped the cushions on the sofa so that no one would know someone had slept there. She left the flat, and as she closed the door she heard Ruby cross the kitchen, open the fridge, pull something out from inside.

On Freelands Road Eliza took in a deep breath and held it till it hurt. She let the air out of her mouth with a shout of joy. She felt light as popcorn, she felt scrubbed and new. She was in the mood for a stroll so walked to the centre to buy a coffee. She was sleep-deprived but happy, and soon she began to notice that her delight was not reflected in the faces she saw around her. Oxford was hung with an eerie calm as it had been the day before, except that today the atmosphere was more that of a funeral than a coronation. Eliza knew Remain had lost, but part of her hoped it wasn't true, that in the hours she'd been asleep things had turned around.

In the café she ordered a bagel with her cappuccino and asked to borrow a phone charger. She was halfway through her breakfast when her mobile finally powered on and she was able to read the news.

It was official, the country was leaving the EU. Cameron was long gone. She turned on Radio 4 on low volume and listened to it with the phone pressed against her ear:

the newsreaders were talking in cracked voices like they'd been hitting the town all night. She was just starting to eat the second half of her bagel when the messages from Ada flooded in.

It took Eliza a long time to recover from the shock of being rejected by Ada so decisively. All sorts of things swung into motion when it happened; Eliza felt horribly unwanted but also surprised, almost to the point of being amused, that she'd so misread Ada as to assume their living situation was making her happy. Once she had established that Ada wasn't joking she felt angry too, not only that she was being chucked out of her home with so little warning, but that Ada was refusing to see her or clarify further what exactly had made her come to her decision, and why she'd not said anything before, given warning signs, had a grown-up discussion about how things were getting on. At first Eliza thought there must be a missing puzzle piece, that something she didn't know must have changed Ada's mind, but then she decided she was looking for excuses, conspiracy-theorising as a way of obfuscating the brute fact of her rejection, and that the simplest explanation was probably true: Ada couldn't abide living with another person so soon after the death of her husband, and Eliza, myopic and young, could never hope to understand.

At eleven Eliza called her mother. They'd communicated so much while the vote was unfolding last night that it felt like the obvious thing to do. Flora didn't even know that Eliza was living with Ada, nor did Rich, but she grasped the fundamentals of the situation soon enough:

Eliza was being kicked out of her home, she was broke and distraught and needed reassurance, as well as an action plan devised by an adult who cared for her.

'Come back up here,' Flora said. 'You've got your room, we'd love you to stay for the summer.'

Rich must have been standing by the phone, because he said something like, 'Yeah, love, come home.'

Eliza's mind was fried after barely sleeping but she forced herself to consider the offer. It would be odd, certainly. She'd feel like an intruder. Perhaps that didn't matter very much. Going up there until the autumn would be good for her, good for all of them. Then she remembered she'd made commitments to Baleotti that she didn't want to renege upon; she was meant to be helping set up his outreach programme, she couldn't let him down again.

'I can't,' she said. 'I'm sorry. I've got to spend the summer in Oxford.'

Rich seemed disappointed but Flora rallied, made some calls to Eliza's college and found her a room that a visiting scholar from Berkeley was meant to be living in, only he'd had to stay in California unexpectedly. Flora could be a tough negotiator when it came to it, and she managed to secure the room for peanuts: Eliza would be paying just a fraction more than she had to Nick the developer in Swinburne Road.

At noon George, Sam and Judy came over to Swinburne Road to help Eliza pack up her things. She was grateful but also acutely embarrassed at the situation: how could it not seem that she'd behaved badly towards the old woman who'd opened her home up to her? She refused to touch the bank notes Ada had left for the removal men in the kitchen; looking at the pile actually made her feel ill – as if Ada had found a use for all the money she'd stockpiled from Rent-a-Gran, and was using her earnings to pay Eliza off. Judy was furious, kept saying how fucking cruel it was of Ada to turf Eliza out when she knew she'd had a rough year. Eliza was too weary to marshal much of a defence, though any anger she had was increasingly turning inwards into a sort of blithe self-hatred. 'It would never have worked,' she said whenever Judy exploded with rage.

They stopped packing every few minutes to listen to the news or check their phones; Britain was being ripped up by the referendum result, heads were rolling, journalists licking their lips at the story of the decade and politicians scurrying into configurations they hoped would pitch them into power. George was shell-shocked. Eliza wasn't much interested in any of it. The dust would settle. The vote hadn't gone the way she wanted but things often didn't. Judy kept saying that she couldn't believe it, that she'd never felt more alienated from her country, that she would apply for an Irish passport (her father was from Cork). Sam just shook his head sadly every half hour or so. Once Eliza had gathered all her things, they loaded everything into a taxi and drove to the centre. Eliza thanked them all and sent them on their way; George was sticking around Oxford for the summer, but Sam and Judy were due to fly to Jamaica the next morning.

Eliza spent the rest of the afternoon blearily arranging her belongings into the college cupboards and drawers. It was an undergrad room with pin boards and cheap mirrors that made her feel like she was stepping back in time to freshers' week. Finally, at eight, exhaustion defeated her. She went to sleep on the hard narrow bed, a choir practising in the room underneath. They were singing 'And So It Goes', over and over, and Eliza cried for the first time that day. The tears ran into her mouth, into her nose. She slept eventually and dreamed that she and Ada were sitting in the kitchen in Swinburne Road having a pot of Lapsang, only it was too hot to drink and it didn't seem to be cooling. They didn't talk, they just stirred their tea, round and round, their spoons tinkling against the porcelain, their eyes on one another's hands.

Chapter Twenty-Nine

Eve lived in a red-brick semi with her daughter Gwen near Preston Park in Brighton. The house was large enough for Ada to have her own room, a bathroom that had been converted into a tiny box room by the last owners.

The night she arrived, Ada realised she hadn't slept in a single bed in decades. Though she kept almost toppling to the ground it felt gratifyingly appropriate, like she'd had it coming. She didn't tell Eve what had happened with Eliza, the situation was too complicated to trawl over and anyway, Ada still felt mortified that she'd assumed Eliza had been enjoying living with her, that there had been more to their friendship than convenience. There was also the problem that Ada was already missing Eliza more than she thought she'd be able to articulate. No one else made her laugh as much or feel as good. Eve could see some emotional crisis had made her sister leave Oxford, but they had been respectful of one another's instincts for privacy for decades. She didn't ask questions, or not many. Ada was grateful.

Ada had never spent so much time with Gwen, her niece; usually they saw one another once a year or so, for a day out in London or a lunch in a restaurant. Living with her was quite another matter. Ada was relieved to see it confirmed that Gwen was a nice woman and her own children, Ali and Tom, were not bad either. They seemed remarkably at ease with the idea of an old woman they barely knew moving into their home for an indefinite amount of time, and Ada was touched by their openness. But the difference between life in Swinburne Road with Eliza and life in Brighton with the family was stark: there was never a let-up from the frenzy of getting the children sorted for school, fed, entertained, ferried to bed. They woke, like Ada, at the crack of dawn, except that they didn't proceed to read quietly in bed: they ran around madly. It took some adjusting to. Since Gwen's partner had left her, she had come to rely on Eve totally. Ada was interested to see how such dependence functioned. She didn't blame Gwen in the slightest, though it did mean that quality time with her sister was shaved to almost nothing, the occasional late-night hot chocolate, or snatched chats in the kitchen while the children were doing their homework.

One week into Ada's stay, Gwen returned from work with a set of keys. Ada was embarrassed: she feared it was a tacit hint that she was outstaying her welcome.

Gwen insisted that the opposite was true, that she wanted for Ada to stay for as long as she wanted to, and that having keys would help her feel more independent.

'The happier you are, the more likely you are to stick around,' Gwen said.

Ada tried not to narrow her eyes. But the impulse came from a place of habit, not belief: she could tell Gwen was being truthful, that she really did like having her aunt in the house.

'Thanks,' Ada said. She took the keys and jangled them. 'I'll go exploring tomorrow.'

Every day after that, she left the house having eaten breakfast and walked to the centre of town, or out of town, or into the countryside, often in the direction of a church or a coffee shop or an antiques emporium that she'd been recommended. She noticed that a lot of the young people she passed on the pavement paced while listening to things beaming into them from headphones: she valued the silence of her walking trips. She could think. She could hear birds. She could smell the swaying of the verdant summer trees. The walking also made her feel closer to Michael: when he'd been alive that was the only concession to physical activity he had made, and though walking without him made her ache with sadness, it quenched her soul as well.

As the weeks began to pass Ada's affection for Ali and Tom grew. Once the children had overcome their reserve around Ada, they made her laugh with their frankness and jutting ignorance, the questions that were so philosophical she couldn't help but smile ('Why is why?', 'What's the point in thinking?') Their bodies were remarkable – so quick and spry, so full of charge until suddenly they were not, good only for being lifted into bed or a bubble bath. Ali was remarkably clever and spent all her time reading – cereal packets, dictionaries, science fiction, comic books, even at one point a copy of *The New Yorker* that somehow made its way into the house.

'Are you called Ada and Eve after Adam and Eve?' she asked one morning.

Eve looked at her sister. Ada looked back. They were both stricken. The thought had never occurred to either of them.

'That might well be the case,' Eve managed to say. She stroked her granddaughter's hair fondly. 'How very intelligent of you.' Ali rolled her eyes. She always wore green, literally refused to don clothing of any other colour, an affectation that incensed her mother but which Ada rather admired.

Tom meanwhile was quieter, more interior, harder to draw out. He was tiny for his age and constantly bashing his knees and dropping plates. Initially he was reluctant to talk to his great-aunt, preferring to direct questions or comments for her at Eve or his mother, who would repackage them and send them Ada's way. Things shifted when he drafted Ada into building a train set his father had given him years ago when he was far too young for it. Now, at the grand old age of nine, he'd come into the gift, only his dad wasn't there to watch him play with it.

It was clear to Ada who Tom was building the train set for, and sometimes that made her feel so sad she wanted to step out of the boy's room for a bit, get some air and shake the image of his solemn concentration from her mind. But she never left his side. Rent-a-Gran had toughened her up more than she'd noticed. She and Tom carried on fitting the parts together, now building a station, now a little lift-bridge, more and more each day when he got back from school, and for hours and hours at week-ends. He told her one Sunday afternoon, in a voice that indicated a great secret spilling over, that his dream was to one day build a model village.

'And my model village will have a model village in the middle of it,' he said, his eyes huge and fanatical. 'And in the middle of that model model village, there'll be . . .'

'Let me guess,' Ada said. 'A model post office?'

'NO!' shouted Tom. 'A model model model village!' And he threw his little body onto a beanbag, triumphant.

Ada knew she couldn't stay in Brighton for good: it would feel like surrender, like she was sinking what she had left of her own life into the lives of her family members. She loved Gwen and Eve and Ali and Tom but she wasn't ready to do that. After a couple of months, the things she expected to tug her back to Oxford began to exert their pull – the suspicion that there were overdue bills piling in the hallway, the fear that her garden had become a jungle after weeks of rain and sun. It would be good to be back in a place of silence, to read again, to watch television programmes she had selected herself, to write and sit undisturbed.

'Are you happy with us?' Gwen asked her one evening.

'Yes,' Ada replied.

'You're welcome to stay. As long as you like. Forever, if you want to.'

'Thank you.'

'But you won't?'

'Not yet.'

'I thought so. The children will be devastated when you leave.'

'I'm sure they'll bounce back.'

'Possibly, but please visit again soon.'

Ada promised to. When leaving day arrived her sister offered to drive her to Brighton train station. Ada declined:

she wanted to walk there via the beach one last time; she had gone to the seaside a lot over the past few weeks, and enjoyed it. 'One of the drawbacks of Oxford,' she explained to Eve, 'is that it's far from the coast. I never see a flat horizon.' In the end Eve won, sort of: it was decided that a couple of hours after Ada had left the house, Eve would drive her bag to the station. They'd say goodbye then.

It took Ada a little over half an hour to walk from Gwen's house to the shore. It was an overcast Tuesday in August but even so the town was lively, full of hipsters that Gwen had taught Ada to identify by their clothing and demeanour. It was quite painful for Ada to see them; so many of them had hair like Eliza's and a similarly waify look. She'd been thinking of Eliza a lot, and a suspicion that she may have done her wrong, been too harsh and injudicious, was swelling uncomfortably within her, gathering substance every day. Yet whenever Ada wanted to act on that suspicion – reply to one of Eliza's texts, say, or give her a call – her motivation to do so was throttled by something larger and crasser, like humiliation. 'You silly old crow,' she scolded herself. 'You mad, stupid biddy, of course she only wanted to live with you because you weren't charging her rent.'

Ada reached the water's edge. The beach was fairly busy. People were doing what Ada remembered them doing when she'd gone to the Devon coast as a child: eating fish and chips, shooing gulls, lying back on their towels for all the world as if they were feather mattresses. It wasn't even slightly hot but people were in microscopic bikinis, trying to coax colour from their bright white bodies. Ada looked at the water, the grey waves, the vague grey rim of the sea. She remembered her and Eliza's conversation in the garden about their parents, how Eliza had been avoiding talking to her father, then sent him a text and thrust her fingers into the soil. Had Eliza gone back to live with them for the summer? Part of Ada hoped so, though something less noble hoped not: she wanted to be the most important adult in Eliza's life, even now.

After a few minutes Ada felt too self-conscious to continue contemplating the horizon. She left the beach and walked back through town. She got to the station slightly early and bought a coffee as she waited. Eve arrived with her carpet bag and hugged her tightly when they said goodbye. Ada promised she'd come back in September, it was Tom's tenth birthday and he'd asked her soberly to return to the house for it because he was having a 'ginormous party'. There wasn't long to wait.

Gwen turned up; she worked for an accountancy firm not far from the station. They hugged. Ada got on the train feeling that she was leaving people who would miss her, who would talk of her fondly when she'd gone. When she looked in her carpet bag she saw that Gwen or Eve had slipped in a packed lunch – a Cheddar and Marmite sandwich and some chocolate buttons. She opened the packet of chocolate buttons at once, sucked them slowly and deliberately one by one as the train drew north-wards to Farringdon. She would have to cross London on the underground, a daunting prospect, then it would be another train from Marylebone to Oxford, a taxi at the other end – and finally, home.

Chapter Thirty

Eliza knew that Ada had left Oxford for a while because she found herself returning to Swinburne Road every day, just to walk past the house. Her room in college wasn't even close by Oxford standards: it was a ten-minute cycle away. She felt embarrassed about her compulsion to go back and justified the excursions by telling herself that the true reason for them was that she wanted to continue doing her groceries at the shop on Iffley Road, where you could buy the most luscious dates in Oxford and the men at the till said mad things like 'Nice to see you' when they scanned your purchases. After picking up bread or a banana, Eliza would idly cross the road, meander to her old street as if by accident and walk the short distance to the house with the bright yellow door. But the building was empty and stayed empty for weeks.

The curtains in the sitting room were always open and it was unsettling to see the living room inside exactly as Eliza had left it in June; the blanket Ruby had pulled onto herself that night in a pile by Ada's armchair, the empty bottle of champagne on a side table. Once, Eliza gave up all pretence – she pressed her face against the glass and drank in the sight of her old home. She could just make out the glint of Primo Levi's copper-wire owl on the table. She had her keys still, she could in theory let herself in, but something deep within her told her that it would be wrong to enter the house again without Ada's consent.

On such expeditions Eliza often held her phone in her pocket, as if she were about to pull it out to give Ada a call. She missed her. Yet it was a strange missing, freighted with bewilderment and resentment. The questions she'd asked herself the day she'd been chucked out had widened and deepened; Ada's decision now seemed majestically unfair, a whim so despotic it was almost laughable. Once or twice she had wondered whether Ada had overheard her talking to Ruby about her, but that seemed improbable: Eliza would surely have seen her by the door, and anyway Ada wasn't the sort of person to creep around eavesdropping. Yet even as Eliza continued to find what had happened unfair, she knew she'd already forgiven Ada. So she continued to miss her, more and more as the days accrued, in a messy way she didn't quite understand.

Things in her life were not collapsing. In fact, they were going fairly well. Living in college had its advantages: she was bang in the centre of town, everything within reach. She walked everywhere, apart from when she cycled to Swinburne Road. When she wasn't reading around her thesis, she helped craft the programme Baleotti was spearheading, read reports on university access, studied why so few students from areas like Carlisle thought to apply to Oxford. As it turned out, the work was paid, and generously, so gradually she accumulated enough money in the bank to feel she was no longer tiptoeing by some great ravine. She was asked on to the local radio to talk about the outreach programme one morning and nearly threw up from the nerves right before, but it seemed to go fine, and Rich texted her afterwards to say he'd been listening as he did a patio in Cummersdale, and that he was bursting with pride.

On the first weekend of August she took him up on the offer he'd been making for months, and went back home. She didn't go first class this time. She had no desire to stay long, just a Friday evening to a Sunday morning, but in the end the trip went too quickly. Flora was huge and very happy; her baby was due in late September. Rich fussed over Flora in a way that Eliza was surprised to find inoffensive. She made the three of them dinner, a giant cauliflower cheese that would have fed a family of six, and thanked them for helping her out when Ada had asked her to leave Swinburne Road. Flora had been brilliant to negotiate the room in college. Both Rich and Flora waved their daughter's gratitude away. Eliza thanked them again. She felt grown-up, like the last few months with Ada and the weeks without her had handed her the keys to an adulthood she would never previously have imagined being ready to unlock.

Eliza and Flora hadn't fallen into some gooey love-in now that they were talking again, the mother–daughter bond was still frayed and twined with historic bitterness, but Eliza felt that progress was being made. She was even calm about Ruby, who had called and messaged her endlessly after the night they'd spent together. On a whim, the morning Eliza was due to return to Oxford from Carlisle, she spoke to her mother about it, who knew nothing about the relationship or its ending, but had solid advice anyway: 'Cut her out'. So Eliza blocked Ruby on all platforms and deleted her number. It was satisfying: she felt like the old woman in *Titanic* when she walked to the edge of the boat and threw her diamond into the water. She felt lighter, she felt softly free. She felt like the contours of her personality were being strongly drawn, now, in thicker pen with every passing day, that she had more agency than she'd ever had to decide who to be, and who to be with.

Ada's journey back from Brighton to Oxford was tiring. She supposed it was a mark of her great age. It was disconcerting to find herself wrung out by the trip across the city to Marylebone, she'd never clicked with London and it seemed to have absorbed more people since she'd last been, even at lunchtime her tube carriage was heaving. She saw three young women with pink hair, and every time her attention snapped to them ravenously, her chest sparking with hope that it was Eliza, that they had run into one another in some dingy underground corridor on London's transport network. But none of the women were her.

In Oxford the day was warm and humid. It felt strangely normal, stepping back into the house on Swinburne Road after so long away. Maybe it was because she'd not prepared it for her absence – she'd left in June in a whirl and everything now looked reassuringly untidy, as if she'd just popped out to the shops and was home again. But of course, small disasters had befallen since she'd gone: the contents of the fridge were jungly with mould, the roses in the kitchen had shrivelled to horrifying shrunken heads, the garden was indeed the chaos she feared it might be.

The house smelled fusty and needed a good airing out so she threw open the back door to coax in the late summer air. She looked gingerly in the bin, expecting to find it crammed with rotting food, but it was empty, with a fresh bag inside. Eliza must have taken it out before she'd left. Ada felt her throat tighten at the thought, and she stood staring at the bin dejectedly for a moment. Then she told herself to get a grip. There was work to be done and a house to be re-spruced. She put on some Bach, as loud as she dared, and set to it.

Ada didn't particularly like cleaning; when Michael had been alive he'd always insisted on paying someone to do it to save them the trouble, but she wanted to restore the house to order herself now; it would help her settle back in. When she turned her attention to the rooms upstairs, she got a shock: there was a fat gob of a spider in the bathtub, with thick black legs tented around its body. She actually screamed Michael's name, a reaction so built-in she'd clearly not kicked it. He didn't come to the rescue, and Ada was amused that she'd bawled in so undignified a manner, but in any case, the problem remained: the spider. She found a tumbler, coaxed it in with an old CD and released it into the garden, shuddering as she shook the glass out to make sure the bugger was gone.

Other than the cleaning, the major task she had to deal with now she was back was all her emails. She'd not touched a computer since leaving Oxford, and the quantity of messages she'd received in the interim was quite alarming. Some of it was spam but there was Rent-a-Gran correspondence to deal with as well as poetry business. James had called her when she was in Brighton to ask why she wasn't replying to Harriet her editor; Ada explained primly she was having a 'digital detox'. She'd learned the term from an article.

James seemed rather wrong-footed.

'Well,' he blustered. 'Detox be damned, Harriet's been worrying you hate her edits. I'll tell her to call you instead.'

Had Ada not been holed up in the study parsing through her emails, she may have noticed Eliza walking past the house every afternoon. Eliza, for her part, knew that Ada was back almost the moment she returned: the curtains were hung differently and the blanket on the floor in the sitting room was folded away. She didn't linger by the ground-floor windows as she used to, but walked past quickly, half yearning for Ada to see her, half fearing what might happen if she did.

Only once did Ada think she saw Eliza – she was reading in the sitting room on her armchair and looked up at Swinburne Road, with the intuition that eyes outside were fixing on her face. Someone with Eliza's features and hair seemed to dart past. When Ada got to her feet and went to the window to check, there was no one on the street.

In fact Eliza was there, she'd ducked in front of a car to conceal herself. Both women were motionless for a minute, the same feelings of loss and shame pulsing through them, then Eliza crept away, hunched and abashed and desperate not to be seen, and Ada, heartsick, returned to the sofa and failed to read her book.

Chapter Thirty-One

The day before Ada was due to go to Brighton to see Tom on his birthday, she confronted the suspicion she'd been ducking for weeks. The time had come for her to apologise to Eliza and have a frank conversation with her about what she'd overheard on the staircase. She didn't dare ring Eliza up, so she decided after her lunch to draft a preliminary email by hand. She sat in the living room, glancing up every so often at the blue and white sky as she wrote; it was one of those days where a week's worth of weather seemed to be crammed into several hours: now sunny, now dank, now so windy the window panes made grinding sounds as they heaved against their frames.

Ada was in her nightdress still, though she knew she ought not to be. She had a pile of paper on her lap, on top of a couple of dictionaries to lean on. She felt rather childish, writing a few sentences then crossing them out, finessing the language so vigilantly it reminded her of composing a poem, but she knew it was the right thing to do; Eliza deserved an explanation and the remorse and regret were becoming too much for Ada to bear.

She was trying to articulate how her vanity had been

bruised by what she'd overheard, when there was a knock at the door. She got to her feet, surprised; she wasn't expecting visitors.

Two police officers were standing on the doorstep. They must have been in some special unit as their uniform looked peculiar, actually they looked more like costumes.

One of them took off his hat and said with a smile, 'Are you Miss Ada Robertson, ma'am?'

She said she was.

Her blood seemed to thin, to frisk through her more rapidly as she looked into the man's pale grey eyes; the last time police officers had come to her house had been when Michael had died – who was gone this time? She thought it must be Eve, or Gwen or maybe all of them, gunned down in some grisly Brighton shoot-out she'd not heard about yet. She could barely breathe, she felt the air drawing into her lungs was thick and haired.

'May we come in?' the police officer asked.

'Yes, please, of course, at once,' Ada heard herself say.

She opened the door wider to let them pass her, noticing there was a big white van parked right in front of her house. The street was deserted and for a moment Ada took the humdrum sight of it in and held it to her, aware she might remember this moment later when everything was lost. Then she turned back inside. The two officers were walking down the hallway.

The second man was pulling a vast suitcase. It was rather strange: his big pale hand had a piece of paper in it, kind of scrunched around the suitcase handle as if he'd been holding the sheet before he set off to come here. Ada could tell it was her Rent-a-Gran advert, one of the ones she'd stuck up all around Oxford, with the picture of the beautiful old woman from Google Images and Ada's postal address at the bottom in case clients wanted to get in touch.

'Let's talk in the sitting room,' she called to the men. Her voice sounded parched. She realised she'd not drunk water since breakfast.

She heard the men go through to the sitting room. She shut the front door. She looked at herself in the mirror before going through to join them; she looked pale and old.

In the sitting room, one of the men had placed the suitcase flat on the ground and opened it. Ada saw it had lots of other bags inside, the vast woven plastic bags you might use to transport a duvet. She also thought she saw a measure of rope, earplugs and a bundle of black clothing. She didn't have time to question the suitcase's contents before the other officer said, 'Is there anyone else in the house?'

'No,' she replied.

'Anyone due to come here today?'

He took off his hat; he had very short blonde hair, shaved almost to the skin. Perhaps there were robbers in the area and the police officers had come to warn her.

'No!' Ada said.

'Not your husband?'

'I'm widowed.'

'You live alone?'

'I do now, yes.'

The police officer didn't reply. He caught the other man's eye. Ada was terrified: there must be bad people in the vicinity, some poor pensioner a few doors down had been butchered and his killer was right this minute prowling around for his next victim.

'I presume you've installed panic buttons and so on, to protect yourself from harm?' the police officer asked.

'No,' Ada said shrilly. 'Of course I bloody well haven't!'

She stepped closer to him, desperate to hear what was happening. Then the man's freckled hand did something unexpected. It curled into a fist, pulled back, hung in the air for a moment then swung at her face.

The fist collided with her nose. Ada heard the shatter. There was a split second before the pain kicked in, where she simply marvelled at the bizarreness of what was happening, at the heat of the blood coursing out of her face and onto her front. Then the fist pulled back again and the man's eyes narrowed. He was aiming. He punched her on the cheek. The second man was behind her now, not to catch her, she realised, but to ensure she didn't escape. She collapsed backwards. Her body hit the ground.

She must have struck her head, because when Ada next came to, everything looked different. She could only open one eye and once she'd managed to do so she thought for a few disorientated seconds that she'd been transported somewhere; been moved to a bunker or some grim torture basement. Then she realised that she was at home, only the sitting room had been devastated. It looked as though a great hand had enveloped the house and shaken it roughly like a snow globe: everything loose was on the floor, books had been pulled from their shelves, even the closed curtains were slightly ripped. There were bulging bags by the door that Ada recognised from the suitcase. They were full of her and Michael's belongings. There were also other containers filled with things, including her own carpet bag, which seemed stuffed with kitchen appliances. Ada was still too woozy to make sense of any of it, then slowly she remembered the men that she'd let in must have caused this wreckage, they can't have been the police officers they'd seemed. The more clearly she managed to think the more scared she became, and she realised with horror that her hands and feet were tied up, and that she was wearing earplugs and her mouth was full of material. She couldn't hear where the men were, though vibrations coming to her through the floor suggested they were upstairs. She tried to shunt herself towards the door but all the strength had been beaten out of her; the pain was immense. She knew her nose was completely mashed because it felt sickeningly open and when she looked down at it she couldn't see the slight smudge of bone that was normally there. The rest of her body ached too, like she'd been kicked when she was unconscious. She realised she was urinating. She began to cry, the one eye that could see oozing blood and salt onto her cheek.

The men came back downstairs. Ada closed her eye and pretended she was unconscious. They were talking in low polite voices to one another, straightening out the logistics of their plunder. Their voices came to her dimly through the earplugs, like she was underwater. 'D'you find a safe?'

'No.'

'Nor me.'

'Lots of jewellery though.'

'Yep. I have her wedding ring too, got it off her finger.'

'Well done. Got the computer and music system. They're really old.'

'Yeah. Think the TV's not worth taking.'

'Mm.'

'Her wallet – did you find that?'

'Yeah, yeah. Passport too.'

'Good.'

'I found a ton of cash in her study, then more in the kitchen.'

'It's like she was expecting us.'

'We'll sort it later.'

'Of course.'

Ada was amazed: it was the sort of discussion crooks had in films, yet she was hearing it live. She opened her eye a tiny amount and saw that both men had taken off their police costume, they were just in trousers and T-shirts. They looked muscly, to be sure, but other than that, normal. It frightened her. She was about to close the eye again, to ensure she didn't attract their attention, when she saw something that filled her with reassurance. The owl. They hadn't taken Primo Levi's copper figurine. It was on the floor, nudging under the skirt of one of the tables, a little flattened perhaps but mostly unscathed. Ada stared at the animal, feeling her breathing become steadier, as she took in its dear little body, the wings of golden wire, the mild-mannered expression Levi had somehow been able to coax from its face. Then one of the men snapped his head down at her, saw she was conscious and walked over, stepping carefully through the debris. She felt him sit her up against the wall, then she watched his right knee bend. His foot, encased in a massive Timberland walking boot, swung at her stomach. She was winded utterly. She slid down the wall. She heard a voice somewhere saying, 'Alright, alright,' then she felt nothing at all.

Chapter Thirty-Two

On the first of September Eliza very nearly didn't go to Swinburne Road at all. She and Nat had lunch together in the Handle Bar Café in the centre, and she had such a pleasant time that she thought, for once, she could forego the pull of her old home.

She'd been seeing Nat casually for a month or so. Nat's home was up in Summertown, and mostly Eliza just went there to see her. Nat had four siblings, all younger, and they were home for the summer, some of them about to start school again. Nat's mum Nicola was a solicitor originally from Barbados, and her dad Tim was from Kent and headed up some charity based in Tadley. When Eliza first came over she assumed they knew nothing about Nat's sexual orientation or what kind of role Eliza was playing in her life, then over dinner one of Nat's brothers said something like, 'So are you the new girlfriend then,' and everyone started sniggering and looking at one another.

'Um, dunno,' Eliza said, looking at her napkin ring.

'No one liked her last girlfriend,' said another sibling. 'You seem alright though.'

At this point Nicola stepped in, told the children to zip it and eat their vegetables, and Eliza felt Nat squeeze her thigh apologetically.

They slept together on their second date. Nat threw her bedroom window open and the sweet August air kept rushing in, blowing goosebumps onto their bare shoulders. The sex was kind of wonderful, languorous until suddenly it changed pace, before arcing back to something slower. Nat had been burnt by hot tea as a child, and a lot of the skin on her stomach and back was shiny and crinkly, like light brown cellophane. She said Eliza could touch it, if she wanted; the skin had healed long ago. Eliza ran her fingers over her. Her skin was impossibly soft. She kissed it lightly, tongued the glossy ridges. When Eliza slept with other people she found the transition from normal interaction to sex quite hard to manage, like she suddenly had to become some erotic temptress, whisper sexy things in just the right hoarse tone. She felt no compulsion with Nat to confect such a personality, they just took what they wanted from one another's bodies. There was something generous in the taking.

Eliza told Nat all that had happened with Ada. The story involved Ruby, tangentially, and it was jarring to realise that the sting had come out of talking about her, so she did, a little, when she felt like it. Nat too had women to talk of, but mostly they spoke about books they liked and films they went to see together, crappy summer block-busters full of sound and fury, which delighted them both.

After lunch in the café, Eliza said she wanted to go over to Iffley to buy some milk. Nat raised her eyebrows and smiled. She knew why Eliza kept going there, and Eliza knew that she knew and smiled as well.

'Maybe I shouldn't,' she said. 'Maybe it's getting weird now. Is there a word for someone who just stalks a house, not the person who lives there?'

'Just go, whatever,' Nat said. She put her hand on Eliza's. 'There are worse compulsions. Anyway you are legit running out of milk, I know that for a fact.'

Eliza laughed gratefully. They got the bill. Nat went to the Pitt Rivers Museum to meet a friend and Eliza swung onto her bike to go to Iffley. The weather was changing from one minute to the next. Over Magdalen Bridge, Eliza was nearly tipped over by a ruthless shove of wind; she gritted her eyes and pushed the pedals laboriously until it died down. This part of town was quiet now, the undergraduates wouldn't arrive for three weeks at least. She locked her bike up outside the fish and chip shop and walked a few doors down to buy some milk. Muhammed, the owner, was reading the *Financial Times* at the till, stroking his beard, he looked like a sage from the first century. There was a crate of fresh figs by the boxes of gum, ripe and silvery blue, their skin splitting. Eliza bought a few and bit one as she left the shop. The flesh was silken and sweet. She walked towards Swinburne Road, watching a big van do a hurried U-turn at the end. It was about three o'clock. The van managed to do the manoeuvre and hurtled off. Eliza kept to the other side of the street, unwilling for Ada to spot her. She watched the house for a second, barely registering the building right behind her, which she had lived in for months. Then she saw that one of the black bins near Ada's front door was on its side. It was a windy day and she supposed it had been knocked over; all the same, some instinct for tidiness kicked in and she crossed the road to lift the bin upright. As she did so she saw that the curtain in the living room looked odd. It was drawn, which in itself was strange given it was mid-afternoon, but some of it was hanging down like someone had yanked it. Eliza contemplated it for a moment. She decided to inspect the window closer up; if Ada saw her and rebuked her, so be it.

She stood outside the sitting room. It was hard to see inside the house; the glass windows were so reflective. She wondered what someone would think if they walked past and saw her lingering. She gave up trying to look nonchalant and pressed her face against the glass. Inside the living room was chaos. There were no lights on but the configuration of furniture Eliza knew so well was gone; the ground was a mess of upturned lamps and broken vases, picture frames on the floor like dropped playing cards. She took in the chaos unfeelingly for a moment, then terror gripped her. She realised she was shouting Ada's name. There was something that looked like legs by the fireplace, only she couldn't see more, she couldn't tell if it was Ada's body or something else. She fumbled in her backpack for her keys and wanted to scream when the zip caught, and finally she gripped the keys and ran to the front door. The hallway had been stripped of its paintings; the mirror was still there but it was smashed in one corner. Eliza rushed into the sitting room, feeling disconnected from her body, like some cold part of her was watching the scene unfold, assessing her response to the emergency. Ada was slumped against the wall in her nightdress. Her face was pulped. Eliza pulled open the curtains to get more light in and called 999, bending by Ada's body, pulling her small frame to her, checking she had a pulse: she did, though it felt weak against Eliza's fingers. She had no fucking clue how to put her in the recovery position, but she pulled the material out of Ada's mouth and yanked the earplugs from her ears and cradled her while she talked to the emergency services, telling them all that she could about the situation, following their instructions, arranging Ada's limbs to better help her breathe. Ada's right eye kept opening and closing, and every so often she made a sound. Eliza rocked her, trying not to cry. The older woman felt light in her arms, she could feel the nobbles of her vertebrae, her shoulder blades cutting out like wings. She realised Ada was trying to say her name, only her mouth was full of blood and too crushed inwards to handle the vowels.

'I'm here,' Eliza said, again and again. 'I'm here, my love, I'm here, my love, I'm here.'

An ambulance showed up, but Eliza was unsure whether it came late or quickly. She talked to the paramedics and to the police who arrived too, telling them the same thing: that she was Ada's friend, that she had no idea how Ada had got into the state she was in, that they had to do all they possibly could to make sure she was alright. They took down her phone number and someone began powdering parts of the house to look for fingerprints.

'They razed it,' Eliza heard one of the police officers say. 'They've taken everything.'

She wondered why the thieves couldn't have just tied Ada up, kept her body unharmed. She went to the garden and leaned against the trunk of the cherry tree. Its leaves were turning, some green still, others a luminous amber.

At one point Ada was taken to hospital. Eliza asked to ride with her but someone told her she couldn't or shouldn't, it wasn't clear which. Nat came over, then Nicola her mother arrived and gave Eliza a crushing hug that made her feel, briefly, like things would be fine. The police disappeared, leaving Nat and Eliza in the wrecked sitting room. Eliza didn't have much to say, she could barely think. Nat held her hand. The scale of the destruction was daunting. They unearthed the kettle from the kitchen floor, it had leaked its water everywhere. The tap was broken but the hose outside was fine. Nat made them tea. They sat in the garden with their scalding mugs for a while, then went back indoors. Dusk was falling. Eliza said she wanted to start putting the house to rights. Nat asked her if she wanted help. Eliza thanked her but said she wanted to do it alone. Nat seemed to understand. She told Eliza she'd be in touch and not to stay too late. 'I won't,' Eliza said. 'Thank you for coming.'

Nat left, saying her mother was trying to find out which hospital Ada had been taken to, and that she'd text her when she found out.

Alone, Eliza restored the living room to something approximating order. She found Levi's owl in the skirt of one of the tables and put it back in its place in front of the picture of Ada and Michael. The frame's glass had broken but apart from that the photo seemed untouched. She picked up the books and piled them by the fireplace. She found a few loose sheets of paper cramped under a couple of dictionaries and got a shock when she turned them over and saw that they were drafts of letters addressed to her. She read them avidly. She was moved by the remorse they bore but she also didn't understand. She pocketed the notes all the same, because they attested to Ada's affection.

As Eliza worked she kept checking her phone to see whether Nicola had found the hospital yet. It got dark. Eliza turned on the overhead light in the living room; she'd never used it before as Ada always insisted on lamps, but they were broken or gone. At ten Eliza found some peaches in the kitchen and ate them directly from the tin, then drank the syrup, discovering she was ravenous. The robbers had turfed out the contents of a corner cupboard in the sitting room that Eliza had never even known was there; it looked rather like a panel in the wall and it didn't have a handle or anything, you just had to grip the right edge to swing it open. Eliza didn't think Ada had known it was there: before it was opened and emptied by the thieves, it seemed to have contained boxes from when Ada and Michael had moved from Manchester. There was a cardboard rack full of old Italian comics, their pages chalky from having been stored away so long, and a zip-up bag of make-up that looked ancient, the eyeshadows cracked and powdery.

Right at the back of the cupboard Eliza could make out a black velvet box that was barely visible it was so deeply thrust in. She got on her stomach to pull it out. It seemed like the kind of box you'd store an embossed tumbler in, or a medal. She opened it curiously. She felt a kind of stillness settle over her body when she saw what was inside.

The box contained one small object.

It was a golden owl, twisted from industrial copper wire.

The bird in the box looked slightly larger than the one Eliza knew so well, and this creature's head was upturned and it had a sharper beak. Its wings looked like they were preparing for flight. Eliza went to the little table where she'd put the other owl earlier. It was clear that the two copper-wire models were a pair.

She pulled the owl out of its box, her fingers weak. The wings of the wire sculpture Eliza had just found curled perfectly around the back of the other; the two models slotted together, so obviously fit for one another she sighed in satisfaction, like she'd come to the end of an unending calculation and found that it all checked out, it worked, she had done everything correctly. She lay back on the jumble of belongings cluttering the carpet and held the owls to her chest, lightly and tenderly, a laugh in her throat like song.

Chapter Thirty-Three

By the time Eliza found out what hospital Ada had been sent to she knew it would be too late to visit her. Before setting off the next morning, she dug around in the wrecked study and found Ada's old address book. She knew Ada had a sister in Brighton and she thought she should probably know what was happening. Eve picked up on the first ring, she was very nice on the phone, though she didn't seem to know who Eliza was. Eliza heard a boy shouting in the background but Eve quietened him and listened to Eliza's news. She said she would take the next train up.

Ada was being looked after at the John Radcliffe hospital, about twenty minutes from Iffley by bike. It took Eliza a while to find out precisely where Ada was, then finally she was given a floor and a ward by a receptionist, and she set off. The corridors were overlong and lit white, sweetened with the smell of ill health. The lifts were uncannily large, to accommodate beds on wheels presumably, and every so often Eliza would see a patient roll past, their eyes closed, strung up to bags of quivering liquids. She hated that Ada was here. At another reception, she was asked who she was and she heard herself say 'Next of kin'.

There were seven or so beds in the ward, all of them occupied by old women in varying states of harm and undress. By the door one woman was sitting up against her pillows, staring indifferently ahead, her hospital-issue nightdress so askew one of her small low breasts was exposed. Eliza went over and said hello. They spoke for a minute: the woman was called Beth, she'd had a fall, she didn't know if anyone was coming to see her or when she'd be out. Eliza pulled the fabric of her nightdress gently over her chest and kissed her on her cheek.

Ada was in a bed next to the window, overlooking the broad beige Oxford suburbia. There were no doctors or nurses tending to her and she had no cards or belongings or flowers in the vicinity.

Eliza wanted to cry when she saw Ada's face, but she managed not to. Her right eye was invisible, folded under billows of red flesh. Her thin face was so puffed up she looked like a cartoon of an injured person. The hair she brushed until it shone was matte and tangled with blood, and a patch behind her left ear shorn to the skin. The rich colours of Ada's bruises made Eliza feel ill, she had to hold her own hands tightly and fix her gaze on the edge of the bed to stop her mind from freewheeling around her skull.

Ada was sleeping. It wasn't clear if it was induced or not. Eliza had brought a book with her so she hopped onto the windowsill and began to read it to the equable beeps of the room's equipment and the quiet voices of other people visiting other women. Opposite Ada's bed there were a couple of children holding their gran's hand, showing her drawings they'd brought from home.

Ada stirred. Eliza put her book down. She picked up two items that she had brought from Swinburne Road which she thought would make Ada more happy than if she came with flowers. She felt suddenly nervous: she and Ada had not talked in months, there was no knowing how Ada might greet her.

Ada opened her good eye and began to shunt herself higher up on her pillows. It was clear that she thought she was alone. Her brow ploughed up with the effort of the movement. Eliza could feel a pulling at her heart as she saw how fragile Ada was, how much pain she was in, how much resolve it took for her to adjust herself on the mattress.

Eliza called her name softly. Ada looked round, trying to place the sound. She saw Eliza on the windowsill.

It really was her. It was absurd, but it was her.

Eliza was smiling anxiously, swinging her legs back and forth, in her ripped jeans as usual. They looked at one another for a long minute.

'You found me,' Ada said at last.

The words didn't come out as she intended, her tongue was too thick to carry them cleanly, her lips swollen. But Eliza seemed to understand.

'Just about,' she replied.

She swung off the windowsill, landing lightly on her feet, and walked around the bed so that she was on the side of Ada's good eye. There was a chair in the middle of the ward. She brought it over and sat down.

'You weren't in great shape,' she said.

'No,' Ada said. She closed her eyes. She was in agony. 'Idiotic. I let those men in.'

'Not your fault.'

'Is everything in the house destroyed?'

'Not everything, though I think quite a bit's been nicked, including your Rent-a-Gran loot.'

Ada tried to chuckle, then winced. 'Ah well,' she said. 'Serves me right. Won't be able to spend it on drugs and a convertible then.'

Eliza laughed. Ada fixed her in the eyes, her mouth unsteady.

'I'm sorry, Eliza,' she said.

'We'll talk about it all at another point.'

'I'd like that.'

'There's no need to now.'

'Perhaps. But I am so sorry, my darling.'

Eliza shook her head.

'One positive thing has come out of all this, though,' she said. 'There was chaos when I came into the house, everything was turned upside down. I found some things I don't think you've seen in years.'

Ada waited for her to continue. Eliza showed her what she had on her lap: the two wire owls made by Primo Levi and treasured by Michael Robertson, and by his wife: perfectly intertwined copper models, united after too long apart.

Ada gazed at the little figures, like she would never want to look at anything else. Tears formed in her open eye, blooming silver until they broke and fell down her cheek.

Then she tore her eyes from the copper sculptures to look at Eliza's face. Both women smiled at the same moment, tried to say something, stopped and smiled again, knowing neither of them could say a word.

Chapter Thirty-Four

It was the last day of October. They decided to rent a boat from the Magdalen Boathouse. Summer was still in the sunlight, though leaves were gathering on pavements and around trees like copper snow. They'd watched the weather report that morning and seen it would be the last mild day of the year: rain was due tomorrow and the days were losing time.

Ada gasped theatrically when she saw how expensive the boat hire was, but they rented one anyway for a few hours. Eliza was carrying a couple of blankets, a thermos of coffee, Pringles and some raspberry biscuits she'd made in Swinburne Road, studded with small white nubs of marzipan. The biscuits were warm from the oven still, wrapped in foil.

Ada had two delicate wire figurines in her handbag: she'd said she wanted them to get some fresh air.

Eliza did the rowing. She wasn't very good at it. For the first ten minutes they bashed from one side of the river to the other. Then she smoothed the ridges of the zigzag they were tracing and found her rhythm. The air smelled vegetal and ripe. There were trees draping their finery into the slow green water, insects skittering on the surface. Ada watched Eliza from her seat opposite, saying encouraging things like how natural a rower she was, how skilfully she was manoeuvring the boat.

They passed canoes, punts, houseboats. University rowers in long thin titanium tubes that Michael used to love, the cox bundled up at the end like a Christmas present. They spoke idly of Eliza's new brother, Caspian: he'd been born one week ago; she'd gone to Carlisle for the birth. He was small and pink and lovely. Soon they had no idea where they were but it didn't matter: there were hours until sunset, they had provisions, there were always people around to help.

Ada was still recovering. It had been two months since the men had come to the door to steal her belongings and beat the resistance from her body. She had a few cracked ribs that were being belligerent but her eye was better and every day that passed made her feel sturdier. There were treasures in the house that were gone forever, but the losses were becoming easier to bear.

Eliza had been by her side for nearly all of it. She still had her room in college but she visited Swinburne Road each day, and they'd discussed her coming back to live there in the new year. There was no rush for Eliza to make the decision, so she hadn't yet. One of the joys of the past few weeks had been that she had come to know Eve and Gwen and her children, who came up from Brighton as often as they could to visit Ada. Once they were all there in the house, putting it fully to rights after the burglary was easy, as Eve had a better memory than Eliza for where things had lived before. When Ada returned home at last, three weeks after she was admitted to hospital, she found the house busier than it had ever been, more homely. It wasn't better than when Michael had lived there, but it was nice, and it was different. Gwen slept in the guest bedroom with her children and Eve was staying in Eliza's old room. Tom was ecstatic his great-aunt was better and jumped on her the moment she stepped inside the house, to show her pictures of his finished train set.

Eliza stopped rowing. They were in a deserted pocket in the river now, just past a junction where some of the water pathways conjoined. No other boats were around.

She lay back, her arms pumping their tiredness. Ada unscrewed the flask and poured some coffee into two china cups she produced from her handbag. There was a willow on the bank, its branches moving languidly in the breeze.

'So how are things progressing with Nat?' Ada asked.

Eliza sat up, beaming.

'Really well,' she said. 'She's lovely.'

Ada nodded, giving her a cup. 'I think she's a very impressive young woman,' she replied.

Nat had spent a lot of time in Swinburne Road since Ada had returned, and she and Ada got on well, partly because Nat was also obsessed with daytime television so a topic for conversation could reliably be found.

Eliza drank some coffee. It was scalding still but thick and creamy. It cooled fast in the October air.

'And she's being good to you, I mean, not like that witch?' Ada asked. She didn't need to say Ruby's name.

Eliza nodded. 'They couldn't be more dissimilar,' she said. 'Before Nat I'd not realised that when you're with someone they should probably make you laugh. Now I laugh all the time. She's funny and cleverer than me and quite a weird person, which I'm only just finding out now.'

'Laughter is the fuel of love,' Ada said, in a grand voice like she was a Shakespearean actor. Eliza smiled. Ada dipped her hand in the river.

'I'm pleased you've found her,' she said quietly. 'It's so rare in life for one to like someone and for them to like one back. And on top of that, for that person to be good news.'

'Yep, Nat's good news I reckon,' Eliza said.

She began unwrapping the foil from the biscuits and offered Ada one, taking one too. They were pale, fragrant things, steaming their sweetness. Eliza wrapped the other biscuits back up quickly so they'd stay warm.

'I know you know this,' Ada said, 'but you've saved me many times this year.'

She looked at Eliza steadily. She was radiating affection. 'I was so isolated before we met. Even once I'd got my business up and running. I was completely alone.'

Eliza broke off a piece of her biscuit. It was warm. She could taste the honey in the crumb.

'So was I,' she said. 'When I walked over that night, the first night, I don't think I knew even then how lonely I was. I sometimes feel that you were the one who found me, who came out looking for me, not the other way around.'

'I don't know. That makes me sound more sophisticated than I was. I just opened the door and there you were.'

'You rescued me just as much as I rescued you.'

'Maybe. I feel now I know well the difference between being alone and feeling alone.'

'Yes.'

'Even when I'm not with anyone now, I don't feel alone. Or if I do, it doesn't feel important.'

'That's how I feel.'

'Good.'

'Yes, that's probably on balance rather good.'

They both laughed at the same moment, tooting biscuit dust. Then Eliza looked around, gripped by a sudden panic.

'Shit, where are the oars?' she demanded.

Ada looked around too. They weren't in the boat. They weren't anywhere to be seen.

'Did you pull them in?' she asked.

'I have no idea!'

They twisted round, moving the blankets and crisps and coats. It was clear the oars were gone. They gave up searching and began to laugh again, first guiltily then wildly, as the afternoon sunlight goldened and the willow branches kissed in the breeze.

Acknowledgements

Where to start. Laura Macdougall, my agent at United, has been brilliant from the get-go, long before Eliza and Ada were even twinkles in my eye. I'm deeply grateful for her support and for the Pageturner Prize that brought us together.

Katie Brown, who edited this novel, has been a dream to work with. The edits she suggested were exactly right for the book; I couldn't have hoped for more. Everyone at Trapeze and Orion has been dazzlingly skilful. If anyone reads or listens to this book, it's thanks to them.

I'd also like to express my gratitude to Ian Thomson, the author of the best biography on Primo Levi to date. His guidance has been invaluable. Robert Gordon supervised my dissertation on Levi. He is a preposterous font of knowledge – his writings on Levi, and much besides, are worth seeking out. Hugo Azerad, my tutor at Cambridge, is one of the cleverest and loveliest people I've met. I'm grateful to Magdalene College and to Cambridge University's brilliant modern languages department. Thanks to the Henry Fellowship too, which sent me to Yale for a year. Without that experience I can't see how this book would have come into being.

Former colleagues at *The Times* and the *Sunday Times* have been steadfast in their encouragement, particularly Ellie Austin, Megan Agnew, Hannah Evans, Daniel Finkelstein, Graham Paterson and Adrian Fernando, who cheered me up so often in the lobby.

I'd like to tip love over my siblings, Alex, Kate and Alice. My grandmas, Jean and Daphne, and my step-grandma Valerie, have been an inspiration. Love to Bumpa too, and to Nigel and Julie. And to Jake, whose contribution to this book runs deep. The Thorolds. Carolyn Soakell who introduced them, and by extension me, to Tumbling Bay.

Some friends have been particular book life-savers and more. Dom McDonald, the driest, smartest, kindest man. He is so missed. Eric Hambro, who got me going on another writing project, which got me going on this project. Everyone on Arbuthnot Road. George Kenwright. Harriet Fitch Little. Jess Gibson. Ali Grodzki. Ella Robertson. Nikita Bernardi. Radhika Seth. Yvette Dickson-Tetteh. Love to you all and to everyone it would be overkill to list here. You have my heart.

Credits

Trapeze would like to thank everyone at Orion who worked on the publication of *Looking for Eliza*.

Agent
Laura Macdougall

Editor
Katie Brown

Copy-editor
Laura Gerrard

Proofreader
Jenny Page

Editorial Management
Holly Harley
Jo Whitford
Charlie Panayiotou
Jane Hughes
Alice Davis
Claire Boyle

Audio
Paul Stark
Amber Bates

Contracts
Anne Goddard
Paul Bulos
Jake Alderson

Design
Loulou Clark
Lucie Stericker
Joanna Ridley
Nick May
Clare Sivell
Helen Ewing

Finance
Jennifer Muchan
Jasdip Nandra
Afeera Ahmed
Elizabeth Beaumont
Sue Baker
Victor Falola

Marketing
Lucy Cameron

Production
Claire Keep
Fiona McIntosh

Publicity
Alainna Hadjigeorgiou

Sales
Jen Wilson
Victoria Laws
Esther Waters
Frances Doyle
Ben Goddard
Georgina Cutler
Jack Hallam
Ellie Kyrke-Smith
Inês Figuiera
Barbara Ronan
Andrew Hally
Dominic Smith

Deborah Deyong
Lauren Buck
Maggy Park
Linda McGregor
Sinead White
Jemimah James
Rachel Jones
Jack Dennison
Nigel Andrews
Ian Williamson
Julia Benson
Declan Kyle
Robert Mackenzie
Sinead White
Imogen Clarke
Megan Smith
Charlotte Clay
Rebecca Cobbold

Operations
Jo Jacobs
Sharon Willis
Lisa Pryde
Lucy Brem

Rights
Susan Howe
Jessica Purdue
Louise Henderson
Richard King
Krystyna Kujawinska

318

About the Author

Leaf Arbuthnot, 27, is a freelance book critic and journalist. She has written for the likes of the *Sunday Times*, *The Times* and the *Spectator*. Subjects of her interviews include Hilary Mantel, Prince Charles, Jilly Cooper and Ellen Page, and she is a judge for this year's Forward Prize for Poetry. She studied modern languages at Cambridge and lives in south London.

Q&A with author Leaf Arbuthnot

1. Grieving for her husband and the life they once had together, Ada decides to offer her grandmotherly services as a way to connect with people. Where did the inspiration for Rent-a-Gran come from?

From a mix of places. Many countries have traditions involving paid mourners – people who get a reward for putting on a bit of a show at a stranger's wake, at their funeral, at their gravestone etc. The strangeness of that cultural phenomenon had been playing on my mind for years. I'd also read about the boom of rentable family members in Japan, and wanted to imagine how that could work in a British context.

Nowadays you can pay people to do just about anything for you – change a lightbulb, look after pets, whatever – and I was curious to see what would happen if you tried to sell something more intimate, like companionship. Particularly in wealthy parts of the world, that's the only thing people can't buy – but often most need.

2. Primo Levi and the motif of his owls is prominent in the story. Why Primo Levi, and why those copper sculptures?

I've loved Levi for years and wrote my dissertation on him when I was at university. His works are unabashedly interested in ethics and in investigating what it means to be human. They're also very funny (or some of his books are – *The Periodic Table* for instance). I return to Levi regularly and wanted his ideas to be wound into my own story.

When I learned that he used excess copper wire from the factory where he worked to create these strange little sculptures, I felt very moved. It seemed to embody something vital in Levi – that he found the value in things that others overlooked. Ever since knowing about the sculptures I've wanted to own or hold one, so I imagine there was a bit of wish fulfilment going on there too, as Michael, Ada's husband, buys two in Turin.

3. **Another theme present in the book is that of loneliness, and the difference between lonely and alone. Was this something you intended to explore?**

Very much so. Loneliness is one of the biggest problems of the age and I wanted to look straight at it, without sneaking it in as a side-theme. I've felt immense loneliness in my twenties, and believe lots of others from my generation do too. But we don't talk about it.

It's more widely accepted that elderly people are vulnerable to loneliness, though sometimes the conversation around that experience can lack depth. While Ada and Eliza are lonely for different reasons, the actual emotional ride they're both on is comparable. I wanted to show how something can be recouped from the awful experience of feeling, rather than being, alone.

4. Eliza is an incredibly refreshing character and the way she navigates her past trauma feels so real and nuanced. How did you go about developing her as a character? How do you want the reader to feel about her?

I'm a bit old-fashioned and generally like books that give me characters to fall in love with. Ideally I want the readers of my novel to feel empathy with Eliza and to like her, in spite of the emotional paralysis she often puts herself in. She's both formidably capable, as an academic and thinker, and remarkably blinded – she doesn't always know what's best for her, and doesn't have the resolve to make her life better. I felt from the start that I wanted a character that was living a fairly recognisable millennial life, but someone complicated enough to be worth spending a whole book with.

She's an inveterate outsider – she was in Carlisle when she was growing up, she was at school, and she certainly is at Oxford where she's studying for her doctorate.

5. *Looking for Eliza* is your first novel. Are you planning another one, and if so, what is it about?

I am planning another one. I don't want to reveal too much in case the house of cards comes tumbling down, but the next book will be about female friendship and is going to be set in a school in the UK, at university and in various glamorous locations around Europe (so that I can vicariously live through my characters).

Help us make the next generation of readers

We – both author and publisher – hope you enjoyed this book. We believe that you can become a reader at any time in your life, but we'd love your help to give the next generation a head start.

Did you know that 9% of children don't have a book of their own in their home, rising to 13% in disadvantaged families*? We'd like to try to change that by asking you to consider the role you could play in helping to build readers of the future.

We'd love you to think of sharing, borrowing, reading, buying or talking about a book with a child in your life and spreading the love of reading. We want to make sure the next generation continue to have access to books, wherever they come from.

And if you would like to consider donating to charities that help fund literacy projects, find out more at www.literacytrust.org.uk and www.booktrust.org.uk.

Thank you.

*As reported by the National Literacy Trust